Keeper

Keeper

JESSICA MOOR

VIKING
an imprint of
PENGUIN BOOKS

VIKING

UK | USA | Canada | Ireland | Australia
India | New Zealand | South Africa

Viking is part of the Penguin Random House group of companies
whose addresses can be found at global.penguinrandomhouse.com.

First published 2020
001

Copyright © Jessica Moor, 2020

The moral right of the author has been asserted

The publisher is grateful for permission to quote from the poem 'School Note'
from the collection *Between Ourselves* by Audre Lorde, copyright © 1976, 1997.
Reproduced here by kind permission of the Audre Lorde estate.

Set in 12/14.75 pt Dante MT Std
Typeset by Jouve (UK), Milton Keynes
Printed and bound in Great Britain by Clays Ltd, Elcograf S.p.A.

A CIP catalogue record for this book is available from the British Library

HARDBACK ISBN: 978–0–241–39684–1
TRADE PAPERBACK ISBN: 978–0–241–43102–3

www.greenpenguin.co.uk

for the embattled
there is no place
that cannot be
home
nor is.

    – Audre Lorde, 'School Note'

Death?

Seen him. Loads of times.

Average height. Brownish hair. Couldn't tell you what colour his eyes are but I can tell you he's nothing special to look at.

Death's just a bloke.

He doesn't look angry or sad or evil. Just a bit bored.

At the end of the day, he's a guy with a job to do. So what happens is he comes up to you and he opens your mouth and then he just pulls the life out of you.

It's like a dentist pulling out a tooth.

Imagine that.

I.

Then

Katie leans over the bar. She shouts her order in the ear of the
bored-looking bartender, whose long ponytail is as pretty and
silky as a girl's. She and her friends have only been in the club
for an hour; the watery assault on the senses and calculated
euphoria have started to wear off, but they aren't yet so drunk
that they've been enveloped by generosity and money has
stopped mattering. It's a wrench to bellow the order for seven
drinks.

She's starting to feel a bit sick. She didn't have dinner.

Along the bar, a boy is smiling absently at her.

He's the kind of boy she'd never normally look at uninvited.
His face looks like it was painted in bold brushstrokes – blond
hair, almost cherubic features. Yet the soft-full lips and long
lashes are assembled against high, flat cheekbones, languid
bedroom eyes. He looks like he was composed with a purpose,
rather than being, like everyone else, the product of random
genetic entropy.

He's beautiful. So beautiful that Katie doesn't bother to ask
herself if he's her type. He's everyone's type, surely. An object-
ive work of art.

He smiles at her more distinctly, his eyes coming into focus.
They're green, not the expected blue. They cut through the
club-haze, looking straight at her.

Or maybe not. Maybe that's just a trick of the light. Katie
looks hurriedly away.

'Forty-two pounds, please.'

The barman holds out the card machine. *En garde.*

By the time Katie's finished fumbling with her PIN and has returned her debit card to her bra, the beautiful boy is gone. She takes the tray of mojitos to the cramped grouping of leather pouffes where her friends sit, two to a pouffe. She yells above the noise that she's going outside for a minute, and leaves, taking her drink with her. She can sense the disgruntled looks shooting from smoky eyes and catching into her back.

She feels guilty. They haven't all been together like this since they graduated and came back home. Most of her friends are on day release from their relationships – serial monogamists, all of them. Seven years at a girls' school will do that to you.

It's February. The quiet, wintry air settles Katie's senses, a cooling shower on her overheated skin.

She drifts towards the edge of the smoking area. Really, it's just a section of alleyway behind the club with a couple of empty glasses on the floor. For years it's been ruled over by the same gregarious Polish bouncer, who used to remember her name. There are no ashtrays or seats, only men in sweaty polyester shirts and squeaky brogues, smoking roll-ups and leaning unnecessarily close to speak to eager-looking girls. Their edges seem blurry against the night, as if they might float away like large, pale balloons.

Katie watches it all. No one seems to see her.

She has always done this – wandered off by herself on nights out. Her friends are used to it. Perhaps it's an odd thing to do, but it helps her and it doesn't seem to harm anyone else. It soothes . . . something. To call the something an anxiety attack would feel too self-absorbed. But there is definitely something in her that needs soothing. Especially today.

Being here – being home – drags Katie's heart down, but for now she doesn't have a choice.

'Home' is on the outer fringes of what can reasonably be considered London, though the association is more by map than spirit. It's a twenty-five-minute train journey from the centre of things, although rush hour stretches out that time-span indefinitely. Here, a lone suicide on the train tracks can throw a whole swathe of London's workforce into an agony of grumbling, packed as they are on to the slender margin of a single railway line. People move here for the good schools, and stay because the property prices dart upwards, just as surely as gravity pulls everything else down. Fresh graduates return to their parental homes like flocks of migrating birds.

Nothing can go too badly wrong here. It's difficult to leave. Or maybe it's just easy to stay.

Being home means being out. *Out*-out, even though this group of friends made far more sense in the context of ibuprofen in school bags, borrowed class notes, a seemingly endless sense of imprisonment. Being in a bar with them, drinking the alcohol they'd once coveted so distantly, wearing the short skirts they'd been forbidden from – it doesn't feel quite right.

But they've all trickled back home, so here they are. Every day they head into the City to populate Excel spreadsheets in different offices, telling themselves that it's somehow connected to their degrees, or else just that it's *experience*. Going out-out seems like the obvious thing to do with these early pay cheques. Now Christmas is entirely over, they might as well come to terms with the fact that this, for the time being at least, is where they are.

Katie doesn't smoke, but she wishes she did. It would give her something to do, and save her from wondering if people think she looks odd out here by herself.

'Hi.'

The man who steps in front of her, seemingly from nowhere, is thin and dark, maybe an inch or two taller than her. His build is wiry – he probably weighs less than her – but he seems to take up space in a decisive way that she's immediately drawn to. He looks at her with a directness that makes everyone else's eyes seem veiled.

'I'm Jamie.'

He smiles at her, holding out his hand with a formality that she assumes is ironic.

'Hi, Jamie.'

She feels like she's being set up for a joke that won't include her. She waits a couple of beats too long before replying.

'I'm Katie.'

He doesn't say anything further, but seems to wait, his mouth smiling and his body relaxed, his eyes following the lines of her face as if examining a map. She shifts, her ankles twisting slightly above her pencil heels. She wonders if her face is red.

'I didn't see you inside.'

'No.'

'I wasn't enjoying it much. Came out here. I'm guessing you were feeling something similar?'

She nods.

'But you must have been enjoying it a bit, or else you'd leave.'

She smiles, because that's an answer in itself to statements like those.

'Maybe going to clubs is worth it,' he says, 'even if only so you can find the people who aren't into clubs either.'

She laughs. She doesn't find his comment funny, but he grins as if he's expecting a laugh, so she provides it.

They amble in the usual circles of half-drunk conversation. She asks the usual questions. *Come here much? What do you think of this DJ?* She forgets his answers almost as soon as he gives them, focusing instead on the timbre of his voice. It's deep and strong and very discernibly male, accented a few layers of privilege below her own.

'What do you do?'

The question slips out just a second or two before she's thought about it properly. She shrinks inside. That question wasn't on the setlist. She's made this mistake before, and men have looked at her with seasoned disappointment, as if she has just signalled to them a fundamental incompetence at living in the moment.

But Jamie doesn't seem to mind.

'I'm a prison officer. Well. Juvenile facility.'

He folds his arms. His movements have the studied sharpness of a newly trained actor.

'Yeah?'

Maybe this line of conversation is an unexpected rope that she can pull herself along.

'Do you like it?'

'No. But the pay's decent.'

'Yeah.' She laughs. 'I know the feeling.'

'That's life, I guess. But it'll get better, I know it will.'

His eyebrows are thick and surprisingly black, which gives an air of resolution to all his expressions. He seems like someone who keeps his ideas hard and simple, like daggers that can be drawn cleanly from their sheaths.

Katie likes that.

They keep talking. Her attention, such as it is, sways when the beautiful boy from the bar comes outside and stands alone at the other end of the smoking area. Half is caught following the disintegrating column of ash between his long fingers. Maybe Jamie will excuse himself before it burns away completely.

But he doesn't, and the beautiful boy doesn't linger, and Katie and Jamie talk on.

At a break in the flow – if you could call it a flow – she suggests that they go back in. Jamie frowns. She wonders if she has somehow misread him.

But then, to her surprise, he takes her hand and leads her back inside. His grip is warm and dry and firm.

As they go down the stairs together, her mind works through a series of possibilities, like trying a set of keys in a lock.

She could abandon Jamie now and go back to her friends.

She could accept one drink from him and then make an excuse.

She could drink with him into the night. Dance with him, her hands resting on his slim shoulders, a fuzzy heat growing between her thighs as she allows herself an occasional glance at the beautiful boy.

She could get a taxi home with her friends, like they all agreed at the beginning of the night.

She could go home with Jamie.

She could take him by the hand and lead him to a dark corner of the alley behind the club. She could sink to her knees before him and let his hands rest on her head as she takes him in her mouth, like he's giving her his blessing for a religion she's not yet sure she believes in.

Jamie taps Katie on the elbow. She turns around and he hands her a glass of clear liquid over ice. He didn't ask her what she wanted so she's not sure what it is, but she smiles at him and takes a sip, identifying only something strong and chemical.

'I got you a double,' he says.

She resolves, before she's too drunk to resolve on anything, that she's going to keep drinking, and that she's going to fuck him. She decides it now, before she can get too caught up in the question of whether or not it's what she really wants.

They talk. Or rather, he talks. She says little, focusing on enunciating her few words clearly. She nods and smiles and occasionally lets her hand brush against his thigh. He doesn't seem to understand what she's inviting him into and looks her square in the eye every time they touch. It surprises her how unimpressed he seems. He doesn't appear to particularly enjoy her touch, but he doesn't step away either. After a few minutes he puts an arm around her shoulders, continuing to yell something that she can't hear over the music.

Then, without warning, he puts a hand on the back of her head and crushes his mouth against hers.

She opens her lips, as if obeying a cue. His tongue makes a measured, inspecting progress around her mouth. Her body seems prepared to let him in.

He doesn't keep buying her drinks. He doesn't even keep kissing her for long. Once the terms of their embrace have been set, he goes back to talking. About how he's thinking about going into the army.

Katie is sobering steadily, but she doesn't let the ebbing warmth around her eyes force her to consider whether she's making a mistake.

Over Jamie's shoulder, she sees her friends swaying towards the exit and disappearing up the stairs.

They return a few seconds later, their faces dressed up with expressions of pantomime horror. They gesture at her to join them. She flaps a hand at them behind Jamie's back as if to say, *Go on!* Her friends leave, eyebrows raised. Katie allows the same hand to slide around Jamie's waist and pull him closer.

Jamie frowns at her.

'You know, I'm not that kind of guy.'

Her hand, which was sliding down towards his bum, stops abruptly.

'And you don't seem like that kind of girl either.'

The pause is filled by the throb of the music. Katie feels a slow cascade of shame burning through her chest. She withdraws her hand, and Jamie catches it. He takes it in both of his own and spreads the fingers, inspecting it carefully as if assessing its worth. He looks at her and smiles. For the first time, he seems really good-looking.

'Let me get to know you. Properly.'

Katie doesn't say anything. It didn't feel like the kind of request she needs to answer out loud.

'Can I walk you home?' he asks. He laces his fingers into the hand he's captured.

She doesn't want to walk home. She's wearing high heels and it's over a mile. Besides, she isn't sure what they'd talk about on the way. Suggesting they get a cab would feel somehow tone-deaf, and she doesn't think he'll want to sit with her on the night bus, exchanging the banalities of increasing sobriety while she tries to avoid spearing McDonald's chips on her heels.

'Trust me. I'll be worrying about you if you go off by yourself.'

She laughs, but he doesn't.

'Look, I'm not going to try it on with you, if that's what you're worrying about. Just want to deliver you to your door, safe and sound.'

Why is she making this so much more complicated than it needs to be? If there was anything to worry about with Jamie, then she shouldn't have accepted the drink he gave her. But she did, and there's no harm done.

'I can get a cab,' she says, even though she doesn't mean it.

'Not a chance. Do you know how many women are raped by unlicensed minicab drivers?'

She makes to take a little step from him, but his hand is resting in the small of her back and it seems to stop her from moving, though he's not actually exerting any force.

She nods, though she's not sure what part she's agreeing to. 'Let me just go to the loo quickly.'

He grins and leans forward to kiss her lightly on the forehead. It feels more abruptly intimate than all their previous contact.

There is no quickly, of course.

Katie stands in the queue for a single bathroom stall, watching as the girls around her, clearly strangers, move into a slurring sisterliness as they wait. One of them puts a little white pill in her mouth. She catches Katie's gaze and holds out her hand. Katie shakes her head.

She stands in front of the mirror, looking deep into her own irises. To see if they are any different from usual.

But she sees only herself – only the usual blankness. Her eyeliner has flaked off and is lying in the creases of skin underneath her eyes. Her face looks greyish in the bathroom light, underneath the red flush from the hot club. The swaying glow is nearly gone.

She steps back, rocking on to the balls of her feet to see her outfit better, how the tight (too tight?) black top blends into the black polyester skirt, which has started to go a little grey. She notices that a part of her flesh – her flank? The part between the waist and the buttock – is bulging a little, like a joint of beef before the string has been snipped off. She wonders if she ought to take off her knickers, to smooth out the line.

She can tell she's going to have a hangover tomorrow. She's a little dizzy and holds on to the sides of the basin to keep herself standing firm.

'Do you need to go into the cubicle, babe?'

She looks into the mirror at the girl standing behind her. She's tall – she'd be over six feet if she weren't wearing heels, which she is – and has the vertiginous limbs of a drag queen. Her tiny dress is a slash of silver, covering only the essentials. Katie shakes her head and the girl steps into the bathroom stall, her long body carving a swaying diagonal.

'Thanks, darliiiiing,' she says, stretching out the second syllable with a sensuous yet impersonal smile.

As Katie leaves the bathroom she nearly collides with the beautiful boy she saw earlier. He smiles again, and this time she knows for certain that it's directed at her.

2.

Now

It was Whitworth's corpse. So to speak.

The body had been found the previous day, washed up downstream of Widringham. The location, the current, the lividity – all these suggested that the victim had come off the old bridge, which was on DS Daniel Whitworth's patch.

It was a popular local spot for suicide.

Whitworth had always expected that he'd get over the first bolt of shock on seeing a dead body, but so far he still hadn't.

It was the way they so intimately resembled people, yet weren't.

Whitworth had hoped to retire without having to deal with another corpse. Sod's law, too, that it was a girl. Older than his Jennifer, but not so much older that he didn't think of her primarily as *someone's* daughter. The smooth young skin was drained of colour, the eyes unframed by crow's feet. Death had no business on those faces.

At least this girl – Katie Straw – hadn't been in the water too long. Her features weren't wrecked. It was bad enough that her boyfriend would have to identify her. He didn't need the shock of seeing that pretty face bloated into a pale monster.

Whitworth noticed crumbs of something black around her eyes. The pathologist said it was eyeliner.

His daughter's eyes had been dirtied with the same black stuff when she'd rolled them at him that morning. It had been the usual rows – getting into the car, in the car, exiting the car.

Jennifer had justified herself in shrill tones over the tinny babble of the radio and drum of the rain, full of sixteen-year-old outrage.

He'd watched her walk away, watched her wait until she thought he couldn't see her any more, watched her angry stomp morph into a sort of waggle.

Whitworth wondered if a man of almost sixty was just too old to be parenting a teenage girl. He had no energy for dealing with her, not now that all the sweetness seemed to have been sucked out of her and this difficult demi-woman stood in her place.

Maureen, his wife, was always on Jennifer's side, of course.

But Whitworth didn't get to feel sorry for himself for too long. The movement of the door handle made him throw the sheet back over the body on the slab like a guilty secret.

His trainee, Detective Constable Brookes, entered the mortuary room, followed by a tall, nauseous-looking young man with a scrappy russet beard. There was a greasy sheen to his pale face. As he approached, Whitworth noticed the brackish smell of spirits.

'Hello' – he glanced at his sheaf of notes – 'Noah?'

The young man nodded.

Normally, in a case like this, you'd look very carefully at the boyfriend. After all, if a woman was murdered, then it was fifty–fifty her bloke had done it.

But Noah apparently had some sort of alibi. A stag do up in Glasgow.

'I'm DS Whitworth,' Whitworth said. 'I'm afraid we have to ask you to identify the body. I think DC Brookes has already had a little chat with you about it?'

Whitworth kept his eyes on Noah, as if propping him upright with the solidity of his gaze.

'Ready?'

How could anyone be ready? But Whitworth had to say it.

Noah nodded again. Jerkily, like a marionette.

Whitworth picked up the corner of the sheet between his thumb and forefinger and drew it back as carefully as he could.

Noah stared down for a few long moments, then abruptly seized the covering and gracelessly yanked it back into place.

'That's Katie,' he said.

Most people went pale when they saw a dead body, but Noah had gone bright red, as if embarrassed.

Whitworth had a feeling he'd seen Noah about before, hovering around the edges of things. Pub fights, pissed-up messes, silly bollocks involving traffic cones. Always arse-over-tits drunk, of course. Probably not terribly bright, but not necessarily a bad kid.

'Do you have a way of contacting Katie's family?'

Whitworth was using his kind voice. The voice he always used on people whose futures were crashing down in front of them.

Noah shook his head.

'Katie's parents are dead. No other relatives.'

Then his shoulders started to shake.

'She's all *alone*.'

It wasn't clear if he meant she had been alone in life or that she was now alone in death. There was always that funny in-between period when folk weren't sure if they were supposed to talk about the dead in the past tense.

Either way, it made Whitworth breathe a sigh of relief. No need to tell a mother or father that their little girl was dead. Maybe by her own hand, maybe by someone else's. As a parent, he wasn't sure which would be worse to hear.

Now Katie Straw could become a memory. A pile of paperwork.

Noah's quiet sobs had turned into a kind of wailing. He

didn't look like he was going to be much help to the investigation, for now at least.

It seemed to Whitworth that young men *cried* so much more these days.

The door opened and Rachel, the pathologist, stuck her head in. She glared at Whitworth, then hurried forward to take Noah by the hand.

'Come on, love. Let's get you a cup of tea.'

Noah allowed himself to be led away from Katie's body. As he left the room he seemed to convulse slightly. Whitworth wondered if he was going to be sick.

Brookes shut the door behind Noah, then strode forward towards the slab. He brushed the sheet back, studying the dead face.

'Always sad, sir. Suicide.'

Whitworth nodded. It was true.

The body had all the hallmarks of a mundane, self-inflicted death. Your standard-issue female corpse.

There was barely a mark on her, apart from the bold, professional post-mortem wound which slit her from collar to crotch. But her face had miraculously been spared. Lying on the slab, she looked like a painting, marble-white and perfect. Virginal.

'Noah's upset,' Whitworth said.

'He's hung over,' Brookes replied flatly.

'What does that tell us?'

'Nothing. In itself.'

Brookes tugged at the sheet to cover an overhanging lock of Katie's hair.

'He said he was in Glasgow?'

'Right.'

'And he didn't raise the alarm when he didn't hear from her?'

Brookes was still holding the corner of the sheet, as if he couldn't quite let it go.

'He did not.'

'Bit weird, isn't it?'

Brookes paused diplomatically. 'It's . . . it's not what I'd do.'

'But the other lads say he was there the whole time?'

'For what it's worth.' Brookes shrugged. 'I don't consider fif-teen pissed-up guys much of an alibi. He could have sneaked off.'

Whitworth made a humming noise of consideration. It felt almost as if he were performing for Katie. For Katie's corpse. Showing her he cared.

'You want me to check out the alibi?'

There would be endless CCTV to trawl through. Witnesses to interview, travel records to delve into. They didn't have those kind of resources and the only way to get them would be to start making noises to the DI about murder.

Katie Straw was young, which did make her death very sad. But she had no life insurance or significant assets, which made it unlucrative. When all was said and done, Whitworth's gut told him that this was just an unhappy young girl who'd taken the easy way out.

'Hold that thought for now,' he said. 'Go and sort out Noah. Send Rachel back, would you? Need a word.'

The pathologist's report was not particularly helpful.

'Cause of death was drowning, that's clear. No sign of a struggle . . . no sexual assault . . . not much by way of unusual marks. Wear and tear from being in the water, like you'd ex-pect. Scar tissue on the arms, I'd say from burns, but it's a few years old. And . . .'

She peeled back the sheet, like a hotel maid stripping a bed.

'More scarring. Tops of the thighs. Here – and here. From the placement and the precision, I'd say they were self-inflicted. But again, they're old.'

She pulled the sheet back over the body, covering it to the neck.

'Doesn't tell you much,' Whitworth muttered. 'Self-harm's fashionable these days.'

Brookes was right. As it stood, they had no better theory than suicide. People did kill themselves, after all. It was a fault in their brain chemistry, he supposed.

Noah had reported Katie missing when he got back from Glasgow to find her gone but all her things still at the home they'd shared for the past year. Investigating officers had found an arsenal of antidepressants in her bathroom cabinet. Citalopram, paroxetine, sertraline. Milligrams upon milligrams.

It wasn't exactly a stretch to think she might have taken her own life.

Noah hadn't known what the drugs were. According to Brookes, who had been there at the time, Noah had seemed to think they were for some kind of opaque gynaecological problem.

It sounded like she had been a clever girl. Graduated with a First from the University of Exeter, or so her employer seemed to think. No one had tracked down a degree certificate yet. She had worked in Widringham's shelter for battered women. A professional do-gooder.

Spending all day soaking in other people's relationship problems, then going home to Noah. Whitworth wondered if she'd died of middle-class disappointment.

Whitworth let himself out of the mortuary room and walked down the hall to the car park. Brookes was standing by their unmarked car, peering at his phone. He had transferred to them from Manchester, and Whitworth occasionally got the impression that Brookes wasn't impressed with the calibre of crimes they dealt with in Widringham.

'Noah get off okay?'

'Called him a minicab. Cabby didn't look too keen to take him.'

'We'll get him in for a chat tomorrow, once he's over his hangover,' Whitworth said. He didn't need to elaborate on why. It was standard procedure to grill the boyfriend when a woman died. 'Any luck with the victim's employer?'

Tasks like getting in touch with Katie's boss made Whitworth glad he could pull rank. He had never personally had to deal with Valerie Redwood, the woman in charge of the women's shelter where Katie worked, but she was known in the station for having all the cooperative spirit of a wet sack of concrete.

'Melissa told her we were coming,' Brookes said.

'Got the address okay, did she?'

Brookes looked blank for a second, so Whitworth clarified.

'They keep the locations of these places need-to-know. You know.'

'Of course. Yeah. Melissa got it for me.'

'Smart of you to get one of the girls in the station to ring her up,' Whitworth commented. 'She's not too fond of' – he swung heavily into the passenger seat and shut the door with a thud – 'you know. Menfolk.'

He gave a little grunt of laughter. Brookes didn't.

''S'probably just her job,' he said.

Whitworth felt embarrassed. It was the same kind of embarrassment as when Jennifer told him that his jokes were past their sell-by date.

'Well. You're probably right. Still, no harm in a joke. She's not got much of a sense of humour, by all accounts. You'll need to watch yourself.'

As Brookes wound the police car around the slumped shoulders of the hills surrounding Widringham, Whitworth found himself yawning.

He was meant to be relaxed, restored, loved-up, after whisking Maureen off to the Yorkshire Dales for the weekend.

Twenty-five years of marriage.

But the hotel sheets had been damp, the eggs at breakfast had been claggy, and when Maureen had made her advances on him he had grunted that his back was too bad and rolled away.

That was what marriage was, of course. Good parts, bad parts. In between the good and the bad you had to keep the faith. Whitworth did have the capacity for faith, but he used it all up at home.

Just as well, really. How much faith could you have in anything when you had to look down at a dead girl's face on a Monday morning?

3.

Then

The beautiful boy turns towards Katie, sweeping his eyes across her face with choreographed elegance.

'Hi.'

For a few moments her drunkenness seems to reassert itself. She takes a step towards him then trips slightly on her heels. That little lurch brings the world back into focus and she imagines how she must look to him. A dull-faced, off-balance girl, her makeup smeared, her hair lank with the night's sweat.

She converts the little stagger into a wide arc, which takes her back to where Jamie stands, waiting.

It's one in the morning. The thin crowd has swelled into a living body. The music was cool five years ago, but to Katie's ears it now sounds clunky and echoing.

She watches Jamie exchange a brief goodbye with the group of men he's with ('Work guys. Don't really like them,' he explains dismissively), and they set off.

They're holding hands. Anyone who saw them would think they were a couple.

Before long she's limping a little, but he doesn't seem to notice.

After ten minutes or so she takes her shoes off and lets them dangle from her hand by the straps.

Jamie frowns.

'There's a lot of broken glass here.'

'I'm being careful.'

'You should put your shoes back on.'

Katie dawdles for a few seconds, uncertain.

'Look, you're making me worry about you. Just put your shoes on.'

She does it.

He has stopped talking about himself. Instead, he tells her how beautiful she is. The way he says it makes her feel like he's talking about someone else.

They lapse into silence. He holds her hand.

The night is cloudy, the sky like oxidized iron, betraying in patches a deepest blue and a scattering of stars.

'Look,' Katie says. 'There's the North Star.'

Jamie follows the uncertain line of her finger.

'Oh, yeah.'

'Or . . . I don't really know. Is it Mars?'

'Maybe.'

'Or it could be a satellite, I guess.'

Jamie says nothing. He re-laces his fingers with hers. Their hands slot together with ease.

'So, you live with your mum?'

She thinks it might be the first question he's asked her about herself all night.

'Yeah.'

'Me too.'

'It's just for now.'

'You're moving out?'

'No.'

It's the first time she's grappled with how to say it out loud.

'She's . . . she's not well. She might not . . . she's got cancer.'

'Oh my God.'

'She had it before. A few years ago. It went away but then it came back.'

She tries to keep talking but her voice splinters.

'You're the first person I've told. I don't know why I'm telling you. I wanted to tell my friends, but it just didn't feel right, somehow. We thought it was gone. We found out this week.'

'That happens.'

'I didn't think it would happen to me. To her, I mean.'

'And your dad?'

'He's dead.'

'Shit. He got ill too?'

'No.'

'Oh.'

'I guess . . . I mean, some people say alcoholism's an illness.'

'Right. I see.'

'But no one made him drink-drive. He went into the back of a lorry.'

'I'm sorry.'

'I'm just glad he didn't hurt anyone else.'

'Of course. He's responsible. You can't put it in the same bracket as people like your mum.'

'Yeah. Exactly.'

Katie's worried that she might cry, so she heads off the possibility by saying, with a little smile, 'Sorry to be such a massive downer.'

'Don't be sorry. I mean . . . thank you. For sharing with me.'

Sharing doesn't feel like the right word, but it's the only word he offers, so she accepts it, and they keep walking.

He says goodbye to her at her mother's front door. He doesn't make any indication that he wants to come in, and she's grateful for that. Her mum sleeps odd hours.

He asks for her number. She gives it to him.

Katie isn't sure if what she's feeling is hunger or anxiety, so she hedges her bets and makes tea and toast.

She checks her phone. Nothing. It's 1.58 a.m.

She puts her phone on silent and eats sitting at the table, staring at the jumble of pill boxes, plastic bags and old detective novels that covers the table-top. Her mother has left the TV on with the sound muted, which lends the faces onscreen a kind of weariness.

The fuzz of alcohol has worn away completely and left a hollow feeling in its place. A small part of her head, just behind her fringe, begins to ache.

She crosses to the kitchen cabinet to take down one of her dad's old pint glasses and fills it with cold water. Then she throws away the packaging for the microwave moussaka her mum must've had for dinner and washes the dirty dish in the sink.

She checks her phone again and switches it on to vibrate before turning off the lights and going upstairs. She avoids the creaking floorboard outside her mum's room.

She takes off the remaining smears of makeup, puts on a pair of clean pyjamas and gets into bed.

She feels the same sense of anticipation she did on the day she left for university, and, perhaps perversely, on the day her dad walked out on them. There was even a shameful note of it when her mother told her about her diagnosis, although that quickly gave way to a metallic chill that she now carries daily at her core.

Her phone fusses on the bedside table. She counts to five, then picks it up to look at the screen.

It was great meeting you tonight. J xxx

4.

Now

They drew up to a street lined with Victorian houses in the posh part of Widringham, the part that made tourists think it was a nice town.

Parking on the roadside, Brookes crossed to one of the large houses. Its gravel drive was oddly carless and the recycling bins were overflowing. Whitworth followed him. They climbed a set of stone steps, then pressed the button to the entry videophone.

There was a long pause. Both men glanced sideways at the beady camera lens. Then the door cracked open enough to reveal a short, fat woman. She had turquoise horn-rimmed glasses, a slash of red lipstick on lips so dried out they resembled a cat's arse, and black hair dyed far past the point of believability.

'You were supposed to meet me by the pillar box,' she snapped, instead of a hello.

She inched herself out of the front door piece by piece, never opening it any more than was absolutely necessary, then thudded it shut with her back. Once the door was closed she began to advance on the two men, forcing them down the stone stairs one by one.

'Oh, it's all right, love. We didn't want to come in anyway.' Whitworth made a show of blowing out his breath, emphasizing the frosty vapour that it formed in the February air. 'Don't worry about us. Brrr.'

He stamped his feet on the crunching gravel and a tiny puddle of muddied ice cracked beneath his shoe.

The woman didn't smile. She held out her hand imperiously.

'Credentials, please. If you are who I think you are.'

Whitworth sneaked a look at Brookes, who was smiling blandly. He reached into his jacket pocket and withdrew his police badge, wordlessly presenting it for the woman's inspection. Brookes did the same.

The woman narrowed her eyes as she read, folding her arms across her heavy chest. Whitworth was reminded of a school dinner lady.

'We take no chances here. Not with the kind of characters we've had poking around. With the threats we've been having. Certainly not after what's happened to Katie.'

She moved towards Whitworth without extending a hand or a smile.

'I'm Valerie Redwood. Chief executive.'

The way she said her name made Whitworth think she was in the habit of announcing herself.

'I'm not sorry for obstructing you,' she continued, not giving Whitworth a chance to reply. 'I make no secret of the fact that I'm a difficult woman.'

Her vowels sounded like they had been forced into the contours of a local accent, but there was a fruitiness underneath that suggested an expensive education.

'This is a female-only safe space. I make no apology for that.'

She gestured at the two men.

'For all I know, you could both be perpetrators. My job is to protect women, not necessarily to help the police.'

Whitworth was used to ungrateful attitudes towards the Force. Perhaps some people really couldn't help it – it was just the environment they'd been brought up in. But women like Valerie Redwood ought to know better. He couldn't stand the self-importance of it all – the way posh women like her mined past history to convince themselves they had problems. It made him think of his mother, quietly earning her factory wage, ruling over four children and a drunk husband with an iron fist. Yeah, his dad had given her the odd backhand when he got home from the pub. She'd clocked him right back. It was the way it was.

'Well, Mrs Redwood.'

'Ms.'

'Well, Valerie.' Brookes stepped in. 'You say you want to protect women. That puts us on the same side, doesn't it? If Katie was killed by some . . . you know' – he lowered his voice – 'some unstable character, then we need every bit of information you've got to put him away and make this town safer for women. Besides' – he jerked his head towards the front door of the house – 'we don't want to take you away from your vital work at what must be a very difficult time.'

She seemed to soften slightly.

'This is Detective Constable Brookes,' Whitworth said.

She pursed her lips, tilting her head to look up at Brookes, as if she were trying to decide what species he belonged to.

Then she turned wordlessly, producing a bunch of keys from the pocket of her leopard-print raincoat, and led them back up the stone steps to the front door. She made to put the key in the lock, then paused and dropped her hand, turning back to the two detectives.

'I should emphasize to you that this is an absolute exception,' she said, each consonant thrutting out spittily between her teeth. 'We never usually permit males in a refuge. *Never.*'

'That's understandable.' Brookes shot a glance at Whitworth.

'These are exceptional circumstances, Valerie,' Whitworth said.

Valerie Redwood's scarlet lips tightened over her teeth for a second, then she turned her back on the two of them, as if to attend more closely to the lock.

'Please comply with any instructions I give you as we move around the refuge,' she muttered to the crumbling paint of the door. She seemed to steel herself for a minute, then turned the key. The door swung open and the three of them entered.

As Whitworth stepped over the threshold, following Val Redwood, a wave of central heating hit him, carrying with it the smell of stale cooking and own-brand fabric conditioner. Mother-smell.

He found himself in a narrow hallway with all the beige internal doors closed. On the wall hung a corkboard with fire-safety regulations, a list of house rules and a cleaning rota. There was little inside the building to distinguish it from anywhere else.

Valerie called out to the house. 'It's Val. Just letting you all know that I've got two male police officers with me.'

The house made no reply.

Whitworth glanced at Brookes, who gave the faintest indication of a shrug before smiling jovially and following Val into a pokey office. The walls were decorated with children's drawings, with the words 'thank you' spidering across the pages in coloured pencil. One of them was unmistakeably a portrait of Val herself – black hair, red lipstick, massive bosom and all. Some of the pictures were yellowing and curling at the edges.

'I've prepared Katie's employment records for you to review,' Val said, gesturing towards the desk, which was clear except for a slim cardboard file. Beside it sat a much thicker wad of papers, zealously highlighted and spiked with coloured sticky tabs.

'Also, for your convenience, a copy of the evidence I submitted to you several weeks ago,' Val said. 'Maybe now you'll take it more seriously.'

Whitworth managed to stop the question 'Evidence?' slipping out of his mouth, but Brookes was less discreet, craning his neck to see the pile of paper.

'Oh . . .'

It seemed to be a collection of emails and . . . screen grabs, were they called? – from Facebook, and the other one. Twitter.

Could @valredwood please tell us how much of the money raised will go to male victims of domestic violence, since she claims to care about 'all victims'?

Interesting that @valredwood never replied to my simple request for information. Her misandry shows through once again

@valredwood feminism is cancer

1/? Ideology-driven lesbian bitches like @valredwood and the rest of them at @widwomensaid serve to trivialize REAL rape you can't just change your mind on a whim then cry about it in court

2/? Women these days are encouraged only to think about themselves (the nasty side of so-called female empowerment) and have no regard for the men whose lives are being ruined by reckless accusations

3/? The facts are plainly apparent that men are being scapegoated

4/? Yes all societies have their problems but to claim that there's some epidemic of violence that only affects women is unjust and absurd

5/? Most murder victims are men but I don't see @valredwood and her feminist pals speaking out about this I WONDER WHY???

@valredwood women are unbelievably coddled by the modern world even though men are committing suicide in droves it seems these feminists don't care at all

interesting that @valredwood did not attend the PCC engagement event and sent one of her flunkies instead DO NOT BE
FOOLED the feminist lobby is incredibly powerful and will
silence anything that doesn't fit their agenda

this modern obsession with victimhood turns my stomach. If
that dyke @valredwood really thinks all men are rapists then
maybe she'll get what's coming to her

It went on and on, for pages. At a glance, it looked like a difference of opinion rather than a threat of violence, Whitworth
observed, even if the language was a bit crass. If you were
looking for offence, you'd be able to find it, certainly, but that
didn't make it criminal.

'Oh, yes, sir, we've already had this,' Brookes said.

'We have?'

'It's separate –'

'It may very well not be,' Val Redwood interjected.

'They're woman-haters, for sure,' Brookes continued. 'Mum's-
basement types, in my experience. Sorry he called you a
lesbian, Valerie. That's really not very nice. But I'm sure it's
just internet chatter. They never actually do anything, this lot.
There's nothing here we'd call a viable threat of violence.'

'And the rape threats?'

'Rape threats?' Brookes looked blank.

'If that dyke Val Redwood really thinks all men are rapists
then maybe she'll get what's coming to her,' Val recited, apparently from memory.

'I'm not saying it's not upsetting. But I think you're reading
into that a bit, maybe,' Whitworth said.

'I don't think I am,' Val replied, her voice shaking. Clearly,
she was pissed off. 'The point is, Detective, that we have plenty
of reasons to believe that the situation has escalated, even putting Katie's death to one side for a moment. We've had strange

cars parked across the street. Side gates left open at night. And' – she leaned forward to indicate the CCTV screens on the back walls – 'one of our cameras stopped working. Mysteriously.'

'Sounds like you might need to maintain your equipment a bit more carefully, love.'

Whitworth knew he was being flippant, but there was something addictive about seeing those cheeks purpling on cue.

'We're not careless here, Detective,' Val responded. 'I don't know what you think a refuge is for, but I can tell you that our number-one job is homicide prevention. We're careful. Katie was careful. Most of the women here have a viable death threat on their heads. They're relying on me to keep them safe.'

She tapped on the front of her polyester jumper.

'Not you. Not the police, not the courts. Me, and my expertise, and this building. On a forty-grand grant, and that's getting cut next year. I sent all this information to your station weeks ago. Do you think I'm having a laugh here, Detective?'

She seemed to swell.

'We've been a bit overstretched –'

'My employee is dead. I'd be grateful if you took my expertise seriously. This is *male violence*. This is –'

'DC Brookes.' Whitworth picked up Katie's employment file and the pile of print-outs, thrusting them both towards Brookes. 'Perhaps you could review this – both of these – while Valerie and I have a chat?'

Val Redwood still looked annoyed, but she didn't seem to be able to find anything specific to disagree with.

'We'll go into the key-work room for some privacy,' she said, after a pause. 'Detective Brookes, I would be very grateful if you stay only in this room. No wandering about.'

Her fingertips were twitching nervously on her set of keys.

Her eyes darted about, checking locked file cabinets, computers, empty desk tops.

'I can vouch for DC Brookes,' Whitworth said.

Val Redwood still looked reluctant, but she nodded.

She led Whitworth out of the office and closed the door sharply, before producing yet another key and turning down the labyrinthine passage.

5.

A door slammed. A voice called out: 'It's Val. Just letting you all know that I've got two male police officers with me.'

The shout was thin, interrupting the denser silence that had lain over the refuge since last night, when Val had sat them all down and told them that Katie was dead and that no one knew why.

If Nazia had learned anything at all since she arrived here, it was that watching TV was the appropriate response to pretty much everything. It flattened life out, dimmed down the urgency. Katie was dead. *Morse* was on.

The two facts just . . . coexisted.

'I've seen this one before,' she said, frowning at the screen.

Nazia recognized the blue waterproof jacket, the large, scared eyes, the brown nineties lipstick – why were they showing such old telly? The woman onscreen might as well have had 'victim' rubber-stamped on her forehead.

Nazia pointed.

'He did it.'

''Course he did,' Sonia said. 'It's always the boyfriend, right?'

Nazia turned to look at Sonia. Her coily hair had been relaxed and was pulled off her face. It made her look very different. Like she was being held together even more tightly than usual.

'Not always,' Nazia replied.

'Husband, then.'

Nazia could hear minuscule noises of irritation coming from Lynne. There were two types of families, Nazia thought.

The type that talks over the TV and the type that doesn't. Clearly, Lynne had grown up in the second type.

The woman onscreen was walking through a car park, looking around frantically. Sonia turned up the volume a couple of bars and leaned forward, as if studying the TV for clues on what not to do next.

'Silly cow. Why would you walk around there by yourself?'

'I've seen this one before,' Nazia said again. Everything here needed to be repeated endlessly, as cyclical and as thankless as a load of laundry.

'Don't spoil it.'

Nazia turned to look at Angie. She didn't tend to speak to the older woman. It wasn't that she knew for a *fact* that Angie was racist, but it seemed like a fair assumption, considering her age and background, and Nazia wasn't interested in doing outreach work to someone who probably thought she was a terrorist. Or rather, that she did a terrorist's laundry. Besides, there was nothing odd in their lack of conversation. Acknowledging each other would have been an acknowledgement that they both belonged there, and no one thinks they belong in the madhouse.

'What's to spoil?'

Jenny rarely spoke, to the point that Nazia wasn't sure that she shared a language with the rest of them. Maybe she didn't. Weren't hookers often from Romania, and places like that?

But Jenny did sound English. It was just that when she spoke the things she said made no sense. You couldn't make a pattern out of her. You couldn't see where her thoughts were going or where she'd got them from.

Christ knew what she was doing here. But Val had some funny ideas.

Since the day she had come to the refuge, Nazia had been doing her best not to stare at Jenny. The harsh lines of her seemed to demand attention; the heroin had evaporated all her surplus flesh and left only eyes and bones.

This morning, Nazia just let herself look.

Jenny's eyes were red. She was the only one who had cried last night when Val told them that Katie was dead.

Maybe Nazia should have known intuitively that something was wrong. She'd been due to meet Katie on Friday morning and make a start on a benefits application. When Katie hadn't turned up, she'd sat in the office alone, angry, tired, bored.

After an hour of waiting Val had called, and Katie had stopped being late and started being missing. And now she was dead.

Nazia felt guilty that she hadn't cried, but the list of things to cry about had just become too long, and now didn't seem like the time to make a start. She'd prayed, though, for the first time since she'd got to this place. She hadn't seen that one coming.

Nazia guessed that Sonia would rather die than show weakness by crying, and Angie probably thought crying was too much like attention-seeking.

But Nazia would have expected Lynne to be the one to cry. Not Jenny.

Jenny had sobbed late into the night. You could hear everything in this building. The large, high-ceilinged Victorian rooms had been divided up with cheap plasterboard partitions that leaked every sigh and bedspring squeak and private phone call.

'So . . . these police officers . . .'

Nazia's eyes swivelled back to the screen, but Lynne was clearly far too nervous to pretend to be watching any more.

'I suppose they're here about Katie's death?'

Some people looked angry or surly when they were scared, but Lynne looked exactly the way you were supposed to – pretty, helpless. White-white skin, huge blue eyes, blonde hair that seemed to glow even when it was unwashed and hung limply around her face. The tension in her frame made her look even smaller and thinner than usual.

Clearly, Val's call had scared her.

You couldn't let Val wind you up too much. That was something else Nazia had quickly picked up on. Nazia quite liked Val, with her liberal swearing and strong cups of tea, and the mixture of wariness and unconditional love that she poured on to every woman who walked through the refuge door. But she definitely got too wound up about things.

'That'll be it, I expect,' Angie said. Angie never looked wound up. Her face seemed permanently stuck in a placid expression.

Nazia went back to pretending not to look at Jenny.

'Can't be dealing with this shite,' Jenny muttered. She glanced at Nazia, who immediately had the sick, flooded feeling of having been caught.

'It's all shite,' Jenny said again. 'I can't be dealing with this. I want a quiet life.'

Nazia nodded. 'Me, too,' she said. 'A quiet life sounds good.'

'Can't we watch something else?'

Now it was Lynne who spoke up again.

'Why?'

'This doesn't feel . . . appropriate.'

'What's appropriate?' Jenny said blankly.

Lynne folded her drapey cardigan across her thin body. 'Never mind.'

'What's appropriate?' Jenny said again, louder this time. 'What's appropriate, eh?'

'Let it go, Jenny,' Angie advised softly.

'Someone's *died*,' Lynne hissed.

'Not *someone*.'

Nazia knew she shouldn't have spoken. She shouldn't be combative – that was the word her dad had always used, chopping it up into its component parts – com-bat-ive. But she couldn't help it sometimes.

'Not *someone*. Katie.'

You've got to name it, Nazia. That way, it isn't in control of you any more.

I don't think that works.

Try it.

Sabbir.

Who is he?

He's my brother. My little brother.

What happened?

It was easier to say nothing, to watch the television, to sink into the fake-leather sofa and let the hot air pull you into sleep.

It was Katie who had brought Nazia into the refuge.

No. That wasn't true. Nazia had brought herself there. But Katie had been the voice on the other end of the phone who took her referral, who told her to get herself north.

To fucking *Widringham*. As if anyone knew where that was.

Meet me by the pillar box.

It was like an impending marriage. The sense of promise, the shy looks, the silent agreement to make a go of living together.

Funny, then, that this was how it had all started. A photograph presented to Nazia by her mother with a wide smile, like it was the best of birthday presents.

A sweet-faced boy. Just a suggestion, her parents had been clear. It was her choice, and always would be. But parents do know their kids so well.

She had imagined that gentle face smiling out at her every morning when she woke up, marking out the moment that she'd have to start pretending. If her parents could only find the perfect girl for her, she would have wanted those same large, bright eyes.

She'd told her mum that she wanted to think about it, and no more was said. For a while.

The young woman walking towards Nazia as she shivered on the Widringham street had a thick fringe. Brown eyes. She stretched out her hand to Nazia.

'Hi, Nazia. I'm Katie. We spoke on the phone.'

The voice was familiar. It had been the final voice in a long chain of voices on the other end of a borrowed phone, in a series of frantic calls made from the toilet of her hospital ward.

The phone had been borrowed from a nurse, who had spoken to her parents in polite Sylheti, and then, when they left, she'd shoved her phone into Nazia's hand.

'You need to get out,' the nurse had said.

'No police,' Nazia mumbled. 'No way.'

'Of course not. Not if that's not what you want. Look. Call this number. They can help you. Go on.'

For a few seconds Nazia just stayed where she was. She could go home, like her dad had said.

'He shouldn't have been so aggressive.'

Nazia's father said the words in his soft voice. He was ballooning in and out of focus with the flow of the morphine.

Aggressive. That was one of the words he used on Nazia when he was trying to get her to back down. *Don't be aggressive.*

She couldn't be angry with him for that. It was a policy that had served him well since he came to this country and it had done its best to shrug him back out. His words made her feel alone, ashamed.

'When you come home we can forget all about it,' he said.

There was no guarantee that Sabbir would ever lay a finger on her again.

But there was no guarantee that he wouldn't.

And, Nazia had realized, as she lay there with the phone in her hand, a grim smile tugging at the side of her mouth, that just wasn't fucking good enough.

So Nazia had made the call, and now here she was, and there was no point in asking herself whether she'd done the right thing.

She took Katie's hand and wanted to hang on to it. She wanted to let this girl lead her somewhere quiet, somewhere safe, somewhere she wouldn't have to start pretending from the moment before she woke up.

Katie said some stuff about Nazia's journey, and about the front door and the security of the building. Then she led her into a house and up some stairs – cream walls, a cheap carpet that was either brown or navy – and down a hall. Doors with numbers on them.

Somewhere in the house a toddler was having a tantrum.

Nazia grasped reflexively at the empty air where a suitcase ought to have been.

Katie opened a door. The room was beige. Grey. Pale blue. A swirl of indistinct colours. There was a single bed and a chest of drawers, both from Ikea. She recognized them from everywhere.

'You've got your own bathroom,' Katie said. As if to prove it, she crossed the room and pulled a cord to illuminate a small wet room with a shower head that flopped down from its fixture.

'The knob needs a bit of a jiggle to get going. You'll get the hang of it, I'm sure. Let me know if you have any problems.'

'Thanks.'

'We've got some stuff ready for you,' Katie said, gesturing down at a pile of bottles and toiletries on the bed. 'I'm guessing you've got no clothes?'

'Nothing.'

Nazia's black jeans, sweater and scarf suddenly seemed terrifyingly insubstantial, as if she might as well be naked.

'That's fine. We've got some spare packs of knickers and PJs down in the office. Come find me there when you're settled and we'll sort some out for you. And we've got vouchers for clothes. Hope you don't mind Next.'

'Great,' Nazia said.

'Do you need any more scarves? Or' – Katie looked like she might have been embarrassed, if she'd given herself the chance – 'like, a prayer mat or anything?'

Nazia shook her head.

'I don't pray,' she said.

'Oh, right. Sorry.'

'It's all right.' Nazia hadn't been trying to make any particular point with her answer. It wasn't some big renunciation, she'd just never been the praying type. But she'd said it out loud because she wanted to taste the truth on her tongue for a second, just to see what it was like.

'Okay. I'll let you get settled, then.'

Nazia didn't know what she was supposed to do to settle in. She didn't have any bags to unpack, so she just picked up the tube of toothpaste from the bed and stood there in silence, holding it in her hand.

'Nazia?'

'Yeah?'

'I . . . I just want to let you know that you're safe here.'

Nazia twisted the cuffs of her sweatshirt over her hands.

'I don't feel safe,' she said.

'We'll work on that.'

The next day Nazia had gone to the barber's with her last twenty quid in her pocket and had what was left of her hair cut off.

She'd googled the word 'lesbian' and waded through the pictures of skinny white girls with long hair kissing on beaches.

It took a few minutes for her to find what she needed. A face free of makeup, glaring out at the world. Cropped hair, like a boy's. This woman was white too, of course. You couldn't have everything.

Nazia printed out the picture from the office printer.

Katie hadn't said anything about it the next time they met. It took her a couple of weeks to say, very shyly, 'I love your haircut.'

It was the ad break, but Nazia was still staring determinedly at the screen. Small claims. Centerparcs. Mobility scooters.

Sonia and the others had drifted away. It was just Nazia and Jenny on the sofa together.

The two of them never really talked. She'd always figured that Jenny would expect her to talk with an Apu accent. Nazia, for her part, could barely manage to say hello to Jenny without imagining the street corners, the ugly men, the purr of a car slowing down. The bones like a chicken carcass, the papery skin, the spiky pubic hair.

Nazia had to say something, just to release the pressure valve.

'Are you feeling any better?'

'Better than what?' Jenny looked blank.

'You seemed upset. Last night. You were crying.'

'Wasn't crying.' Jenny's voice was too casual.

'I thought I heard . . .'

'Nah, babe. Just rattling a bit. It happens, you know.'

Nazia didn't know, but she nodded.

'If you ever want to talk about —'

'Everyone always wants to *talk*,' Jenny interrupted, rolling her eyes. It made Nazia feel dizzy. 'Talkers and cuddlers, they're the worst. We don't need that, do we, babe?'

She laughed. Then she hooked an arm around Nazia's shoulders and pulled her in for a jarring half-hug. She smelled of cigarettes and Dove. Her body was tightly still, like a frozen animal.

'Don't you worry about me,' Jenny said. 'I was rattling, like I said, but my prescription's all sorted now. Got my medication now. Doing great. You're sweet, though. Sweet of you to worry about me.'

'I thought maybe you were upset about Katie.'

Jenny seemed to desiccate slightly.

'Well, it's fucking horrible, what happens to people.'

She looked at Nazia. 'Nothing you can do, though. That's what you learn.'

'Do you think Katie killed herself?' Nazia hadn't meant to be so blunt, but it seemed like the only question worth asking.

Jenny snorted.

''Course she fucking didn't.'

'How do you know?'

Nazia knew that Jenny was only twenty-five – six years older than her – but she looked closer to a bad forty. It must be the drugs and the hard living. But she looked like she knew things. Surely she'd understand why people died.

Jenny shrugged and turned the volume too high on the TV.

'It's what they want you to think, isn't it?' she said in a low voice. 'Always a cover-up. Goes all the way up. Right the way up to the top, I reckon.'

She's paranoid. She can't help it.

But Nazia couldn't help it either.

'Why do you think that about Katie though?'

'This and that.' Jenny shifted and started to chew on her thumbnail. 'She just wasn't the type,' she said. 'You know the type when you see it. The type that kills themselves. It's obvious.'

Was it obvious? For some people, what happened with Sab-bir would have been obvious. Obvious that a brown boy would beat up his brown sister and nearly kill her.

But it wasn't obvious to Nazia.

'So what do you think did happen?'

Why is she dead?

It was the kind of conundrum Google should have an answer for.

'Someone did it. Obviously.'

Onscreen, the next murder was being set up. You could tell from the music. A naked couple were writhing over each other. Jenny grinned and leaned forward. 'He's a right dirty bastard, this one.'

6.

Then

They don't sleep together until their fifth date.

They kiss, and things like that, but then they seem to hit a wall. Every time they stop, Jamie cites a different reason. He wants to get to know her better first. Sex complicates things. She's been drinking. It leaves Katie feeling unsure. Unsure of herself, and even more unsure of whether or not she wants to see him again.

But then she goes home to where her mother lies on the sofa, staring at the TV screen as if it might save her life, and then somehow Katie finds herself surprised to realize that her body has started to long for him before her mind can catch up.

He always circles back to the same old refrain.

You don't seem like that kind of girl.

But part of her *wants* to be that kind of girl.

She realizes now that she had plenty of opportunities to be that kind of girl at uni, but instead she'd spent the first year being the kind of girl who was terrified that her mother was going to die. Then, when her mum got better, being withdrawn had become just part of her personality.

She's had flings since then, of course. Not to have at least something would have been weird, and Katie had no desire to seem weird.

She seemed to attract a certain kind of guy – the kind of guy who took her quietness as proof that she wasn't like the other girls, who liked her as a conduit for intense conversations that stretched late into the night. Sometimes those ended in sex, but the sex never felt like the point.

'It's like they think I'm broken and interesting because my dad's dead and my mum's been ill,' Katie once said to a tangential university friend in a moment of drunken clarity. 'And it's like . . . they think that if they tell me about all their problems, then that'll make them deep too.'

The friend nodded, but Katie could see that she didn't really understand. Katie felt the certainty of her pronouncement drain away and realized that she wasn't even sure if she meant what she said.

The great thing about Jamie was that she didn't feel like she needed to make any of those grand insightful statements, much less ask herself whether they were true or not. Instead, Katie and Jamie's conversations were rooted in real, concrete things. Her day or his. Everything they talked about was framed in the infrastructure of tight reality – how you got to places, how much you paid for parking once you got there. When they talked about their jobs they talked about what had actually happened, not how it made them feel or what it all meant for that nebulous smudge, the future, on which Katie had always kept her eyes firmly fixed.

Always until now, maybe.

Even her mum's chemotherapy appointments were rendered manageable when they were plotted on to the diary of their conversation, and the parking situation at the hospital had been discussed and requests for annual leave had been entered.

Katie wasn't sure exactly when it was that she decided to give a nice guy a chance. Maybe it was the fact that, when they met up, he kissed her on the cheek and asked her how her mum was, all the while making it clear that she didn't need to dwell on the answer if she didn't want to.

Maybe it was the way he pulled her chair out for her when they went out for dinner. Katie knew she should object. She was a feminist, like all her friends.

'Don't give me that independent-woman crap,' Jamie would say with a gently teasing smile when she opened her mouth. 'I can see you're exhausted. Let me take care of you.'

Then he'd ask her about her day and be satisfied with vagaries regarding train delays and being too busy to take a lunch break. Then she'd ask him about his day. Work was the only thing he ever got abstract about, so Katie pushed it, out of conversational habit.

'It makes you think,' he says one time, chewing slowly on a mouthful of spaghetti bolognese (he always orders the same thing, no matter which Italian chain they're eating in), '. . . you think a lot about morality. Like, on the news or whatever, they always tell you that you've got to feel sorry for people. You've got to try and understand them. Well, what's to fucking understand? They do the shit they do because they think they can get away with it, pure and simple.'

'But haven't loads of them had really awful childhoods?' Katie says. She feels compelled to make the case for the opposition, even though she has to admit that Jamie's first-hand experience ought to count for more than her vague middle-class guilt.

'Sure,' Jamie says, shrugging. 'But what about the kids who have awful childhoods and don't pull that kind of crap? The kids who go to school and get their GCSEs or whatever and get some job that pays the bills? What about them? Where's the sympathy for those kids?'

Katie has no answer. The old her might have tried her hand at a bit of sophistry, just to punch the conversation into an easier direction. But she has a different self now, the self that's with Jamie. So she just shrugs.

'It makes you realize that some people just have something in them, and some people don't,' Jamie continues. 'Call it decency, call it respect for the law, call it what you want. Dunno where it comes from, that's not the point. The point is that it's real, and it matters.'

Katie drinks a lot of water so that she has something to do with her mouth. Jamie never orders wine. He says it's pretentious. She finds she's never very hungry around Jamie.

Must be true love to put my daughter off her food, she can imagine her mother saying as she looks down at her still-full plate.

On that fifth date they go for a walk by the river and feed the ducks. Ducklings have hatched and follow their mother across the pond, carving a rippling fan in the sun-flecked surface of the water.

It's easy to meet him here, in a shared nostalgia for childhood.

Katie sits on Jamie's coat with her head on his shoulder. His neck is warm and smells like soap.

They don't talk much. It's good not to talk sometimes. Instead, they look at the ducks and idly comment between silences that the ducklings are cute and the sunlight is pretty.

'Quack quack,' Jamie says. He strokes her hand with his little finger and reaches into the polythene bag of bread. You're not supposed to give ducks bread, but it's nice to pretend not to know that.

Sometimes they speak to each other like this. Teasing, bantering baby talk. It puts them on a level playing field, and there they pretend to play. They pretend she's chasing him and that he's chasing her, but then he catches her around the waist and it's real. Realer than real. It's like an old film, the way they're kissing, before directors learned how to make kisses look photogenic and showed them for what they were – mutual devouring.

There's an intensity to it. A refusal to hold back.

Maybe, Katie thinks in between kisses, she can stop worrying about being one kind of girl or another. Maybe now she's just herself.

He drives her home.

'My mum might still be up,' she says.

'No, she won't,' he says. 'It'll be all right.'

And it is.

She leads him to her bedroom then goes into the bathroom to brush her teeth and take her makeup off.

When she returns to the bedroom he takes her face into his two hands, as if inspecting it for any flecks of grime.

'I love you,' he says.

She frowns a little. Takes a step back. She wants to say *no you don't, you don't know me*. But she doesn't want to hurt his feelings. Besides, maybe he knows her better than she realizes.

'Are you sure?'

'Yes,' he says.

Katie thinks about her mum sleeping across the hall. She's a light sleeper. If they talk about it too much, then they might wake her up.

'I love you too,' she says.

She knows clearly that it isn't true. She knows that more clearly than she knows most things. But it might become true later.

He smiles, his body sagging with relief, then steps close to her. He kisses her, running a hand over the curved plane between her waist and her hip. Katie imagines how her flesh must feel to him. Soft, she knows, but maybe firm, too.

She starts to take her top off, but he catches her hand and says, 'No, let me.' She feels like a gift that's being unwrapped.

He takes off her trousers next. That's a little awkward – there isn't really a sensual way to take off skinny jeans, so she ends up feeling more like a child than anything else. He stays on his knees in front of her. She sucks in her stomach, and he kisses it. She wonders how pale her body must look in the lamplight.

He's still fully dressed apart from his trainers, which he took off carefully as soon as they came through the front door.

He thanks her after he comes.

She doesn't know what to say, so she says, 'You're welcome.'

It's different, she realizes, having sex with someone who loves you – or at least claims to. You have to be there for them in a different way. You have to look them in the eye and treat their pleasure as somehow interchangeable with your own.

He goes to sleep immediately afterwards. She cradles his head in the crook of her arm and studies the lines of his closed-eye face. She thinks about how you can see the face of a child in every sleeping adult.

She can't sleep all that night, not proper sleep. She can't get comfortable, but she doesn't want to disturb him by thrashing about. Her arm cramps under the weight of his head.

As the sky starts to turn a cool blue, that freshness of vision which sleep deprivation sometimes brings descends over her eyes. She decides that she's going to make a go of it with Jamie.

7.

Now

The room they entered was so small Whitworth felt like he needed to tuck his knees under his chin, just so that there would be enough space for the two of them to sit down.

There was a poster on the wall. *Are you afraid of your partner?* A black-and-white photo of a woman slumped in a darkened room, one hand covering her face. There was a menacing shadow thrown on to the wall beside her. One of its hands was raised.

Val Redwood sat like a man, her shanks jutting out at sharp angles from the slacks-clad bulge of her belly. In the fluorescent light Whitworth could see a greasy sheen to her black hair. Her red lipstick emphasized the steep downward curve of her mouth. Whitworth wondered what kind of woman would paint on a blood-red mouth so soon after her colleague had been found dead.

He pulled out his notebook and felt around for a pen. With a deliberate motion, Val Redwood pulled a ballpoint out of her cardigan pocket and offered it to him.

'Er. Thanks.'

He clicked it into life. 'Okay, Valerie. Just the usual sorts of questions here. Apologies if you've already answered any of these.'

'No apology required for doing your job, Detective.'

Whitworth blinked.

'Okay. Good, then. So.'

He propelled himself into the usual routine. 'Could you tell me what time Katie left this address on the ninth of February?'

'Early,' Val said.

'How early?'

'Four o'clock, maybe?' Val shuffled slightly in her seat, like a bird settling into its own feathers.

'How come?'

'She had to go offsite for a work commitment. There was a community engagement event taking place in the church hall.'

She looked at him beadily. 'In fact, I believe it was organized by your office.'

That caught Whitworth off guard, though he did his best not to show it.

He *had* been there that night. Their team had drawn the short straw of outlining the new policing strategy to the Widringham community – which, in practice, referred to a load of hawkish old women. But he hadn't recognized Katie's face when he saw her on the slab. She must have had one of those demeanours that willed itself to be forgotten.

'And you spoke to her before she left, did you?' Whitworth continued. 'Could you describe her behaviour? Anything unusual? Any clues as to her state of mind?'

Val's lips were working furiously against each other, thinning out into nothing then reappearing.

'I was working offsite that day.'

'Offsite too? Where?'

'It was . . . ah . . . publicity work. I was being interviewed about the work of Widringham Women's Aid on local radio.'

'So you were being interviewed while Katie was working?'

'I was working too.'

'Mrs Redwood,' Whitworth said, enunciating clearly. 'I think you know what I'm trying to ask you here. Could you please tell me, unambiguously, whether you did or did not see Katie on either the day or the evening that she went missing?'

Val Redwood was gripping her elbows tightly, as if to hold herself in. Then she inclined her head in a stately movement. The word 'no' was barely audible.

'No, you didn't?'

'No, I didn't.' Her face seemed to slip a bit. 'I spoke to her on the phone in the morning, but no. I didn't see her. Not at all. I'm not proud to say so.'

Whitworth let her words hang for a moment. He knew what he was going to have to say next and couldn't imagine it would go down well.

'Did the ladies – ah, the residents? – here – did any of them see Katie?'

'Yes,' Val said. 'They had a group session with her that day, I believe.'

'In that case,' Whitworth said firmly, 'they're all key witnesses. We're going to need to question everyone.'

Val looked at him as if he'd just proposed to begin the investigation by interpreting the spatter pattern of his own piss.

'I can't possibly allow that,' she said. Her nostrils flared as she drew in her breath sharply. 'It'll re-traumatize them. There's a duty of care.'

'I'm sure they can cope, Valerie.'

'I'm sure they can,' Val snapped back. 'Some of the women here have *coped* with years of abuse. Decades, in fact. The question is not whether they can cope, but whether they should be *asked* to cope. It's not fair on them. This is a delicate, delicate atmosphere.'

'And this is a police investigation into the death of a young woman. Katie's dead. That's not exactly fair either.'

'No, it's not,' Val responded. 'And it's not fair that threats to her safety were not treated with due seriousness when she was alive.'

So she was back on the internet troll again. Jesus Christ.

'Detective Constable Brookes is looking into that as we speak,' Whitworth said, in what he sincerely hoped was a soothing voice. 'We'll get to the bottom of it, one way or another. But in the meantime I'd really appreciate your full cooperation.'

Val Redwood was looking at him very intently, her eyes like black marbles. She held the silence for a long time. Then she spoke, but not in reply to what he'd just said.

'Is this a murder investigation, Detective Whitworth?'

Her tone was bracing, as if she were asking whether she needed a cagoule for the weather outside. Whitworth opened his mouth, then shut it again. He didn't want to revert to the uncomfortable silence, but he hadn't been expecting to have to field this question head on. He was about to mumble something about exploring all lines of inquiry. One of those non-answers he hated.

But before he could fill the air with any unhelpful reassurances, his phone buzzed. Normally, he would have immediately switched it to silent, but glancing down gave him an excuse to stop looking at Val Redwood, so he did.

Urgent. Update on Katie Straw. Call me. M.

'Sorry, got to take this,' he said mildly. 'Mind if I step out?'

Val Redwood sighed, as if this request confirmed the utmost disdain she held him in.

'Why not?' she said rhetorically.

Whitworth nodded and smiled, pretending courtesy, before leaving. He could hear the stillness in the little key work room. No doubt Val Redwood didn't want him moving any further away than absolutely necessary.

'What's the matter now?' he said without ceremony when Melissa picked up.

'It's Katie Straw, Sarge.' Melissa seemed to be in a hurry to get her words out. 'I'm afraid we can't find her.'

8.

Lynne watched her daughter Peony wipe a trail of green snot off her nose with her fist then return to the plastic seesaw in the middle of the refuge's playroom.

They'd had to leave all her nice toys behind – bright, good-quality books, soft animals made from natural fibres, a delicate marionette that Peony was allowed to look at but not touch. Those were all still at home.

'She'll get used to it here,' Katie had said. 'Kids are incredibly adaptable.'

Too adaptable.

'The best thing for Peony is to have a healthy, happy mum.'

Lynne knew she was a fraud, being in the refuge. She could feel the other women looking at her, judging her, could hear her own breathy accent grating like an out-of-tune flute in an orchestra. They all knew, she was sure, that Frank hadn't hit her, not really. Not like they'd been hit.

'He was *physical*,' she'd tried to explain to Katie the day she arrived at the refuge. 'But that's just the sort of man he is.'

A marathon runner, a weekend rugby player. Not sensual, exactly, but always giving the impression that he enjoyed her immensely. And of course that intensity had to come with its opposite. There was always something profoundly physical in his anger.

Lynne believed that everyone's good qualities were the flip side of their bad qualities. Anger was the darker twin of passion; paranoia the double of protectiveness.

One of her therapists had told her that – she couldn't remember which.

The only time he'd ever so much as bruised her was when she was pregnant with Peony. He'd seen her drinking a glass of white wine through the kitchen window (she'd kept the bottle hidden, knowing that she was in the wrong with a baby on the way) and followed her into the bedroom and held her down by the wrists.

She apologized, and the truth was he was right. It *was* bad for the baby, and she'd done it anyway. She had always been selfish.

He forgave her and she cried, and they made love and then went to sleep. The next morning, the bruises on her wrists were stark. More crying – *look what you made me do.*

Then more forgiveness. More sex. More sleep.

There was a cold going around the refuge – Sonia's two had been sniffling all week – and Lynne was convinced that Peony had picked it up from that playroom. She could feel her very skin itching just from sitting there. Lynne imagined the cheap plastic of the toys leaching into and staining Peony's little hands. As her daughter's small pink tongue traced any remainder of mucus from her upper lip, Lynne felt her thoughts slipping along the path to disaster, a path worn smooth by frequent traversing.

She saw Peony coughing wetly, her cold turning into a chest infection that her delicate organs, like little buds, wouldn't be able to shift.

She saw herself in the children's wing of the local hospital, her baby's lungs wracked with pneumonia.

She saw a miniature coffin. One of those gravestones shaped like a teddy bear.

She saw Frank. Such a handsome man. He wouldn't cry

at the funeral; he never cried, except when he was asking forgiveness.

You killed our daughter.

Then –

I forgive you, darling. I'll always forgive you.

She knew she ought to be down on the floor. Ought to be talking to Peony. Ought to be making eye contact, building vocabulary, fine-motor skills. But she was so tired.

Lynne didn't sleep here. She had learned to sleep well when she had been with Frank, and now there was only one way she could sleep – pressed against the solidness of him, his head resting on her neck, her heart pounding so hard it felt as if it wanted to burrow right out of her body and into his.

So instead she sat on the sofa, watching, nursing the cold feeling behind her breastbone.

'I think he's found me,' Lynne had said softly, looking out over the water. It had been two days before Katie's death. They always walked to the bridge together when they had a session.

'I don't know if . . .' Lynne had gestured outdoors on the first day she'd had something called a 'key work meeting' with Katie. 'I'd like Peony to have some fresh air. While it's not raining.'

It had been Katie's suggestion to go to the bridge. It had become a ritual of theirs. An odd ritual to have, since Lynne had come to the refuge at the beginning of November, and there had been scarcely a day of decent weather the whole time she'd been there. But it became the one part of their week where she was guaranteed to go outdoors, and to walk, with Katie, cups of tea in their hands and Peony toddling between them, to the bridge and back.

Lynne generally didn't feel safe going outside – she'd never told Katie, but she felt that perhaps the girl understood none-theless.

But that day was different. Normally the mere presence of a person whose job it was to understand her made her feel a little less like the old cottages of Widringham were going to fall down on her. Or else that she would cut all ties with everything and float off into the blue sky. That was why she liked going to the bridge with Katie. She wanted to see the view, to watch the bold sweep of the swift river, but she didn't want to be there alone or, worse still, there with just Peony.

That would be too dangerous.

That day, the edges of the world felt fuzzy.

'I think I saw a man,' she said to Katie quietly. She expected Katie to dismiss it the way she wanted it to be dismissed, but instead Katie looked up sharply.

'What man?' she said. Lynne felt that perhaps it was her turn to do the reassuring.

The word 'man' was loaded in the refuge, because men never passed the threshold. The dishwasher needed fixing, but the idea of 'getting a man' in to do it never crossed anyone's lips. Instead they reverted to the passive voice. It needed to be fixed. Consequently, it never was. The postman never came to the door – everything was sent to a PO box in the next village, but everyone would hold their breath if they heard a flyer coming through the letter box. Val treated the man who came to read the gas meter like a prisoner of war.

'What man?' Katie said again. Then her voice changed slightly, although Lynne couldn't have said exactly how.

'Do you think you saw Frank, Lynne?'

'I'm always seeing Frank,' Lynne said. 'I just . . . it probably wasn't him. He was too short, I think. Or too tall. Too slim, maybe. Definitely younger. I think his hair was different. But he was looking at the refuge. From a car. He was sitting down. I couldn't see much of him. But he was just . . .'

'Was it Frank's car?'

'No.' *You're hysterical, Lynne.* 'No, it wasn't.'

Frank wouldn't have been caught dead in such a small car.

'I suppose . . . I suppose I thought he might have hired it or . . .' *Or I'm a fucking fantasist.*

'Was there anything specific that you noticed about him?'

'No. Just a man. Looking at the refuge. I couldn't see his face.'

'You think Frank's found you? He's following you?'

Lynne could believe that of Frank.

He was persistent – that was what had been so charming about him at first. She didn't remember the first time he'd asked her to go for a drink. He'd been so much older than her, so much her senior in the organization. She'd probably shaken her head automatically and more or less run away.

Managing professional relationships. She'd never been much good at that sort of thing.

It had become a little joke of theirs – or his – she wasn't sure. A Post-it note on a file – *Let me take you out.* Flirty emails. An aside in a presentation about Lynne's gorgeous legs or killer smile.

Then, one day in the lift, he'd said, 'All right, Lynne, you've had your fun, but the joke's over.'

He'd kissed her, roughly, pressing her against the wall.

She had been able to feel her pounding heart in every cell, felt the cracking chasm in her chest. Sweat pooled in the underwiring of her bra and the backs of her knees.

They went for drinks. He ordered for her. It was exciting – or, at least, that was what the thrum of her heart seemed to suggest. By the time he led her from the bar and across the street to a hotel – the hotel room somehow already booked and paid for – she knew what was going to happen, even if she didn't remember deciding that it was what she wanted.

In retrospect, she wasn't sure why they went to the hotel. It wasn't as if Frank had a wife. In the months that followed they had sex in the toilets, in the locked photocopier room. Frank's office. He'd never been a boyfriend. He went from boss to lover to husband and she couldn't exactly say how the transitions took place.

She couldn't recall when it was that they agreed she'd leave her job either, yet the resignation letter had materialized on Frank's desk. She didn't really remember writing it, but it hardly mattered. It was a joint decision.

He told her he accepted her resignation, and then kissed her hard.

Katie was still looking at her intently. Was there anything stranger than the idea that someone was being paid to listen to her? That she could take her time, without having to dash into the nearest possible excuse?

Lynne realized that she hadn't answered the question. *Did* she think Frank had found her? It was hard to know what she thought. She wasn't in the habit of asking herself.

'Not Frank. Not exactly. Frank would make more of a fuss. But I'm sure I saw this car. I'm sure I saw *something*.'

There were whispers. Maybe Lynne had been the first to say something – maybe she'd been the one to mention the side gate to Val – she wasn't actually sure. But now the fear lived independently of any one of them, sliding along the corridors and prickling at the backs of their necks. Nobody ever put everything together and said it out loud, but there had been little nods, little tightenings. They cut through Val's bulldozer utterances about something called 'safeguarding'.

The side gate had been found unlocked and a little ajar one morning. Nobody admitted to having used it the previous day. In a normal home, that would have just been one of those funny things, but a refuge isn't the same as a home.

'I'm sure it was nothing, but I'll mention it to Val anyway. She can decide whether it's worth flagging to the police or if we'll just keep a close eye on it.'

Katie reached out and squeezed Lynne's hand.

'I don't think he's found you, Lynne.'

'He doesn't need to find me,' Lynne replied.

Katie didn't say anything. Lynne sighed.

'He does love me a lot, you see.'

'Control can feel like love,' Katie said.

'I don't know if I ever understood the difference.'

'I think . . . I think we're taught that there isn't a difference. Especially . . .' Katie gave an apologetic little smile. 'Maybe . . . especially as women.'

Lynne felt something inside her pucker. She wasn't the drum-banging type.

'It's the nature-versus-nurture thing, isn't it?' she said lightly. She wasn't keen to come down on the side of either.

Katie fiddled with the zip on the cuff of her coat, pulling it back and forth with a rhythmic *click click click*.

'Maybe,' she said.

Lynne didn't dare lean on the bridge itself. It would be straying too close to the edge of something unnameable.

The two of them watched as Peony flung twigs on to the frozen surface from the edge of the bridge then dashed to the other side. She kept doing it for a long time, always seeming to expect the next attempt to turn out differently.

It was too cold in the garden and too warm in the house. The air had that kind of density that festered colds, dried out faces and lips, sent volleys of static across the surfaces of cheap fabrics. The sliding doors into the garden always gave a gentle sort of scream as they moved along their runners.

'Didn't know you smoked, Lynne.'

Lynne glanced down at the cigarette between her fingers, its thin line of smoke rising away from her then flickering into nothing.

'I don't,' she said, glancing quickly at Sonia then averting her eyes just as quickly. It was true. She didn't *identify* as a smoker, not exactly. She had once, when it had seemed to fit the image of who she was trying to be. She had started as a way of ingratiating herself with her boss during those brief breaks, shivering on the concrete planes of the City. She'd stopped when Frank told her that he hated the smell of it on her.

So she didn't smoke. But she was having a cigarette now. She admitted that.

Her lips were so chapped they burned as she puckered them around the damp shaft of the cigarette. Her foot started tapping of its own accord, skidding off the wet paving stones.

'I don't either,' Sonia said. She raised an expectant eyebrow at the packet in Lynne's hand and took a cigarette, without smiling. 'Not since the boys.'

'You don't want them to see you.'

'No. Though with some of the stuff they've seen, it can hardly do any more harm.' Sonia laughed, then coughed. 'Oof. I've gone all soft. Lungs can't take it.'

'How're you?' Lynne had largely given up asking people here how they were, assuming that they didn't want to answer the question any more than she did. But tonight it came automatically, to fill the space between them.

Sonia shrugged.

'Got my court date coming up. With *him*.'

'I'm sure they'll . . . that he'll get what's coming.'

Sonia frowned. 'What?'

'That he'll be . . . you know, punished.'

Sonia blew out a cloud of smoke. 'It's a custody hearing. Family court.'

'Oh.'

'I'm not putting my boys' dad in prison.'

'Of course not.'

'They don't need that.'

'No.'

Lynne put the cigarette back between her lips, forcing her to unclench her jaw.

'Well, in that case. It'll be fine. Val will give you the right advice.'

Sonia tapped her ash. 'Val's a joke.'

Lynne didn't say anything.

'I mean, don't get me wrong. Her heart's in the right place. But with all this stuff going on with Katie? Police crawling all over? People are too busy covering their own arses at times like these. You can forget about getting any help out of Val, I reckon. I have.'

Sonia flicked her ash.

'She does her best,' Lynne said.

'I know that. But she doesn't really get it. It's all just an idea to Val. It's a shame about Katie.'

The words were said casually, but one amplified itself. *Shame. Shame. Shame.*

'I can't believe . . . I can't believe she killed herself.'

Lynne wasn't sure what she meant by that. That she didn't believe that Katie had killed herself, or that she did?

'I can,' Sonia said quietly. 'I can see why someone would do that. It's different when you've got kids. You just can't let yourself even think about it.'

'Yes,' Lynne said. She wasn't sure that she understood exactly what Sonia meant, but the word 'shame' was still lying limply between them on the wet patio.

'She got it, Katie did,' Sonia said. She stubbed out her cigarette and stood up. 'Don't know what it is – *was* – about her, but she got it. That the hitting isn't the worst part.'

Lynne nodded. Sonia kept looking at her. For just a second too long. The heat from the tip of her cigarette was starting to nip at Lynne's fingers.

'Too fucking cold up north,' Sonia said. The f-word seemed to crack out of nowhere, and Lynne winced automatically then recovered herself quickly enough to give a little knowing smile, a nod. Sonia patted Lynne on the arm.

Lynne knew not to flinch, but she wasn't used to being touched so cavalierly. In her mind, no one touched her but Frank. Certainly no man, and women weren't necessarily any safer. The nature of the touch mattered less than the fact of it.

'I've never got used to it,' she said. 'We moved up – oh, just before Peony was born. It seemed like a better place than London to raise a child. Cleaner air. You know.'

9.

Then

Those evenings and weekends with Jamie give Katie a sense of shape to her week, something to think about while she stands packed on to the commuter trains, someone to call in her lunch break as she hovers on the comfortless, swarming street outside her office in the City. Nobody wants to be single in London. Friends live too far away to fill any void; the cattle effect of the daily train, two hours round, makes her ache to have her personhood caressed.

The first time he calls her 'my girlfriend' she feels like she's being lassoed, drawn into his side so that his arm can encircle her waist. But there's no denying that she acts like his girlfriend and does the things that a girlfriend would do, so it becomes true.

He starts to buy her jewellery. Blue topaz. White gold. A silver pendant shaped like a leaf. That's for their one-month anniversary – the month after their fifth date.

He buys things for her birthday, for their two-month anniversary, for 'just because'. She gets the impression he thinks less about whether she'll like the gifts than how they'll look on her, but that feels like a silly distinction to make out loud. Nobody has ever bought her jewellery before.

Him meeting her friends turns into a bit of a fuss.

He's very keen to meet them properly – he says that being in the same club doesn't count, and she can't really argue with that. He wants to meet them as soon as possible.

'They're important to you, so I want them to see that you're important to me,' he says.

So she invites him to their next set of girls' drinks. It isn't such a controversial move – there's often one boyfriend or another tagging along these days. The evenings have become more like a homage to the times they used to have together in that pub than the real thing – the wine-smoothed, blissfully easy conversations of the sixth form.

So she doesn't really mind that Jamie insists.

Before they leave for the pub he spends what feels like hours deciding where they are going to park. Katie figures it's a manifestation of his nerves. She's a little nervous herself, actually.

'We could get the bus, you know. Then you could have a drink.'

'I don't need to have a drink.'

'Right.'

He isn't really a big drinker. That's on the roster of things she likes about him. She'd never had sex sober before she met him.

'We don't need to rush to get there,' she tells him. He's driving on the edges of the speed limit. They're in his car – a small but determined turquoise Vauxhall Corsa he seems to see as an extension of his own body. It jerks at every traffic light and seems to be trailing the car ahead a little too closely. But Jamie's a good driver, and Katie has never even had a lesson, so it isn't really for her to say.

When Jamie sees the cost of the car park he swears under his breath. Katie can't help but smile at him. It's just a teasing smile, but he frowns.

'What're you laughing about?'

'Nothing.'

He holds her hand firmly on the walk between the car park and the pub, grasping it in a way that feels both more and less than affectionate. She leads him towards an empty table in the beer garden and sits down, moving over on the bench so that he can sit beside her. But he remains standing.

'Four glasses, right?'

She blinks. 'Right.'

He returns from inside a few minutes later, with a pint of Coke in one hand and the tangled stems of four wine glasses in the other, a bottle of white clutched to his side in a cooler. Katie glances at it. It isn't their usual house white.

'You didn't have to get the expensive one,' she says.

'I wanted to make a good impression.' He smiles and pulls her close, his kiss warming her forehead. She lingers for a moment, crushed into him. Then she sits up, wraps her scarf again around her neck and nestles into it, scanning the entrance to the beer garden. Jamie cuddles her to him, feeling her shiver.

'Why're we sitting outside? You're cold.'

'Some of the girls smoke.'

'So?'

'We always sit outside. Even in the winter.'

They have been waiting for the best part of half an hour. The wine bottle still sits unopened in the cooler, the glaze of condensation gradually dissipating from its surface. Jamie stares determinedly at the dancing surface of his Coke without taking a sip. Katie glances at her phone occasionally as the messages begin to trickle in on the WhatsApp group.

Be there in fifteen minutes.

Sorry, bus problems, see you in twenty!

OMG haha so sorry I just woke up from a snooze but will be there ASAP KATIE I CAN'T WAIT TO MEET THE NEW BOY

'They'll all be here soon,' Katie says.

'How soon?'

'Five minutes.'

When they do arrive, one by one – Ellie, Lucy, Lara – the noise in the beer garden seems to amplify tenfold. There's the usual exaggerated kissing, the eager compliments, the tight hugs that hark back to their schooldays, when they were each others' main source of physical contact.

'Jamie got a round in,' Katie says, gesturing towards the wine bottle in the middle of the table. Lara turns around to where Jamie is sitting. He stands up and she sweeps forward to kiss him on either cheek. Katie sees a slight frown crossing his face.

'That's *so* lovely of you,' she says. 'I'm actually in more of a red mood right now, so I'm just going to pop in to the bar. But we'll definitely drink yours later. *Thank you.*'

Though Lara is nominally straight, she always seems to have more girls on the back burner than Katie has ever had boys. She's currently shooting the occasional winning smile at Jamie as she recounts her current knotty involvement with both halves of a married couple. Nothing's happened. Not yet. Katie knows it's a matter of time. Lara's boyfriend doesn't know.

'So the thing that I'm trying to figure out for myself is – is it still cheating, even if it's with a girl?'

The others suck on their cigarettes and look contemplative, but Jamie jumps in immediately.

'Yes.'

There's something in the quality of his *yes* that seems to cut through the smooth, blurry mood. Katie begins to shiver and Lara glances over at her.

'You cold, babe?'

Jamie's head snaps round to look at Katie, and within a few seconds his jacket is off and wrapped around her shoulders. It has something of that swaggering-teenage-boy smell, with the too-strong deodorant. But it's warm from his body.

'Yes,' he says again, pulling the zip of his hooded sweatshirt to under his chin. 'Yes, of course it's still cheating.'

'Why?' Lara's face is lit up with a half-smile, her eyes film noir. '*Why*, though?'

Jamie shrugs. 'Why not?'

He seems to retreat from Lara's gaze and instead turns to look at Katie. 'I can't explain it,' he says. There's something slightly panicked in his face, something appealing that makes Katie feel like she needs to defend him.

'I can't explain why I think it, it's just what I think. I think it's just as bad. If anything, as a guy, I think it's probably worse.'

He angles slightly back towards Lara, but without really meeting her eyes. 'You know, you've got your morals, I've got mine, that's cool. But I reckon that if you actually asked your boyfriend how he felt, he'd probably say the same thing.'

Lara's current boyfriend – she always has one – is a floppy PhD student who always seems far more interested in discussing the semiotics of sex than in actually having it. He says he thinks the distinction between the intellect and the libido is arbitrary. Lara has said in the past that he watches a lot of porn.

'He's not so big on monogamy,' Lara says, gesturing the idea away with a flick of her cigarette. 'You know. In theoretical terms.'

'Okay.' Jamie shrugs. 'I guess it's cool, then.'

Lara keeps looking at him for a second, as if she's expecting him to say something more. Her forehead creases into a picturesque frown. But then she shrugs and stubs her cigarette out, turning her head to look at Katie.

'Come to the bar with me, lovely?'

Katie glances at the bottle of wine in the cooler and realizes that it's empty, though she has only had one glass herself. She doesn't like to drink too much around Jamie. The others have poured themselves half a glass here, a drop there, and now Jamie's offering is gone.

Katie drains the last mouthful of her own and makes to stand up, but Jamie cuts her off.

'I think it's probably time for us to shoot off, actually,' he says.

He reaches over and takes Katie's hand, scratching the back of it lightly with his short fingernails.

'Oh.' Katie leaves her grip slack. 'Maybe we could just stay for one more?'

Jamie glances around them, as if slightly embarrassed, and then leans forward, saying at only a slightly quieter volume, 'We need to get back to your mum, Katie.'

'Mum's okay,' Katie starts to say, but the sympathetic looks have already started and Ellie has risen to her feet to squeeze her in a tight hug. Lara stands up, too, and walks around the bench, her heels asserting themselves against the concrete in a sharp *tock tock tock*. She hugs Katie, enveloping her in a cloud of Chanel No. 5.

'*So* lovely to meet you,' she says over Katie's shoulder to Jamie.

Then she kisses Katie once on each cheek and then, very lightly, on the tip of her nose, her breath leaving a wine-scented trail.

'Oh, you are just looking gorgeous. *Glowing*. It's so good to see you.'

Katie's used to Lara. She knows that her friend is just in the habit of seduction and that whenever there are no strangers around to catch in her tractor beam she'll always let it fall on her friends.

Jamie has stood up sharply, and there's something different about him. He's become a wall of silence. He accepts the array of hugs and kisses and the two of them walk away from the beer garden and through the passage, back on to the main pedestrianized street. Katie pushes the cuff of his jacket on to her wrist and makes to take his hand, but it's rigid and does not return her grasp.

She says nothing.

It's only once they're back in his car that she allows herself a little sigh. She isn't sure whether she meant him to hear it or not, but by the way his head snaps around she feels she must have sounded a klaxon.

'What?' he says.

'Nothing.'

'I don't know what you're blaming me for,' he says as he swings the car out of the multistorey and on to the main street. There isn't much by way of traffic and he starts to pick up speed, though you couldn't exactly call it speeding.

'I'm not blaming you. Blaming you for what?'

'That.' He drags his eyes backwards towards the town centre via the rear-view mirror. 'All that talk about . . . what she gets up to.'

'What about it?'

'It made me uncomfortable.'

'But that's just Lara,' Katie says. 'She takes a bit of getting used to.'

'Don't really want to get used to that. She's a slut.'

The word stings, but Katie lets it sink in for a moment. She waits too long before replying quietly, 'Don't say that about her.'

'Why not? I'm not calling her a bad person. But you can't deny that her behaviour's really slutty. You can't blame me for calling it how I see it.'

'Maybe that says more about you than it does about her,' Katie mutters.

For half a second she thinks about telling him to stop the car, that she can get out and walk home. She doesn't know what implications that would even have, but it feels like the right thing to do right now.

But then she's thrown forward, her seat belt cutting into her bare neck and shoulders.

Jamie has slammed the brakes on and stopped dead in the middle of the road. He's looking at her with statue eyes.

She stays very still. There's a fear in her. A fear that is as old as she is, familiar as breathing, that fills her ears in the silence the engine has left.

'What was that?' he says. His tone is perfectly mild. His hands are clenched on the steering wheel. In the harshness of the light from the street lamp Katie can hardly see anything but those white knuckles.

'Get out of the middle of the road, Jamie,' she says softly.

'What was that?' he says again. Nothing of him moves. Even his voice seems disembodied.

'Nothing. Sorry.'

The *sorry* is automatic. Almost like a tic. The structure of him seems to ease at the sound. The fear slackens. There's a rush of something like euphoria. She's a child again, even though now she's in the front seat.

'We'll say no more about it, then,' he says. They drive on.

IO.

Now

Brookes drove the two of them back to the station.

He wasn't the chatty type and, if Whitworth were honest, that was probably one of the main reasons he'd warmed to the boy. Melissa always seemed to be dissecting things out loud, and Whitworth found that irritating. He needed chunks of quiet in his day so that he could switch off his conscious mind and let the facts of the case stew together.

The car eased out of the posh part of town and through the terraced streets where Whitworth had grown up and raised his family.

Whitworth fancied himself a bit of a local historian; he admitted it. His knowledge had been sharpened by his time as a beat copper, when directing tourists had turned into chats about topography and architecture. People had those sorts of conversations with policemen back then.

He knew every single inch of this little town. Yet there were some days – days like this – when it could still leave him at a loss. Like when a girl turned up dead and she seemed not to truly exist.

Soon it would be his sixtieth birthday, which would mark the end of thirty years of service in the police force. Then – no more crime, no more suicides, no more of the murky areas in between. Instead, he would spend his days doing walking tours for tourists. Just for tips. For the pleasure of it.

Now that the rain had passed over, the day was cold and

bright. Police work felt like such a waste. Whitworth had long ago stopped believing that there was any point in trying to exorcize evil and exact justice. Better to just get on with your own life, taking the good with the bad.

And there was bad in this town, of course. Drugs, and crime, and ruined lives. But they were mostly confined to a group of seventies concrete blocks on the other side of the valley and so lay out of sight and mind. They didn't detract from the charming impression that a first glance of the place always invoked in visitors. They came by train, on the graceful set of grey arches which had been built by the Victorians in a more hopeful time.

The river, which cut its way through Widringham at a bold angle, was bisected by a medieval-era bridge on three low, humped arches. That view – the view of the place where Katie Straw had gone to her death – was the mainstay of the postcards and the shortbread tins. It was Widringham keeping up appearances and, for the most part, it worked. The town was starting to get glowing write-ups in the magazine supplements of Sunday papers. Some preening bloke who Whitworth distantly remembered from his schooldays had become a celebrity chef and had returned to the town to open up a boutique hotel.

That was supposed to mean, everyone knew, that they were on the rise. But on days like this it was difficult to believe that anywhere *really* changed.

The first time Whitworth had been sent to a domestic-violence case, he had been new on the job and a bit of an idealist.

The woman, who had called the police herself, had been tiny, maybe four foot eleven. Irish, like Whitworth's mother. One of those who'd started out in Liverpool and washed up in Widringham with a bloke who'd seemed like a good bet at the time but had proven otherwise.

She'd been torn to shreds, that little scrap of a woman, with her braying voice. Her flowered dress had been spattered with blood.

Moved to fury, Whitworth had punched the husband square in the face. He had been a bigger man in those days and, generally speaking, the police had been able to get away with a little bit more. The husband splayed on the floor. Whitworth stood over him. Really angry. Fit to kill.

But then he'd felt a faint, ineffective pummelling in the region of his kidneys. He turned to find the little wife, her face made ugly by the stretch of swelling, in an ecstasy of rage.

'How feckin' dare you? Don't you lay a bloody finger on my husband!'

How feckin' dare you?

It was then that Whitworth had learned never to guess at what was going on in other people's relationships. That the words 'my husband' held some kind of unaccountable magic. That you couldn't just blunder into people's lives and assume you had the measure of them.

He had seen that same man sobbing on his knees, his arms around his wife's waist, while she patted him on the head distractedly, as if she were soothing a small child.

How did women like Val Redwood account for *that*?

A couple of years ago they'd had domestic-violence training at the station. Whitworth had managed to beg off most of it, citing his heavy workload, but he'd still had to sit through a tedious, ancient video. A couple of drama students affecting the working-class accents of some unspecified region. Men chucking plates about. Women weeping and cowering.

Whitworth couldn't think of a single woman in his life who would ever cower like that. Some women allowed themselves to be dominated, maybe. But some didn't. And those that didn't . . . oh, they could wear you down.

Or maybe that was just what marriage was.

'Hold on a sec . . .' Whitworth raised his hand to get Brookes's attention. 'Pull over here, would you?'

The car was about to cross the bridge. *That* bridge.

The forensics team had already swept the area, but they hadn't found anything of interest. A few fibres that appeared to match the victim's trousers, but there were plenty of people in Widringham who wore Primark jeans. The bridge probably had hundreds – even thousands – of fibres and skin cells in the crevices of its grey-black stone. Yes, Katie might have stood there recently. But so what?

Whitworth got out of the car and stood, listening to the white noise of the water.

According to the pathologist's report, the freshly thawed river had been just two degrees Celsius at night. It always had a vicious quality at that time of year, barging its way down the valley.

Of course, you could never assume, but Whitworth thought it was safe to rule out the possibility that Katie – if that really was her name – had just fancied a late-night swim.

Could she have fallen in?

Sure, if she had been completely reckless, and had no sense of balance to boot. But he couldn't imagine that this girl – this sad, reserved girl, whose own boyfriend seemed to have barely known her – had been dancing along the top of a bridge late on a February night.

Her body had been carried along by the current for well over a mile. Out of town. It had probably taken her no more than thirty seconds to actually die once she had entered the icy water. She would likely have been paralysed by the shock of the cold, that shock giving way to euphoria, and the euphoria to nothing at all, then carried along by the early-spring rush.

76

Whitworth walked over to the bridge wall and pressed its height into his body, leaning forward as far as he dared. It didn't come up even to his hips. For Katie Straw, it would have been around waist-height.

He hinged forward, looking down into the water. It appeared harmless, even inviting, churned into a feather-soft foam which glazed the jagged edges of the dark rocks. You'd never know, just from looking at it, how cold it was. That its clarity concealed a chilly bite; that it could extinguish a human life in half a minute.

Drowning was an unpopular method of suicide, Whitworth knew that. It was too imprecise for most people. Too hard to commit to.

The pathologist had found a quantity of mud underneath Katie's fingernails. His best guess was that she had clawed at the riverbank as she was dragged along by the current. But that didn't necessarily mean she hadn't wanted to die. Maybe the desperate grasping was just the reflex of a dying animal.

Whitworth got back into the car, and Brookes drove on.

As soon as they arrived back at the station, Melissa dashed towards them, awkwardly pulling down a skirt that was just that little bit too tight. Her face was red and her hair was already escaping from its ponytail.

'Where's the fire?' Whitworth joked, but Melissa didn't laugh.

'This is what I've been able to gather on Katie Straw. Or rather, the victim. I don't know . . . Obviously, we don't know what her real name is.'

Whitworth took the papers she was thrusting at him. Scanning them, he saw that Melissa was right. It seemed that, to all intents and purposes, Katie Straw didn't exist.

She had cropped up in Widringham two years ago, working

in some caf and volunteering at a care home for the elderly for six months. After that she'd started her employment at Widringham Women's Aid.

'What about her house?' Whitworth probed, frowning. 'Passport? Birth certificate? Bank statements? Surely there must have been something?'

'Nothing.' Melissa shrugged. 'It's crazy.'

It is bloody crazy, Whitworth thought grimly. *I can certainly foresee a crazy amount of faffing around with computer databases instead of working to find out what actually happened.*

He dreaded the thought of talking to DI Khan about it before they had all their ducks in a row. But, he supposed, at least he had the joy of delegation to fall back on. Let Brookes deal with it. Young people found this sort of thing much easier, anyway.

He poured hot water over his instant-coffee granules and, without bothering to stir it, carried his mug over to Brookes's desk.

'There's your open-and-shut suicide case,' he said, dropping the pile of papers on to Brookes's desk. Brookes grinned, eyeing Whitworth's mug.

'That for me? Sweet of you.'

'Fat chance. Find this girl and I'll consider making you a tea. Only consider, mind.'

'What do you mean, *find* her?'

'She's got no . . .' Whitworth found himself struggling to explain the extent of the absence. It wasn't just that Katie Straw had no paperwork, no back story. It was that she seemed to have achieved something that was supposed to be so impossible in this day and age. True anonymity.

'. . . She's got no . . . no footprint in the world.'

Brookes picked up the papers, scanning them, and whistled.

'She's not even on Facebook.' He looked up at Whitworth. *'Everyone's* on Facebook.'

Whitworth snorted. 'We've got no legal record of her on any database in the country, but never mind that. She's not on bloody *Facebook*.'

'What can I say? The robots are taking over.'

'Speaking of tech and all that,' Whitworth continued abruptly, Val Redwood's face jumping unbidden into his mind, 'for God's sake get one of the computer geeks to work out where all those nasty messages are coming from. I want that woman off my back.'

'Aye aye, Cap'n,' Brookes replied, saluting. He grinned over to where Melissa was hovering ten feet away. 'We've got it covered between us, haven't we?'

Melissa nodded eagerly and hurried back to her desk in a scramble of performative haste. For a few seconds, Whitworth noticed that Brookes's eyes were lingering on her backside.

He could see why a young man would like Melissa. She was fleshy, in that way that irresistibly made you think of what it would be like to grasp at her, but not so attractive as to be un-attainable. Still, Whitworth shot Brookes a stern look. At first Brookes didn't seem to notice but, as he caught Whitworth's eye, he corrected his expression to one of perfect professional-ism. Whitworth breathed a bit easier. He could understand the impulse to look, but he also understood that there would be consequences if there was anything more than looking.

'We'll meet at the victim's house tomorrow morning,' Whitworth said, his tone bright and encouraging. He wanted to encourage the professional side of Brookes to stay at the fore, and apparently Brookes's generation needed plenty of encouragement. 'Hopefully, that'll shed a bit of light.'

He patted the younger man on the shoulder.

'Go on. You head home now. We could be in for a long few days.'

II.

It was a repeat. How could it be another fucking repeat? Why did no one here ever think to change the channel?

Nazia realized that she was tapping out the rhythm of the *Morse* theme song on the arm of the sofa. She forced herself to stop and lay her palm flat. In her mind, she was still tapping.

She wanted to ask Jenny to go for a walk, but she had a feeling Jenny wouldn't want to go outside. She looked like the stripped outline of a tree in winter. It didn't seem fair to subject her to the February wind. Nazia wanted to be considerate. So she went by herself, shoving her woollen beanie on to her cropped head. Her ears were always cold these days.

There were two men standing in the hallway. At first, Nazia just nodded vaguely at them, but then she stopped dead.

It was weird how quickly she'd become unused to the sight of men. The older one made a show of friendly smiling as she pressed her back against the wall of the entryway to allow them past.

The guy looked like a fucking Fisher Price man, all made up of spheres – a shining bald head, a nose that finished in a round pink bulb, weirdly fleshy lips. Red-nosed, blur-featured. Hammy.

The other guy was shorter, darker, slimmer. His eyes were very wide, in a way that made him seem too young to be in a position of authority, but his features were drawn more sharply than the first's.

She didn't bother returning the show of friendliness. She wasn't scared. She just didn't want to have to act friendly towards them.

As she stepped outside the front door she noticed a strange car across the road. It probably belonged to those two cops, she told herself.

She headed down the street. It was a walk she often took. She found that her feet were pounding out the rhythm of the *Morse* theme song, which was dancing tauntingly around in her head.

A few houses down from the refuge she passed a man. Older. He didn't look like anyone in particular, but still Nazia's heart thudded. Angie's old man, maybe? Come to finish her off? She shook off the thought. No need to become paranoid. She'd end up like Jenny if she wasn't careful.

But then again, maybe it was better to end up like Jenny than like Katie.

The last time Nazia's feet had carried her this way – towards the bridge – had been just the previous week. On Thursday. The last day she'd seen Katie. They'd had one of their weekly group sessions, which Val insisted on and which Nazia hated.

Nazia looked to her side, imagining last week's self walking beside her, her face reddened with irritation. She'd like to feel some of that irritation now. Anything was better than the numbness that had gripped her since the news of Katie's death.

Katie had always been very into what Val called 'peer support'. In practice, that meant sitting around the kitchen table while Katie wrote words like 'power' and 'control' in Sharpie on big pieces of paper then looked around at them hopefully.

Those sessions always made Nazia feel like she had wandered into the wrong classroom by mistake. When Sonia had talked about how no one had believed her when she said her husband was hitting her, Nazia's stomach had knotted – it could have been guilt or annoyance, she wasn't sure. What was for sure was that, if Nazia had gone to the police, then no one would have doubted the origin of her bruises. No one would have told her that she must have done something to provoke it. Nobody would think she was capable of provoking anything.

'Who says anything about shared experiences?' Nazia had asked on that final day, after a particularly awkward silence. 'Who says I've even got anything in common with . . .'

She hadn't finished the thought out loud, but her eyes had been on Lynne.

'We've all got different experiences, of course,' Katie had said. 'It's about finding those common threads that exist between all of them.'

Nazia had been shredding a plain Hobnob into the lap of her stiff new jeans. 'You're looking for a link that isn't there,' she said.

'It's about patterns of behaviour,' Katie continued, as if it were an answer. 'So, say that instead of a domestic partner it was your father, for example –'

'It wasn't,' Nazia interrupted. 'My dad's lovely. A sweetheart. You'd be lucky to have a dad like him.'

She hadn't been sure if that was really the truth, or if she were trying to compile a version of her life that was fit for human consumption.

'Okay. Sorry,' Katie continued. 'I didn't mean to imply anything. I'm not talking about any of us in particular. Let's just say a figure of power.'

Nazia snorted again.

'Sabbir's my little brother. He doesn't have any *power*.'

It felt true.

When the two of them were small, Sabbir had followed her around devotedly, mirroring her every move. There had always been a blunt-instrument quality to him; he was totally incapable of delicacy or precision. His hugs were rough and warm.

He always came out with the stupidest things, and really seemed to mean them. That was true for the gym phase, the God phase, the Jordan Peterson phase.

'It doesn't sound like you understand him all that well,' Sonia said coolly.

'Why's it my fucking job to understand him?'

'Well –'

Sonia might have been about to say something insightful, but Nazia wasn't in the mood to listen, so she interrupted out of principle.

'He beat the shit out of me and now I'm the one who's got to put the effort into understanding him?'

'We're all people,' Sonia responded. 'We all do things for a reason. And if you don't understand the reason, then how do you expect to be able to do anything about it?'

'Why? So you can give him an excuse? Like Angie's old man used to do with the booze?'

Nazia jerked her head towards Angie, who was sitting with her head bowed, as if in prayer.

'You said he was really into religion, though.'

'He was *into* religion. He's not *religious*. They're not the same thing.'

Nazia could feel her cheeks burning. She knew her voice was defensive, and she wished she knew just who it was that she was trying to defend. Why should she have to defend anyone?

'This is pointless,' she muttered. Then she stood up and walked out, scattering the plate of biscuits in her wake. No one said anything.

She had stormed out of the house, her chest full of fury. *Fuck* Sonia. *Fuck* confrontation. *Fuck* Angie. *Fuck* Lynne. *Fuck* them all.

That day she followed the sound of the water, just as she was doing now.

'So when's the wedding, then, Naz?'

Fuck Sabbir.

Nazia kicked her trainer into the February mulch that slicked the pavement.

He'd come home from . . . somewhere. The gym or the mosque or the ice-cream parlour, wherever it was that he went to show his better self. Teeth bared like a smile, but not a smile. Maybe if she had pretended to be scared of him, it would all have been fine.

But he was her little brother.

Her mother was convinced that Sabbir was in a gang. The government was probably convinced he was a would-be jihadi. But the only thing that Nazia was convinced of was that Sabbir had never really committed to anything. Not to the protein shakes, not to learning Arabic, not to studying hard at school so he could become a surgeon, like he said he wanted.

Sabbir had never followed through on anything. That didn't stop her from looking around the streets of Widringham now, convinced that he was following *her*.

But there was no one on the road except for some middle-aged man sitting in a car, frowning at his iPhone. Lost, probably. Why else would anyone ever come here?

'*So when's the wedding, then, Naz?*'

'Could ask you the same question,' she had shot back. 'Been hearing all sorts of rumours about you and some Polish girl at school. Oh my God! Does this mean you're going to have a Catholic wedding?'

Maybe that had been cruel. Sabbir's face dropped.

'Turned you down, did she?' Nazia stepped forward to scratch at his patchy beard, like she was rubbing a dog under his chin. 'You know, you're not fooling anyone with *this*.'

That was when he grabbed her.

Even now, a hundred miles away, walking down a road in a town no one had ever heard of, Nazia felt herself being thrown off balance by the force of his movement.

The fractured scream could have been her mother, or it could have been Nazia herself. She could hear it now, blending with the whine of the strong north wind.

Sabbir looked her straight in the eye.

'*I'm* not fooling anyone?'

Even then she hadn't thought he'd hurt her. Even now, she still didn't, though walking this fast made parts of her body ache from the injuries, which still weren't fully healed. Because though the two of them had drifted apart over the years, there were still parts of Sabbir that Nazia understood far better than she understood herself. Because long before she had ever understood herself as *I*, she and Sabbir had been *Us*.

She didn't believe it then; she didn't believe it now. But it had happened.

She had never felt unsafe in her body before. Never felt commanded, crushed by pain. Force and flesh and fist over and over against soft stomach, bone giving way.

Bone doesn't break with a sudden snap. It splinters, slowly.

Then it was over and there was only a distant tugging.

She couldn't move.

That was the part she would never be able to understand. She couldn't *move*. It was impossible to believe now, when her feet were skimming so quickly over the paving stones she could kid herself she could fly.

He had sawn off her plait with a kitchen knife.

'There,' he said, holding it in his hand like a piece of road-kill. 'Maybe that'll teach you a lesson, you fucking dyke.'

So here she was. Leaning on the stone wall of the bridge, watching chunks of ice break away and be carried down the valley by the swift current.

And Katie, too, less than a week ago, before the police, before

Nazia spent the night staring at the ceiling and wondering what it would be like to drown. Katie, catching up, standing next to her on the bridge, the packet of Hobnobs in her hand. Her face had been pink with the cold.

'Sorry about that,' Nazia said, even though she wasn't.

Katie shrugged. 'I think it was probably helpful for you. Setting some boundaries.'

Yeah. Boundaries. As if they were any compensation for what was missing. As if that made it okay that those other women looked at her face and wrote her story for her.

'You don't understand,' Nazia said. She hadn't meant to say it out loud – it sounded so lame, so childish.

'No. I probably don't. We're doing our best, but we're not perfect. I get that.'

'There should be places for people like me. Where we don't have to explain ourselves.'

'There are. Culturally specific services for South Asian women. Indian, Pakistani – you know.'

Maybe Nazia imagined the little jerk of Katie's head towards her at the word 'Pakistani'. But maybe she didn't.

'I'm not Pakistani,' she said coolly. 'My family are Bengali. From Bangladesh.'

'Right. Sorry.'

'So . . . "culturally specific"? Separate but equal, you mean?'

'The idea's that it's easier to recover from trauma when you're not having to explain your background to everyone.'

Nazia's chest clenched. On the one hand, she hated the idea of being filed under 'different' like that. On the other, she didn't think she could bear to hear Val referring to 'your community' one more time, or getting confused about who in her family had beaten the shit out of her, and what barbaric cultural disease had made them do it. Forced marriage, so-called 'honour violence' – it was all the same to Val.

'Or rather, there were,' Katie said. 'They're closing. No funding.'

'That's fucking bullshit.'

'I know. I'm really sorry.'

Nazia didn't quite see why Katie was the one who had to apologize for everything, but she'd take what she could get. For a while the two women just stared out at the river in front of them, and neither of them spoke.

'It isn't what you think it is,' Nazia said after a pause.

'What isn't?'

'I don't know. Call it my story.'

'What is it, then?'

'Don't know.'

Saying those words made Nazia feel defiant. A release from having to have an answer and defend it to the death, regardless of whether or not she believed it.

'What's yours?'

'I don't know either.'

Katie had always been so keen to get everyone to talk. But she couldn't tell any of them what had happened to her. Why she was dead.

Because, despite all that, all the wash of talking, Katie had never really fitted in. Not like Val. She wasn't the type of person who made other people's misery her business. The furniture of disaster.

So why had she been there? And why had she died?

Maybe Jenny knew. Jenny seemed to know all kinds of things that she didn't say.

Nazia pulled her hat down to her eyes and walked away from the bridge, leaving the deadly sound of the water behind.

12.

Now

Sonia was a mum, first and foremost. That was what she'd told the police, and the social worker. That was what she'd tell the judge.

Just a mum, don't worry. No anger against the world; you don't have time for anger when you've got two lively boys like mine. They keep me on my feet. Don't get a moment to think. Ha. Ha. Ha.

'You don't have to just be a mum,' Katie had said. 'It's okay that you wanted to leave him for yourself.'

But it wasn't.

Sonia had gone to the police. They had photographed the bruises. Not a high point for her, but she had done it. She had to, for her boys. That was what she told herself. She'd stood there in her white cotton underwear while the police photographer snapped away, gathering the evidence they said would win her the safety of her children.

'The problem with your skin,' the photographer said conversationally as his camera snapped and clattered, 'is that it's harder to photograph your bruises. They don't show up as easily. They can just look like the natural shadows of your body, if you're not careful.'

Sonia said nothing.

Where is your pride? a voice that sounded a lot like her mother's hissed in her ear.

It's in the posh department store, with all the other things I can't afford right now.

'You're not the one who's on trial here,' Katie had told her.

'Yes I am.'

Katie was sweet, and she was doing her best, but she clearly didn't know the score.

Sonia thought back to one of the women who had greeted her when she first arrived at the refuge. She was gone now, but her story stuck around. The family courts had said that she wasn't emotional enough about her children. They said she was cold, uncaring. Then they had taken her kids away.

Katie had come with them to the school on the boys' first day, just last week. Sonia had asked her to come. She hadn't been able to think of an exact reason, but Katie hadn't seemed to need one.

'Moral support,' she said.

'Yeah.'

The bridge was a natural place to pause.

'Sometimes you need to give yourself a chance to stop and think,' Katie said.

'I think I'd really rather not think too much,' Sonia said, laughing so that Katie wouldn't know that it wasn't a joke.

'What happens when you think?'

'If the thinking part of me was working, then the boys wouldn't be in that school. Away from me.'

'You wouldn't have left them alone?'

'I wouldn't leave them because David won't leave them alone.'

'Yeah?'

'Lynne thinks it's her Frank.' Sonia bit her tongue hard before she could get out the rest of the sentence – *stupid cow always thinks it's about her* – 'but I'm not so sure. Lynne's a bag of nerves, you know that. But following me. Stalking me. Letting me know who's boss before the custody hearing.' Sonia's hand clenched on a bulge of stone on the wall. 'That's exactly the kind of stunt David would pull.

'He could show up at that school and the kids would go straight to him. No bother at all. They always thought he was such a great dad.'

'Even after he hit Lewis?'

Sonia paused, staring into the water, considering. 'I don't know what they think of him now.'

'Maybe it's changed.'

'Maybe it hasn't. Wouldn't surprise me. They're half me, after all.' Sonia snorted bitterly. 'Maybe they still think he's the most wonderful man in the whole world.'

'Is that what you still think?'

'He's the only man . . . the only man I know like that. The only man whose bones I know. And that means I *don't* know. I don't know if he's any better or any worse. And I felt like . . . I felt like it was as good as it was going to get for me.'

'You left him, Sonia.'

'I did. But it was too late. The damage was done.'

Sonia saw the light on in the office. She knocked and entered – Val always said she had an open-door policy. The sound of her movement mixed with a heavy jingle and a drawer hastily slamming shut. Val was sitting at the desk, her cheeks uncomfortably red against the starkness of her black hair. Sonia said nothing but looked – first at Val, and then at the plastic children's tumbler of amber liquid sitting on top of a pile of paperwork.

Val sighed.

'Hi . . . Sonia.'

'Hi,' Sonia said. Val licked at the flakes of red that still clung stubbornly to her thin lips and gestured at the swivel chair that used to be Katie's.

'Have a seat,' Val said. 'Do you want . . .'

She gestured at the closed drawer. Sonia shook her head.

'Got to look after the boys,' she said.

'Of course.'

'Though . . . they're asleep.'

Val said nothing further but reached back into the drawer and brought out a bottle of Johnnie Walker Red Label and an off-white mug with 'Widringham Women's Aid' written on it in pink block capitals.

She poured out what Sonia thought was probably a generous measure – though she wasn't sure; she'd never been a drinker of spirits. Didn't keep them in the house. Not with what they did to David.

Sonia took the mug, wrapped her hands around it the way she would to draw warmth from a cup of tea.

'I don't normally do this,' Val said. 'You know, we're after hours. And it's an exceptional occasion. Those bloody detectives.'

'Yeah.'

'They think they can just wander in, play their macho games, wander out again. Behave the way they would if they were talking to prisoners. As if this was just some . . . *men's* hostel.'

'Right.'

'Poor Nazia was terribly upset by them earlier, I could tell. Lynne's been in here in tears, worried about what it all means. I've been putting out fires all day. Some of the people here are *fragile*. Complex needs.'

'Yeah.'

'Not you, of course.' Val raised her glass as if to toast Sonia. 'Doing a marvellous job with those two boys of yours. Same as always.'

91

Sonia worked her jaw back and forth for a second or two before it could solidify into a hard line.

'Well, you get on with it, don't you?'

'You certainly do. Anyway' – Val raised the plastic tumbler – 'to Katie.'

'To Katie.'

Val took a gulp of whisky and studied her hands intently.

'I keep women safe, Sonia. That's my job. That's the work we do here. Do they think I want to be like . . . like this? Fuck-all money to work with, police coming in and out at all hours, harassed' – her voice cracked a little – 'all day online. Which nobody seems to be paying the slightest bit of attention to, by the way.'

She picked up a piece of paper from the desk and read from it. *'Shut up you sad old whore or you'll get what you deserve.'*

She let the paper slip between her fingers.

'What do you do with that?'

She was asking the room, not Sonia, so Sonia said nothing.

'Not investigate it,' Val continued rhetorically. 'Not treat it as part of an inquiry, that's for sure.'

Sonia took a sip of the whisky, keeping her face calm as the liquid ran a fiery path down her throat and behind her breast-bone, where it wrestled against the shifting flutter of fear that lived in her chest.

She took another sip. The fire started to win.

'My date's coming up,' Sonia said. She'd thought so hard about how to make it sound casual that it came out almost careless. Surely Val would know otherwise. Surely it was her job to know.

But Val wasn't looking at her.

'Come on in, Jenny.'

Val gestured at the door where a tall shape was lingering, wraithlike. 'We're having a little snifter. For Katie, you know.'

She drained her plastic glass and then, in a voice that Sonia had never heard her use before, she murmured, 'Poor girl.'

She raised a hand to rub at her face. In the light of the energy-saving bulbs her face looked dim, reddened. Her eyes were ringed with crumbs of mascara.

'It wasn't your fault, Val.'

Sonia was always surprised when Jenny used full sentences. Her utterances were usually bent out of shape with tangents and clichés, as if she couldn't quite bear to get to the point.

Val looked surprised, too.

'I know it wasn't,' she said, utterly unconvincingly. 'Lord only knows what happened. The police are incompetent. God knows. Even if . . . if it's what they think it is – depression . . . you know. Terrible illness. But in a sense . . .' Val poured herself more whisky. 'There's a duty of care, you know. It's the system. Even down to the sodding background checks. I'm expected to wait weeks or months with no staff for the powers that be to get their act together.'

She turned her eyes imploringly on Sonia, and Sonia felt herself prickling slightly.

'It's a systematic problem, you see. With the resources available to us, structurally speaking, there's no time for what – you know, conventionally . . .' She trailed off and looked back towards the door, only noticing then that Jenny had gone.

'I'll wash these up,' Sonia said, gathering up the mug, the tumbler. Val nodded and locked the drawer of the desk, her keys jangling.

'Better turn in,' she said. 'Was there something you wanted to talk about?'

'My date's coming up,' Sonia said again. Softly this time.

Val nodded.

'We'll speak about it in the morning,' she said.

13.

Then

It's hard to make sense of those first nights together. There are moments of clarity, but they refuse to assemble themselves into sequence. Katie remembers how his skin looked half blue in the faint light of the street lamps outside her bedroom window and how she felt the parallel sensations of being torn and caressed. How he looked at her with great solemnity, as if he had a secret and she knew it, too, and she felt that perhaps she did. It lionized the thing they had into something that might be called love.

Faking orgasms has always been par for the course in Katie's experience – so much so that she didn't think of it so much as faking as putting on the appropriate show. After all, men are aroused by arousal. She is just doing her bit.

None of that matters. Or at least, not in comparison to the flooring sense of eased naturalness she feels when she curls into him afterwards. The boundary of her skin with his offers undeniable proof of his otherness. That she isn't alone, not any more.

She clings to him. So tightly that maybe any other man would be annoyed or spooked, but not Jamie. He has the capacity to hold on to her even tighter than she holds him. How could she fail to love him for that? Jamie makes certain things so *easy*.

It's the comfort of having a vessel to pour herself into, something she can be sure won't break. The set-piece perfection of picnics on Box Hill, wanderings through the South Bank, Sunday-afternoon walks in the park. The sureness that the intensity of his love invites. The singularity of his devotion.

'There are so many guys around these days who don't appreciate an amazing girl like you,' he tells her, before leaning back on to the grassy hill, his face mottled by March sunlight, and pulling Katie down on to the solid step of his chest.

'You're just saying that,' she says, semi-automatically, and he frowns.

'I don't just say things,' he says. 'You're really great. And you deserve to be treated well. Take the compliment.'

Jamie has a tendency to incise the world of men into two – those who treat women well, and those who don't. The former measure time in bunches of flowers, little gifts, money spent with no expectation of being repaid.

It is never clear what those who treat women badly are like, only that Jamie is not one of them. So there's no need to find out.

When her friends ask her how the sex was on the debrief that follows, she replies that she doesn't remember. This makes them worry for a moment, and then laugh for a long time. And then she has to backtrack and says, 'Wait – yes – it was good. Of course it was good. Don't get me wrong, it was really good. Passionate. Urgent. That's what sex is supposed to be like, right?'

And then her friends, who are all at various stages of play-marriage (in rental agreements, at least, if not in spirit), and either live or half-live with their boyfriends, agree that, yes, that's a very good thing. That they wish they still had that.

Yes, the passion does go. Or at least subside. You're lucky you're still at that stage.

'He's kind.'

She's gone for a glass of wine with Ellie after work. Their commutes cross over, so they sometimes meet like this. Sometimes it's good to talk one on one, not in a group where everything falls to a jury verdict.

Ellie blinks and nods and seems to consider.

'Yes,' she says. 'He is. Or it sounds like he is, anyway. He seems like a nice guy. From what you've told me.'

Then Ellie smiles and rolls her eyes. 'We could all do with giving a nice guy a chance, right?'

Ellie's boyfriend *is* a nice guy, but that's all he is. He doesn't seem to have ever been anywhere, done anything or had any interests, but he is undoubtedly devoted to Ellie. Katie has always figured it's not her place to judge, but she knows that she'd pick Jamie's rough edges over that kind of flaccidness any day. She is confident that Jamie is *capable* of doing something substantial in life, even if he hasn't done it yet.

'The point is, I don't want a project,' Katie says. 'I don't need someone who I need to make like me. I think he just *does* like me. The way I am.'

Ellie just keeps looking.

'In fact, I *know* he likes me,' Katie says, and flushes. The words shouldn't mean as much as they do.

'That's good, then,' Ellie says, and Katie feels the fibres of her body starting to relax.

They talk about some other stuff to do with how much they both hate their jobs, now that they're settled into them, but they finish their glasses of wine knowing that the substance of their talk is over.

Katie's phone buzzes.

Where are you?

She hammers out a quick reply.

At home. Talking to mum. Talk in half an hour?

That isn't true, she thinks. She waits a beat, expecting the thought to continue, for the source of the lie to reveal itself. But it doesn't.

'Need to dash off,' she says. 'Work in the morning.'

'Great to see you,' Ellie says, hugging her. 'Let's do it again soon?'

So good to see you last night and talk about stuff. Same time next week? Xxx

Katie looks at the text, then looks at the bed where Jamie is lying.

A shaft of light from the early sunset is falling across his face, airbrushing it. He looks up at Katie and smiles, and holds out his hand.

'Come to bed,' he says, and she does, and she doesn't reply to Ellie's text.

14.

Now

They searched the victim's house the following morning.

Noah let them in and made them a cup of tea, before re-installing himself on the sofa. He was watching some American sitcom (Whitworth vaguely recognized it as one of Jennifer's favourites), with a vast bowl of pasta in his lap.

Brookes went straight into the bedroom, and Whitworth could hear him poking about, pulling drawers open and closed.

'How're you holding up?' Whitworth said to Noah. It was the only thing he could think of to say.

'It's weird without Katie.'

Whitworth did his best to convey concern with his eyes, the way the women officers seemed to do so effortlessly. He hoped that, God forbid, if something ever happened to Maureen, he'd be able to come up with a better word for it than 'weird'.

'Have you got anyone around to keep an eye on you?'

'There's my mum,' Noah said.

'She around much?'

'I'm going to move back in with her. Can't afford the rent on this place by myself, anyway.'

Whitworth wondered if Katie had – if she had indeed killed herself – considered how it might impact Noah. Whether she minded that it would make him regress even further to childhood.

'I've tried to keep it neat,' Noah told Whitworth when he

headed to the bedroom. 'Katie liked it neat. I'm not much good at that sort of thing.'

He wasn't being modest. Everything looked like it had been folded by someone wearing boxing gloves. It felt wrong to paw through all that mess. The idea of Noah trying to restore his dead girlfriend's things to some semblance of order made Whitworth wince. If anything ever happened to Maureen, his own home would fall down around his ears.

Katie Straw had owned very few things, and all her clothes looked newish. Trendy minimalism, or a new life recently begun? She had made a sort of dressing table on top of the chest of drawers, her personal effects crammed into a few square feet of space. The rest of the room was all Noah. Noah's cycling stuff, his camping equipment, his guitar.

It was always odd, seeing a dead person's things. Everything seemed like a tiny corpse, every drawer a mausoleum.

The bed was half slept in. No starfish sprawling for Noah, it seemed. The left-hand side of the bed, the side furthest from the door, looked like it hadn't been disturbed for a while. A pile of folded laundry sat on it. Katie's side.

Whitworth wondered if Katie had done the load of laundry before she'd died.

'Jewellery . . .' he muttered, shoving a little glass box towards Brookes. Brookes opened it, stirring the contents with his finger.

'Nice, some of this.'

'Hm?' Whitworth glanced at the silvery mass where Brookes's finger was nesting. Brookes held up a pendant in the shape of a leaf. Silver, Whitworth thought. Or white gold. He'd never been sure of the difference.

'Bet old Noah didn't buy this for her,' Brookes said. 'I don't think he's the type.'

'You never know. He might be a dark horse.'

Whitworth felt sorry for Noah. He guessed that Katie must have felt much the same.

He thought about the jewellery he'd given Maureen over the years. To say that it had all been a present just for her would be a bit dishonest. It had always given him so much pride to know that he had worked hard to give her nice things. The shy chip of diamond on her engagement ring (they hadn't gone in for big rocks in those days). The brazen gold of her wedding ring. The fine chain he'd bought her on the day Jennifer was born.

Brookes continued to poke through the jewellery with interest.

'You a closet jeweller?'

Brookes laughed, picking up a silver bracelet and holding it up to the light.

'You can tell a lot about a woman from her jewellery, I reckon. Whether it's real or fake.'

Whitworth had heard truisms like that before. Detectives seemed to have an impulse for it – a need to come up with their own little set of laws for how to interpret humanity.

He picked up a pink canvas makeup bag from the chest of drawers.

Inside was a smashed powder compact, a stub of red lipstick, a little pot of black eyeliner. The enforcers of a daily lie: that the world was a little more beautiful than it really was.

There wasn't much else to look through. No suicide note, though that wasn't necessarily a surprise. Notes were more a convenient trope for TV than an actual reality. Whitworth resented that. It made people feel like they were owed a note, and most of them were disappointed. Most of the time, suicide was as inscrutable as cancer.

Brookes was flicking through a box of old photographs.

'Anything interesting?'

Brookes's voice was flat when he replied – disappointed, Whitworth guessed: 'Nothing.'

'Look,' he added, emptying out the photographs on to the bed. 'There's literally nothing. *Look.*'

There were a couple of pictures of a child Katie and then a few more snapshots of her and Noah together. They looked happy enough. Or at least, they looked like they knew how to *seem* happy. What was the difference?

'People don't tend to have many physical photos any more,' Whitworth said.

'Yeah, but she's got *nothing.*' Brookes looked perplexed now. A budding detective's instinct? Or just a rigid sense of how things should or shouldn't be?

'What's bothering you about it?' Whitworth asked. *Probe the instinct*, he thought. *Get it in good working order.*

'Just feels like it's a bit of a pointless case,' Brookes muttered.

Whitworth hadn't been expecting to hear that. He bit back a snappy retort and tried to look encouraging.

'What makes you say that?'

'As far as I can see, we as good as know she committed suicide. I don't know why we're trying to dredge together a reason for it. Why does anyone commit suicide? And instead of tying ourselves in knots, couldn't we be working on a case that actually helps people who're still alive?'

For a second, there was a defenceless look in Brookes's eyes, before he brushed it away. Whitworth wondered if he was trying to sound harder and more jaded than he really was. The boy was pretty new to all this death business, after all.

Noah was still sitting under a blanket on the sofa. He was crying. There was something red raw in his face, as if he'd been scrubbing at it with a flannel. Whitworth wondered whether he should say something. The lad might as well take comfort. Brutal as it seemed to say, Whitworth knew that Noah would get over it eventually.

'I *miss* her,' Noah said. His hand was outstretched at his side, his legs stacked on the coffee table, as if he was used to making room for someone else on the little sofa.

Brookes walked over to Noah and squatted in front of him as if he were speaking to a child.

'Look, mate,' he said, very gently. 'I'm so sorry for your loss. We all are.'

'Thanks,' Noah snuffled. Tears were dripping off his reddened face and mingling with snot.

'You just need to keep remembering that if – *if* – Katie did take her own life, you really can't blame yourself for it. It wasn't your fault, Noah.'

Noah didn't actually look like blaming himself had occurred to him. His eyes grew childish-round, and he started to sob, much louder now.

'I think we'd better go,' Whitworth muttered, feeling a cavern of embarrassment opening up in his chest. Why was Brookes able to convey concern so effortlessly, and when had that become a useful quality in a policeman? 'We'll keep you updated on everything,' he said in Noah's general direction, forming his words very clearly, as if he were communicating with the demented. He couldn't bring himself to look straight at that awful profusion of tears.

'Bit of a wimp, isn't he?' Whitworth said lightly as they picked their way through the cracked paving stones of the front garden path.

Brookes frowned.

'His girlfriend's dead.'

'Right.'

Whitworth knew he'd misjudged things. He really did need

to learn to keep quiet more, he realized. Things just weren't the way they used to be.

They took the car around the corner to the chip shop. Half-way between the church hall and the bridge, it was one of the few places in Widringham where they could be reasonably confident of some CCTV.

'With you in a minute, mate,' Amir, the owner, said. His accent was somehow completely Pakistani and completely Widringham at the same time. It was twelve noon. The first frying time of the day.

Whitworth nodded. 'When you've got the chance,' he said. He settled into one of the plastic chairs and listened to the comforting chuckle of the deep-fat fryer.

He ordered two portions of sausage and chips to go with the CCTV tape from Thursday night, and took them to the car, where Brookes was sitting.

'I'm not eating that,' he said, glancing down at the sausage.

'All right, princess,' Whitworth said. 'Watching our figure, are we?'

'You should be careful about what you put in your body,' Brookes said.

Whitworth raised an eyebrow. 'Fine.' He picked up the sausage with little ceremony and dropped it in his polystyrene container. 'Have it your way.'

Brookes smirked and started to pick at the chips.

'Chips are all right, then?'

'Processed meat is carcinogenic.'

They sat in silence for a minute further.

'So, Noah, eh?' Whitworth said rhetorically.

'Always got to look at the boyfriend, right?'

'He doesn't exactly seem like the kind of guy you'd date if you had much self-respect.'

'You're probably right.'

'That doesn't mean she had to top herself, of course. She could have just left him,' Whitworth said thoughtfully.

'Don't know if it's ever that easy.'

'If you *stay* in a relationship,' Whitworth said, sketching his idea out in the air with a stubby chip, 'you've got to take responsibility for yourself. No one's problem but your own. Try telling that to Val Redwood and her lot, though.'

'That's different,' Brookes said seriously, the chips still frozen in mid-air. 'Those guys they're getting away from are probably nutters. Violent. Some of them must be, anyway. I mean, real men don't hit women.'

'I suppose.' Whitworth's voice was absent, but he adjusted it when he realized how lukewarm he sounded. 'I mean . . . of course. Well said. You know what I mean. On the other hand,' he continued, 'if Noah *did* have something to do with her death, that might make some sense.'

'He's not exactly the wife-beating type, though, is he?'

Whitworth thought of Mr Sullivan, the blundering, burly husband of the little woman in the blood-flowered dress. Even kneeling down, he had been almost as tall as his tiny wife. His meaty arms had looked absurd wrapped around her waist, his big face buried in her stomach.

'Although, I guess . . . what's the wife-beating type?' Brookes folded his arms, staring thoughtfully at nothing. 'He's boozy as all hell. Drugs, too, for all we know. I mean, I've got every sympathy with him being upset and everything. But all those tears could be a cover for something, right?'

'All good points,' Whitworth conceded, glad to see that Brookes was able to keep an open mind. That was the most important part of the job, of course. A good detective had the magic combination – an open mind and a sharp instinct. 'But Noah was in Glasgow.'

'Could have been and come back. Would have been tight, but manageable.'

'Not sure that he's much of a criminal mastermind, Noah. And he's got his mates to vouch for him.'

'They were all hammered. That's not going to stand up in court. Worth pursuing, I think. A girl's dead, after all. Can't help to properly rule out her boyfriend.'

'So you want me to ring up the DI and tell her I'm handing over the case because . . . what?'

Brookes stayed silent.

'We'd better be getting back,' Whitworth said. He drove them on the way back, his fingers making a greasy sausage-film on the steering wheel.

Whitworth spent the rest of the afternoon in meetings, the most important of which was updating DI Khan on the Katie Straw case.

The whole thing wouldn't have taken nearly as long, he would have liked to point out, if she hadn't insisted on having the conversation by video chat, which seemed to cut out every thirty seconds.

'So what is it that we're looking at here, Whitworth?' she asked breezily.

Whitworth started to reply, but the screen froze, leaving the DI's face trapped in a grimace. Khan was about forty, he knew that, but she was the kind of woman who took good enough care of herself to deceive people into thinking she might be a fair bit younger.

'Hello?' There were some odd, disjointed noises coming through, although the screen remained frozen. Whitworth tried again. 'Can you hear me, ma'am?'

'Yes.' The reply sounded as if it were bubbling out from under water. 'I can hear you fine, Whitworth.'

'As far as I can see,' Whitworth enunciated slowly, clearly, 'all the signs currently point to a suicide. Nothing to suggest otherwise.'

'But nothing to prove your theory either,' the voice bubbled back. 'I'd like something a bit more concrete before we move forward into closing the case. You say there was no note?'

'No note, ma'am,' Whitworth replied. 'Although in my experience it can be a bit naive to expect one.'

The DI's face reanimated. Her dark eyes seemed to be fixed on Whitworth's chin.

'Right.' She tapped a pen against her forehead absent-mindedly. 'Do you need me to come in, DS Whitworth? I appreciate you've had limited experience of murder cases over in Widringham, so perhaps it would be useful to . . .'

The screen cut out. A pop-up message informed Whitworth that the connection would resume shortly. He shuffled in his chair, taking the opportunity to steady himself with a sip of coffee. Surely, after a lifetime on the Force, he wasn't still being babysat?

'No, no, ma'am,' he said as the DI's face ballooned back into view. 'No, we know what we're doing here.'

'Of course.' She seemed to give a strange, slow-motion nod, and the image juddered slightly. 'I'm just concerned that, given the question mark over the victim's identity . . .' The sound cut out for a few seconds, but her mouth kept moving, and when her voice was restored she continued, seemingly without noticing: '. . . the next forty-eight hours we'll need to look at sending in a specialist squad for a second opinion. We can't afford to lose evidence if we are looking at a murder.'

'I know that.' Whitworth gripped the arms of his swivel chair and smiled blandly at his own image in the corner of the screen.

Trust Khan to bring up losing evidence.

A couple of years ago a man – mid-forties, recently made redundant, estranged from his kid – had jumped off the bridge. The same bridge. Whitworth had known the guy – had known with all the certainty he had in him that he'd find a note begging forgiveness from his ex-wife, and his affairs neatly in order.

The body had been found not too far from the primary school, and Whitworth couldn't stand to have it near the playground where he'd watched his own Jenny pelt around with her mates. That was the truth of it.

But Khan had gone ballistic that he'd had the body moved before she'd approved it, even though the case had turned out exactly as Whitworth had expected, down to the will placed neatly on the man's desk.

She was a stickler – that was what you needed to know about Khan. Procedure as substitute for experience.

'Forty-eight hours, ma'am. I should think we'll have things cleared up by then.'

'Great.' Her eyes swivelled briefly to the camera and seemed to look straight at Whitworth. 'Looking forward to receiving your update, DS Whitworth.'

He raised his eyebrows and stretched his lips into his acquiescent expression. 'Looking forward to providing it, ma'am.'

When he emerged from the meeting room, well after four o'clock, Brookes was sitting at the desk with his feet up, inspecting Amir's CCTV footage frame by frame. The pixellated impression of the chip shop had stopped looking like a real place and had started to seem like a video game.

But then – 'Wait,' Brookes said. His voice was hard and sharp. The frown he was now wearing seemed to carve up his face into something different. 'What's that?'

Whitworth squinted. He didn't have his glasses on. But through the front pane of Amir's shop he could see a twiggish figure. It was impossible to tell from the silhouette if it was a man or a woman – it was tall and slight and insubstantial.

The figure paused and cocked its head in the direction of the blurry Katie, as if making a mental note of her. Then it kept walking.

'Potential witness,' Brookes murmured. He had a glint in his eye. Whitworth recognized that look – the glimpse of a lead. The possibility that the underlying logic of the world might, after all, be there for the uncovering.

'Whoever it was recognized Katie Straw,' Whitworth said, one of the moments of insight that made him feel a little closer to a TV detective. 'They were following her.'

'They were following her,' Brookes echoed, the sentence somehow seeming to take on a different meaning in the grim-ness of his voice. 'Question is, how long did they follow her for?'

Apart from the chip shop, there was a general lack of CCTV footage in Widringham, particularly the part where the refuge and the pretty old bridge were. Shops tended to be limited to the fudge and tea variety; all the proprietors considered theirs to be family, community establishments with no need for (according to some elderly residents, at least) quasi-Orwellian levels of surveillance. Luckily, the area held no appeal for Widringham's bored and drug-consuming youth, which meant the high ideals of the Widringham elderly hadn't bumped up against reality. They thought CCTV was the end of their personal freedom, that Whitworth and his colleagues had nothing better to do than spy on the spyings of retirees. There were posters against 'surveillance culture' outside the church – an act of warfare, if ever there was one. There was always the chance that someone might have been peering through their net curtains at the right time.

So they went door to door. Or, at least, they sent Melissa to go door to door. Brookes offered to go, too, but Whitworth told him to keep looking for Katie's identity instead. No need to tempt the boy, if he *was* sweet on Melissa.

'Nothing,' Melissa reported on returning to the station, her mouth pressed into a thin line.

'Well, then.' Whitworth paused, arranging his features into what he hoped was a contemplative, worldly look. Brookes and Melissa were looking at him intently. It was an odd one, this case. He was so used to knowing roughly who'd done what and why. The small-town curse of everyone knowing everyone.

He raised his eyebrows. 'Any ideas?'

'We've got to go back to the refuge,' Brookes said. 'If someone followed her to Amir's, that's where we need to start.'

Whitworth sighed, then took out his phone. His personal phone. Just a cheap little thing, which Jennifer seemed to view as an endless source of embarrassment and laughter.

His fingers knew the standard Morse code of apology so well he didn't have to look at the screen.

Won't be home for dinner. Sorry. Love to Jen x

He put the phone back in his pocket, not waiting for a reply.

15.

Then

Love. Love for Jamie.

First, it is carefully cultivated. A fragile stem that Katie doesn't trust to survive on its own, that shrinks back every time he says something wooden or crass. Then, somehow, fed carefully by long mornings lying in bed, skin to skin, the love becomes a vast creeper that covers her entire being.

She isn't sure when that feeling took on a life of its own, when she stopped thinking how convenient it would be if she loved him back and just knew that she did. Loving someone is important – it gives her a sense that, no matter where she goes in the world, there is always an elastic band stretching her back towards a firm centre.

That firmness itself was always attractive. Katie's friends have always lovingly described each other as 'flakey' – it's something of a joke in their group. But Katie had never wanted to be flakey. She finds that, when there is someone as solid and as dependable as Jamie around, part of her personality melts away.

Jamie does odd jobs. Fixes hinges on doors that have hung at odd angles for ever. Tests the smoke alarms. Nails in stray bits of carpet. Large things become no more fixable than they ever were, but small things can change.

The flakey friends seem to melt away a little, too. She can no longer bring herself to haggle endlessly about who has time to meet up when, all juggled around thankless new jobs and live-in boyfriends.

'Don't bother with them,' Jamie advises her. 'If people don't bother replying to messages, then they don't care about you. Why should you care about them?'

'My friends care about me,' she says, more because she feels she ought to be angry at his words than because she actually is.

He just blinks.

'I didn't say your friends,' he says. 'I just said people.'

'I'll get back in touch with them soon. Properly. It's just a lot right now.'

'You don't need to tell me that. What help have they been with any of the stuff you're going through?'

'I can talk to them,' Katie says. It's not true, but it's supposed to be the bastion of female friendship, so she says it.

'What good's talking? What have any of them actually *done*?'

'What *can* they actually do?'

'You tell me,' Jamie says with a shrug.

If anyone were to ask her why she loves him (no one would, of course; that would be overstepping), she imagines her reply – that it's because of his fundamental *goodness*. In a sense, it's old-fashioned. She's trained her brain so hard to think of things like moral relativism and the infinite complexity of things that there is something so honest, so simple, so beautiful, in the way he uses words like 'right' and 'wrong'. Moral truths as hard and simple as darts on a board. He believes in things like honour and pride. Taking care of the people you love.

Besides, her mum likes him, she says he's a sweet boy, and she is glad that Katie is with someone she can rely on. In the past, Katie hasn't taken much notice of her mum's advice, but it feels prophetic now.

Jamie does his part, becoming something of a son or husband for the house. He goes to the supermarket to get the food shopping and refuses to be paid back. He becomes a permanent fixture at the Sunday dinners that her mum still makes without fail, though the myopathy in her fingers is now so bad she struggles to chop the vegetables. She always asks Jamie to carve, even though he doesn't know how and hacks off clumsy pieces of beef and flops them awkwardly on to the waiting plates. He cuts enormous, wedge-like slabs for Katie then winks at her mother.

'She's a growing girl,' he says.

Her dad used to say that.

Katie's dad is gone. That is his defining characteristic, to the point that she struggles to remember what it was like to love anything but the vacuum he left. Everything she was, she had become for him.

He had been a professor of philosophy. An intellectual. He had taught her cleverness like a little parrot, instilling in her the basics of formal logic, then setting her a problem as if he were winding up a mechanical toy.

'Tell me, Katie,' he'd say. 'If all ladies are too fussy, and your mummy's a lady, what does that mean?'

He loved the idea of his clever daughter, loved creating a special club between the two of them. Even back then, Katie's mother was thin, pale, insubstantial. The kind of woman that would always be easy to leave out.

Her parents had been sweethearts from the age of seventeen. When she was little, Katie liked to set photographs of the two of them together into a timeline, from when they were still mostly children. As her father grew, in size, in status, in blooming cheek and belly, her mother seemed to shrink. When they were young, it was noticeable that her mother was nearly two inches taller than him. At some unplottable point in the photographic history of their lives, that seemed to stop being the case.

They had been the two cleverest children in their class at

grammar school, always competing for the best marks. She had done slightly better in her A levels than him and had applied to Cambridge because he had and she wanted them to be together.

She got in; he didn't.

He went to University College London, stayed on and on, eventually became a professor. Katie wondered whether that had been because of his sheer staying power, or just because he had selected a subject for his PhD that no one else had wanted to study.

They had never married. He thought it was too conventional. She didn't push him, she told Katie, because he wasn't the kind of man who responded to being pushed.

Katie remembered overhearing him saying at a party that he could not possibly marry her mother because the only thing they knew about the self was that it was in a constant state of flux. That the very atoms which constituted his being would mostly be replaced in twenty years – then how could he say he was the same person? How could he commit himself to something like marriage, when the self was so ephemeral?

She remembered, after that, him laying a proprietorial hand on her mother's bottom when he thought no one was looking.

In a way that she could never put into words, she had been frightened of her father. At the same time, she had despised her mother for being frightened of him, too. The fright was somehow permanently glued together in her mind with that image of his hand on her mother's bottom – she had been wearing a dark red dress. She never wore high heels, because he didn't like the height difference between them accentuated. She saw the fear in the lines of her mother's body in that moment. The faintest jump, then the determined stillness.

Her father was right about the self being ephemeral, at least. The atoms that constituted his being exploded apart in a car crash. He had been drink-driving. That was an illogical thing to do – but then, he'd never been a consistent person.

He burned. First in the charred wreckage of the car, and then what remained was burned again in the crematorium.

Katie had scattered his ashes in the Lake District. Her father had taken them on family holidays there, telling her about the Romantic poets as her little feet scuttled after him, tripping over themselves to keep up. She thought he probably would have been pleased with his final resting place – although, when second-guessing his wishes, she found that there were great blanks for her to fill in.

She had never been angry with her father. The idea of being angry seemed remote and inaccessible; it lay beyond the threshold of what she was allowed to feel. The person who manned the gate, who exacted tolls from whatever passed through it, that was her father. She wasn't angry with him, because she didn't have his say-so. He had monopolized anger in their home. He never shouted, not exactly. He had seethed, raged, stormed, but never shouted, which made it difficult to lay before him the case that he was the one that infused all the air with such a sense of anger.

I never shout, he would always say, as if it were relevant.

He would have *hated* Jamie.

Jamie doesn't believe in things like philosophy. With the work he does every day, Katie can respect that. Things work, therefore they are.

Her mother isn't the kind of person whose existence was laid out in theoretical terms. Her mother lives in a reality that ignores intellectual protestations.

Katie thinks about the atoms and cells multiplying themselves inside her mother's body, the creation of Katie herself. Later, the gestation of womb cancer, a cruel echo of what had been before.

16.

Now

Charlie and Angie Woods had been married a great many years. Forty-nine.

Two children, no grandchildren. Not yet. But you hope, don't you?

Five pints a night, Charlie, if he could. Two, if Angie had anything to do with it.

One mortgage, paid off three years ago. A business between them, sold off to leave them comfortable. A comic double act all their lives, as far as the rest of the village was concerned, the Jack and Vera Duckworth, bickering away happily, running their village post office.

Charlie beat Angie.

Three days after their wedding, Angie had turned up outside her mam's back door with a black eye. Her mam had let her in and given her a mug of tea and words that were kind but not too kind.

It had been a cloudy Sunday, one of those pallid days when it's hard to hold on to the memory of things.

Mam had put arnica cream on the bruises and sent her home to her husband. The trick was to never let the bruises fully heal, to never remember what life was like without them. Then it didn't seem like too much to bear.

When Angie was a little girl, if she had an apple with a bruise on it, her mam had always told her to put her thumb over the bruise and eat around it. If you thought about it that way, it was Charlie, not Angie herself, who wore the bruises, and Angie who put her thumb over them and loved the pieces of the man in between.

They had house meetings in the refuge. Every two weeks. Angie never knew what to do with herself, always wondered whether she was expected to speak or if she could stay quiet. She felt herself babbling too much these days – she didn't know how to stop.

It had been such a strange feeling when Angie had arrived at the refuge. The way that she could speak freely. She didn't say very much – the other women probably thought she was as dull as ditchwater – but she could say what she liked.

Cup of tea, lovie?

Oh, isn't she just a gorgeous little girl?

So much energy, those boys of yours. It's just fabulous. Wish I could have some of it for myself.

Angie didn't pretend to herself that she had anything new to say. But that wasn't the point.

She was no longer a secret-keeper. She no longer had to examine every little thing she said, checking it for defects, in case some of the truth sneaked through. In case the riverbanks overflowed and the world found out what Charlie was – what Angie was. How terribly she had failed.

She had carried the load for so long it had become part of her. Most days now, she was stretching herself out, exploring the ache it had left. There were only so many times you could spring up and offer to make a round of tea when everything strayed a little too close to the truth.

The meetings hadn't been so bad with Katie. With Katie, it had been chocolate biscuits and cups of tea, the door to the playroom open to keep an eye on the children. Katie had been quiet in the way that she dealt with things, but deal with them she did. Val tended to dissolve under a swelling volume of words about nothing in particular, vague promises that something would be done and a near-fanatical attention to taking minutes.

But last night had been different. At first, they had all been silent, stealing only the briefest of looks at one another before snatching their gaze away to restore it to their cups of tea, to the plate of plain digestives, to the empty seat where Katie had always sat, on the chair that wobbled. She had always insisted it was fine.

Val didn't sit like that. Angie wouldn't have said that Val was fat, but she always seemed to be crammed into whatever space she was occupying.

Once the police officers had left, she had droned on at some length about how she wouldn't let them anywhere near the refuge again, about how there was a duty of care that she took very seriously. About how they were all safe there.

It was astonishing how exactly her repetition of the word 'safe' coincided with the terror growing in the room.

'I know you must all have a lot of questions,' Val said. Angie studied her cup of tea.

'Will there be a funeral?' she asked. A nod to decency, at least.

'I can only presume so,' Val said. 'But that's . . . that's really not up to me. I'll keep you informed as things . . . as it all develops. It might not be for a while.'

'Why not?' Sonia spoke this time.

'It's . . . well . . . if they were to decide to treat the death as suspicious. You know. Can I make anyone another tea?'

'When you say suspicious . . .' Sonia persisted, 'do you think they are treating it like that? You know. Suspiciously.'

'It's really difficult for me to . . .'

'Suspicious as in murder?'

Angie hadn't meant to speak, but the air had built up too much inside her. In her mind's eye, a tall, indistinct figure, half beast and half man, unfolded itself from a dark corner and began to stalk the streets of Widringham.

She looked down so that no one would see her cheeks reddening.

'There are . . . well, shades of suspicion. It could very well have been a suicide. We know Katie was depressed.'

'Not depressed enough to chuck herself off a bridge.'

Nazia never normally spoke up in house meetings. Nazia never normally did anything that might imply she actually belonged there.

'You never know how depressed people are. What's going on for them.' Lynne's cheeks had been flushed as she spoke.

Angie hadn't been looking to find anything wrong with Katie the last time they'd spoken. That was one of the worst things about being a victim. It made it impossible to see anyone else.

Angie opened the door less than a foot and awkwardly distorted her shoulders to squeeze through the narrow gap. The only thing that she wasn't trying to make smaller about herself was her smile, which she turned on Peony.

'Hello, my sweetheart.'

Lynne bunched herself up on the sofa, even though Angie was hardly an expansive woman herself. Surely there was room for both of them.

'Mind if I join you?' Angie said. She felt shy saying it – Lynne was the kind of woman who'd always made her feel a little nervous, but Angie was starting to realize that she could overcome that. In fact, she could overcome all sorts.

'Not at all,' Lynne said, her cashmere-clad body sliding along the sofa with a luxurious whisper.

Angie's phone gave a loud ping. She took out her glasses and frowned at it, holding it in her hand as carefully as you would a baby bird.

'Now, is there a way for me to make that bloody sound go away?'

'There's usually a button . . .' Lynne said. 'On the side?'

Angie prodded for a few seconds, then grimaced.

'There you go. I think I've turned it off by accident.' She rolled her eyes. 'Probably for the best.'

She sat down on the sofa. 'They can be so bloody persistent, men. If you told me my Charlie had learned to text just so he could bother me . . .' She looked up at Lynne quickly. Her voice sounded so silly. Tinkling. 'Sorry, pet,' she said. 'Don't you worry about me.'

'Frank was persistent,' Lynne said. She sounded like she was trying to do a tone of sisterliness. 'He's a very . . . He knows what he wants.'

Lynne's little Peony was sitting on a turquoise plastic see-saw, rocking violently back and forth.

'Not like me,' Lynne said.

Angie didn't say anything. The seesaw thudded rhythmically on the floor of the playroom.

'Do you ever think about going back?'

The police had asked Angie, again and again, why she had never left him. She had left him, she tried to explain, left him dozens of times, but it was only ever for an afternoon or so. She would drive round and round their town, where it always seemed to be drizzling but never properly rained. She would walk through the botanical gardens, clutching an old nylon shopping bag with spare pairs of knickers and the unwashed pillowcases from her children's beds. Then she would pull herself together and go home to make the kids' tea.

'They won't like me saying this. 'Scuse me. Not they. *Her.*'

Angie directed her eyes towards the door and up, towards where they both knew Val's office was. 'But sometimes I think you probably do need to go back. Just to be sure.'

She kept her voice light, like she was talking about double-checking that the iron was really unplugged.

'Will you go back to . . . er, Charlie?'

Angie gave a smile. Her face felt stretched out, like a sweater that had lost its shape. 'Oh, I shouldn't think so, pet,' she said.

Lynne continued to look at her, and Angie felt herself giving in to her gaze, saying a little helplessly, 'I think sometimes in life you just say to yourself, enough's enough.'

'But you never really know, do you?'

Angie folded her arms and settled further back into the sofa. 'Well, I think sometimes you *do* know.' She looked over at Lynne and smiled again. 'But *you* don't know yet, do you?'

Lynne pulled at a loose yarn in her jumper. It bunched up, then gave way a little.

'No.'

Angie laughed, and stood up.

'Oh, you will at some point, I'm sure.'

17.

Whitworth had never done an interview like it – the way Val seemed to need to valiantly defend and carefully document the absolute absence of insight she had to offer about Katie. It was as if she couldn't see the girl as anything other than the extended arm of her own vendetta. She seemed to refuse to see the girl as a person, just something to grind her axe on. Yes, she had seemed troubled sometimes – why should she not? It's troubling work we do here. Had she appeared happy in her relationship? God knows, but if her boyfriend was as useless as most of the young men Val knew, then there was no reason why she would have been.

She was still refusing to let them speak to the residents. That was, she refused until Brookes asked her, with an assumed innocence that Whitworth had to admire, how it was that she hadn't known Katie was working under an assumed name, given, he added in a masterstroke, 'You must surely have run a DBS background check on her?'

Val went very quiet then, and in a constricted voice she said, 'We're on very limited resources here, Detective.'

'Oh, tell me about it,' Brookes said. He gave a bland smile. 'Working on a shoestring budget's nothing new to us in the Force, Mrs Redwood. But . . . and I'm sure you know the legislation and that better than I do . . . but from what I understand, Katie was working around kids, is that right?'

Val Redwood swallowed.

'Not directly.'

'In that case, I'd have thought – and I'd need to double-check here – but I would assume that having an enhanced DBS check would be a legal requirement. What do you reckon, sir?'

He turned to Whitworth, who nodded.

'I think you'd be right there, Constable.' Clever lad.

'It was pending,' Val said, very quietly. 'These things can take six months. I'd been advertising this post for nearly a year and . . .'

'And what?'

'And my instincts towards Katie were . . .'

'But she was around the children on a daily basis?'

'That's right.'

Brookes nodded brightly. 'Pending, was it? Well, that explains that. You weren't to know. These things can take for ever. Tell you what, we can leave it off the paperwork. Don't want anyone getting the wrong idea about your employment practices, do we?'

Val shook her head slowly. 'No.'

'Now, could you bring in the first of the ladies staying here so we can get on with asking our questions?'

Val said nothing, but stood up from the desk, and nodded. Then –

'We've had more nasty tweets, you know.' Her lower lip seemed to wobble slightly. The effect was jelly-like. 'Awful things. Bitch. Whore. Slut. You know.'

Whitworth didn't know, but he felt he could guess well enough to nod an encouraging, 'Yes, love, we're on the case,' and usher her out with his eyes.

He waited until she'd left the room to lean towards Brookes and mutter, 'Well done.'

Whitworth was now waiting for Val to bring in the Asian girl who had raised the alarm on the first day Katie went missing. He had been unwilling to start making concessions to Val Redwood, but he had to admit that two male detectives questioning a traumatized Asian girl might not be the most photogenic option.

'We'll do one-on-one interviews,' he had said to Brookes.

Brookes had looked furious for a second but had quickly smoothed his face out.

It had been something of a relief to give the lad an order after their conversation with Val Redwood – the whole interaction had left him feeling useless. Stupid. He knew Brookes had done a good job. Young talent ought to give him hope for the future.

'Cool,' Brookes said, and smiled. 'Totally get where you're coming from. Don't want any misinterpretations.'

'Don't want to frighten this girl,' Whitworth continued. 'Especially if she's been horribly beaten by her father.'

'Brother,' Brookes said absent-mindedly.

'Father, brother . . .' Whitworth swatted the quibble away. 'Whatever. I think it's best if it's just me.'

'Anyway, gives me a chance to crack on with my research into "Katie Straw".' He used air quotes to sketch his scepticism around the name.

Police work, in Whitworth's experience, was like trying to find your away around a town that is made up almost completely of cul-de-sacs, just on the off chance you might find the one road that leads somewhere.

'Are there really no female officers available to conduct the interview?' Val asked, seemingly as a last-ditch attempt at obstruction. Whitworth had smiled at her.

'None with the appropriate experience, I'm afraid,' he replied, thinking briefly of Melissa, with her too-tight skirt, back at the station.

Val had told them in a thorny whisper that the girl had been horribly beaten because she didn't want to be forced into marriage; that she was *terrified* – her eyes had opened like a set of blinds at the word – of men. That he must. Be. Sensitive.

She offered no further direction on what sensitivity was supposed to look like.

Whitworth had dealt with a few of them in the past. Asians, that is.

He found that they tended to be tough nuts to crack. You're not supposed to generalize, but what was a cop's instinct without the occasional generalization? Besides, it wasn't as though he thought the closed-ranks mindset was a bad thing.

It was all about family for Asians, which was bang on the money as far as Whitworth was concerned. Family honour. Most English people didn't get a sense of things like honour until they were older. Middle-aged, he supposed. The age when you realize family's all you've got.

'I know this is frightening, Nazia,' he told the girl once she had settled, speaking with as much clarity as he could muster. 'But we really need to understand what Katie's movements were that night.'

'I'm not frightened.' The Brum accent was so unexpected it took all of Whitworth's self-control not to look around the room to see if someone else was speaking. 'I want to help.'

He smiled at her. When his voice came out, he noticed that it was oddly slow.

'Could you tell me when you last saw Katie, please, Nazia?'

'Thursday. Late afternoon. Early evening. Fourish?'

He gave her his kindest smile. Get her on side, he thought. Make her think you set some store by her judgement.

'Did you notice anything odd about Katie's behaviour that day?' he asked.

'Well . . .' Nazia paused for a long time, pulling the cuffs of her jumper over her hands so they stretched. 'Maybe she was a bit quiet. Not that happy. But she never seemed very happy.' She shut her mouth sharply and made an odd, reflexive sort of movement, as if to tuck her cropped hair behind her ears. 'But I don't know if this is the kind of job that makes people happy.'

'How do you mean?'

'She mostly just filled in forms. She always seemed tired.'

Like everyone else in the world, then.

Whitworth decided that the best approach was to keep looking kind. People tended to have two broad ideas of police officers – the harsh type, and the kind type. With a witness like this, you needed to make them think that you were the kind type, that they were talking to you because they wanted to.

Perhaps that was what Val Redwood had meant when she told him he had to be *sensitive*.

'Wouldn't have thought this was the kind of job you'd do unless you care about it. Like me, being in the police.'

'Maybe. Maybe there's all sorts of reasons you'd want to do it. Maybe it makes you feel better about things.'

'What, working here or working in the police?'

'Both. Neither. I don't know.'

'Maybe it all got a bit much for her.'

'Maybe it did.'

'Did she strike you as a strong sort of person?' He knew it wasn't a good question. There was no real aim to it. But he'd said it without thinking.

'I'm not really sure how strong people are supposed to strike you.' The counterpunching quality in this girl was growing. She wrapped her arms around herself. 'I'm not sure if there's anything that great about being strong.'

'So . . . would you say that you thought she was weak?'

It was a dangerous question. A dangling question. Anyone who was observing would say that it implied a value judgement, and value judgements were supposedly a no-no. Which was bollocks, of course, because value judgements existed for a reason.

He could see that the girl – Nazia? – was considering whether or not to take the bait.

'I think she was normal. I don't know if that makes her more or less likely to kill herself.' Then, it seemed, it was her turn to be curious. The veiled look lifted away for a second. 'Is there a certain type of person that kills themselves?'

Whitworth remembered that in her culture – he wasn't sure exactly where she was from, but you could more or less guess – they tended to think of suicide as a sin. A mindset like that didn't have much wiggle room for the idea of terrible unhappiness. God was supposed to decide when you died, and it demonstrated a certain kind of uppityness to think that you could weigh in on the decision.

They used to think of it that way here, too, of course, but people had matured out of that idea. Now suicide was a pathology, something that couldn't be helped.

In his bones, he felt the answer – yes, there was a type of person, and that type of person was selfish. But you're not supposed to say that.

Whitworth wondered how much better he'd be able to do his job if he didn't have to spend so much damn energy trying to remember all the different things that you were and weren't supposed to say.

'Yes.' The yes was supposed to stand for 'Yes. People who are depressed. People who just need it to stop, need the pain to go away. Suicide is the cure that kills them.'

A woman like his mother wouldn't have dreamed of killing herself, not when there was a family to take care of.

'I don't know if she was one of those people. But I don't think Katie killed herself, if that's what you're trying to ask.'

'What makes you say that?'

'Just a feeling.'

A feeling. He changed the subject, which made it feel like

an embarrassing piece of small talk rather than a police interview on a suicide investigation.

'So, Nazia, you were the first person to notice that Katie was missing?'

Back on solid ground. The girl was scowling now, resisting. This was good; this meant that he was probing somewhere close to the wound.

'I didn't notice she was missing, I just noticed she wasn't here.'

Jennifer did that manoeuvre sometimes. The truth always had to be on her terms. He wondered if his daughter would ever inspire as much irritation in an older person trying to talk to her as he was feeling now. But his tone remained on track.

'So you weren't concerned?'

'I just assume everyone else knows what's going on.'

It was worth another stab.

'Did Katie say anything to you to indicate that she might not be able to attend her appointment with you?'

'I've got no reason to think that there was anything wrong with Katie.' Nazia shrugged. 'That doesn't mean there wasn't anything wrong, it just means sometimes it's hard to tell. I mean, maybe she was stressed out that day. Plenty of things could have stressed her. That's what it's like round here. Doorbell rings and everyone's heart stops. You hear the gravel crunching and every one of us is thinking, *All right, there he is, he's found me. And that's . . . that's the end. Of everything.*' She shifted in her seat and made the odd movement with her hair again. 'Is there anything else? Can I go?'

'What could have upset Katie. Specifically?'

'I don't know. Work. Work stresses you out, right?'

'Right.'

'And . . . there was a guy that day.'

'A guy? What guy?'

'Just a guy. I don't know. White guy, I think.'

'You think?'

'Didn't see him.'

'When you say there was a guy . . .'

'Yeah. On the street.'

'Doing what?'

'Nothing. Just a guy who walked up and down a couple of times.'

'At what time?'

'Dunno. I didn't see him. Lynne did, though. And Sonia.'

'But he wasn't doing anything?'

Whitworth didn't care to admit it to anyone, but he'd walked past this house a few times over the years and wondered what warranted the small CCTV camera mounted above the door, the expensive padlock on the side gate. The cheap cars outside the swanky house. He'd wondered if it was an old folks' home, or maybe the territory of a former soap star fallen on hard times.

Maybe he, too, had stood there, eyes inquiring, hands in pockets.

Maybe a woman like Nazia had stared back from behind a net curtain, heart thudding.

'Do you think that Katie was a good person?' Stupid question, he knew, but he was sick of navel-gazing. He needed to crack the thought, to say something out loud.

'Yes.' There was a look in her eyes he couldn't put a finger on, a look that he wasn't used to seeing on faces like hers. Defiance.

Then Whitworth did something that he didn't do, something it normally wouldn't have occured to him to do. He put his hand out and covered Nazia's with it. She jumped slightly.

'Then keep believing that,' he said. 'We all just need to find our way to muddle through the day.'

She nodded in the kind of way that he interpreted as not

agreeing with him, and it seemed that whatever was taking place between them – whether it was powered by the force of confidence or compulsion – had drawn to a close. He became aware of her small stature and the cashew-creaminess of her brown skin.

The girl was giving him a look he couldn't give a name to, a look through wary eyes that gave him the urge to fold his arms across his chest and look away, to cut off her gaze. He grunted that the interview was over.

She stood up, and he felt some odd desire to see her out of the room. Perhaps it was a paternal thing. He wanted to say something kind to her, to tell her that it would be all right, somehow, even though he knew the odds were that for a girl in her position it wouldn't be.

All the more reason to say it, he supposed.

When he opened the door for her he nearly collided with a tall, bone-thin, colourless woman hovering outside the door. *Junkie*. The thought was automatic, as was the impulse to tell her to move on.

'What do you want?'

The woman shrank back, hovered, sidestepped, looking past him to where Nazia's face was, several inches below his shoulder.

'Nothing, all right?' She seemed outraged. 'Just . . .' Her face sliced into a smile that looked like raw meat. 'Just wondering where Naz was. Wanted to check on my girl. Hey, Naz. All right, Naz?'

'Yeah, thanks,' Nazia muttered. She hurried past Whitworth and stood next to the junkie. Though separately so fragile, the two of them standing together looked like a wall.

'Cheers,' Nazia muttered to Whitworth. 'See you later.'

He gave a blunt nod and shut the door.

★

Whitworth exited the room a few minutes later, after scribbling a couple of notes. On his way out he asked Val Redwood – who was hovering outside – to call in the next resident. The woman's features yanked into their habitual scowl.

'I wasn't aware that, in addition to single-handedly running this refuge, I was also operating as your secretary, Detective.'

He smiled at her good-humouredly. It was his go-to response for dealing with difficult women. Maureen was wise to it, but Val wasn't. Not yet.

'We appreciate everything you're doing, love,' he said blandly. What he didn't say, though he was longing to, was *How could you not notice that your own employee was using a false name, you stupid, incompetent, blinkered woman?* Cutting corners was a bad look for anyone, but it especially grated on him with this drum-banging parody of a feminist, with her red lipstick, her arsey condescension, her sad dead employee.

Val was looking at him coolly. He smiled at her.

Nazia had receded into the labyrinth of the refuge. There were endless doors in that building, doors that always looked the same and no doubt opened into the rooms of women who were all the same, the same retelling of the same story.

Whitworth had the idea, just for a second, of calling Nazia back and telling her that she would be all right. That she might be wrong about Katie not being the type to kill herself, but that was okay. She was still young, and she had the right to make her own mistakes, and she should seize and enjoy every one of them.

But she had already gone.

Brookes slouched around the corner.

'Noah's in the station making his statement,' he reported, eyeing his phone screen dispassionately. He looked up at Whitworth. 'Might be time for that chat.'

'Chat,' Whitworth echoed mechanically.

Nazia's face. *I don't think Katie killed herself.*

Reflexively, Whitworth folded his arms.

'All right. We'll head off, then.'

'What about the rest of the interviews?'

'We'll come back later,' Whitworth said. After all, it didn't make sense to linger here too long when the smart money was usually on the boyfriend.

18.

'There's a man outside!'

Sonia had to admit that her heart thrummed at Val's words, for a second. She hurried to the window faster than common sense could kick in.

White. Old. Sixties. Grey hair. Fat.

Not David.

He raised a hand in greeting, his fluorescent jacket flapping in the wind. The other hand was holding the blue plastic recycling box.

It was the fucking bin man.

Trust Val.

She had already dashed out the front door and was advancing on the poor guy.

'Sorry, love, we've run a bit late this morning,' he said, his words carrying through the open front door and into the lounge. Val was darting around him like an overweight Border collie, producing words that didn't resolve into sentences, shepherding him off the driveway.

'Yes . . . thank you . . . enough . . .'

When Val returned it was clear that she had lost the thread of their conversation. Not, Sonia suspected, that she'd ever had much of a grasp on it to start with.

'These men can often try to intimidate you in a courtroom,' Val interrupted, when Sonia tried to launch into her pre-prepared speech again. 'But I'm sure you won't let that affect you, Sonia. We all know how strong you are.'

Sonia winced, but quickly absorbed the shock and restored her face to its canvas calm.

Val blinked.

'Oooh, I do like your new hairdo,' she said, before giving a queenly nod and shuffling off down the hall.

It was all Sonia could do not to lean against the wall of the corridor and let herself slide to the floor, but she managed to resist. She'd never much liked the look of the carpet in this place.

She had spent such a long time trying to explain to Katie that strength wasn't what she needed,. but something softer, warmer, milkier, for her moment on the stand.

It was impossible to explain to Katie, let alone Val, exactly what that something was. Easier to get the bus to Manchester, then another bus to Moss Side, to get her hair relaxed. Thank God Angie had offered to babysit.

'We all need a bit of a pamper now and then,' Angie had said. Sonia knew she was trying to be kind.

Sonia had let them leave the relaxant on long after it began to burn her. The strength of the pain in her scalp seemed to push everything out, even the fear of seeing David again.

He'd look handsome in a suit. Probably the same suit he'd worn to their wedding, if she knew him – and know him she did. He hadn't gained an ounce since the day they got married. Sonia wished the same could be said for her.

He'd flash her that grin – that special grin, the one that was just for her – when their eyes met. She could already see it starting to form, in her mind's eye, as she stared into the salon mirror. He'd go in on a charm offensive. That was always how he got what he wanted.

The boys would tear away from her and run straight into his arms. She was sure of that, too. She wasn't sure if it was because they were more scared of him than of her, or they loved him more than her, but they always flung themselves into his arms in a way they never did with her.

They acted out with her because they knew it was safe to do so. A social worker had told her that, and it had made Sonia feel better, for moments at a time. Her boys could push away from her, cry, wail, frown. It didn't mean they didn't need her at the same bone-depth that she needed them.

But she was too susceptible to a flashed smile from a shining face, a pair of devoted eyes. She always had been. That was why she was in this mess.

Then the hairdresser had sculpted her hair into blameless waves.

'Like Michelle Obama, yeah?'

'Yeah,' Sonia agreed, staring into the mirror. 'Exactly.'

19.

Then

Jamie picks her up. Her mother asks him in, but he says no. He waits in the car until Katie is ready.

She is wearing a carefully selected knee-length dress. Most of her clothes are at least knee-length now; Jamie says he isn't keen on her dressing up too much. The words he uses are 'getting all dolled up', but with Jamie sometimes you have to read between the lines. She is sure it means nothing more than looking what most boys refer to as 'fake'.

'I like *real* girls,' he says.

So she finds it easier to wear what he wants. He doesn't exactly say anything, but she prefers the evenings when she isn't wondering if her dress has ridden up too high or if her top is too low.

When she gets into the car he barely glances over at her. Usually when they go out together, he tells her that she looks pretty, but now he only says, 'Okay,' then releases the hand-brake, frowning into the rear-view mirror as if something is chasing him.

Katie's phone buzzes.

'Who's that?' Jamie asks.

It's Ellie. *Cheeky midweek wine Wednesday night? x*

'Vodafone,' Katie says. She deletes the text before she can consider replying.

They pull up to a small, ugly semi-detached house in a part of town that isn't exactly poor, but not as affluent as where Katie lives.

The front gardens are maintained with a degree of neatness that Katie knows her dad would have referred to as 'lower middle class'.

A black-and-white cat comes out of the back garden. It miaows raucously at Jamie as he leads Katie down the front garden path. He bends to scratch it behind the ear.

'Hello, missus,' he says to the cat, with more attention than he paid Katie over the course of the whole car journey.

He takes out a key. It seems odd to Katie, to think of Jamie having keys to somewhere. She's so used to him standing on her doorstep, ringing the bell. Her mother has suggested that they give him a key, for ease's sake, but Katie said no, not quite knowing why.

At the very first sound of the key scraping in the lock, a small, slim figure starts to move behind the swirled frosted glass of the front door.

At the same time as Jamie pushes the door open, it's pulled back. A neatly dressed blonde woman, shorter than Katie, stands in the hallway. She smiles determinedly at Jamie, and he scowls back at her.

'Hi, Mum.' His voice is without inflection.

Katie knows he's nervous. His mother seems to know that, too. She turns her smile on Katie like a rotating camera.

'Well, hello,' she says.

She extends her hand with a formality that Katie feels compelled to mirror.

'Aren't you going to introduce us properly?' she asks Jamie, after a few seconds of silent hand-shaking.

He raises his eyebrows. 'Christ, give me a second, will you?'

Then he seems to relax, and a careful smile appears on his face. 'Mum, this is Katie. Katie, Mum.'

'Karen,' says Jamie's mum. 'So lovely to meet you at last, Katie. Jamie's told me all about you.'

'No, I haven't,' Jamie mutters under his breath, then follows his mother through the hallway.

He doesn't hold out his hand or gesture in any way for Katie to join him, but she follows anyway, wiping her feet ostentatiously on the mat, then, after a few seconds of dithering, taking her shoes off. She follows him into the living room in stockinged feet.

In a small dining area, the table is set for three. Two candles are burning, though it is still light outside and all the house lights are turned on. Karen hurries back to a kitchenette that rears unexpectedly away from the sitting room.

'We've had an extension put in,' she says, and seems a little embarrassed by it. 'It's only tiny, but it helps us.'

Katie nods.

'It's lovely. Great' – she gestures around – 'space.'

'It's just a roast, I'm afraid,' Karen says, bending down to open the oven, as if the comment is an apology. 'I hope that's all right with you.' For a second, she looks stricken. 'You're not a vegetarian or anything, are you?'

Katie shakes her head.

She wants to say something cleverer than yes or no, but the words aren't there. Jamie still hasn't so much as looked at her.

She shuffles a little closer to him, her feet seeming incredibly loud on the thick carpet, and hooks her arm around his. He makes no response that would indicate he's noticed her presence.

She leans up to kiss him on the cheek and he bends back, away from her.

'Not in front of my mum,' he mutters.

Katie sits down at the table, thinking that it probably isn't worth waiting to be asked.

'This is lovely,' she says.

The candles are bright blue and have already started to drip into white ceramic holders, which look brand new. She wonders whether they've been purchased specially for the occasion.

A bottle of Jacob's Creek screw-top stands in the middle of the table, with the top off, as if to aerate the wine.

Karen comes back into the dining area and seems to catch Katie looking.

'I'm not a big drinker, I'm afraid,' she says. Katie isn't sure if she's heard Karen say anything yet apart from her own name in a way that's neither a question nor an apology.

The roast is served. The carrots and roast potatoes are shrivelled and the beef is what Katie's dad would have called 'well done', with a rolled eye and the closest thing he ever gave to a snort.

Karen reaches over to the bottle of Jacob's Creek.

'Wine?' she asks Katie.

Katie smiles. 'Just a little bit, please.'

She barely allows the splash to land in her glass before saying with a sharpness that she does her best to dilute, 'Oh, thanks, that's plenty for me.'

Karen reaches over to pour some for Jamie, but he puts his hand over his glass.

'Not drinking tonight, Mum.'

It's rarer for Jamie to have a night when he *does* drink, Katie is starting to notice. He always wants to be in control – she sees it when the two of them go out together.

Or maybe he just doesn't like the taste of alcohol. Whatever his reasons are, it looks like self-control to her, and she likes that about him.

She wishes she could have a little bit more of the horrible wine.

'I'll just have a taste,' Karen says, pouring herself a drop even smaller than that in Katie's glass. She smiles down at it, as if it's done something to please her. 'Goodness, that's lots for me.'

She is wearing a white linen button-down shirt, the kind of thing that Katie would never dare wear because it would only get rumpled and stained. But Karen obviously isn't going to let a single drop of red splash it.

There is nothing to do but eat the food, and as she does she wishes that she hadn't inherited – for it must have been inherited, surely – that constant inner monologue which makes her feel she needs to pronounce on things one way or another. Why, she wonders, can she never just *be*?

Jamie's mum speaks little, seeming to form all her sentences in advance, with vowels so smooth and rounded they seem like they've been polished on their way out of her mouth.

She asks Katie what she does for work – though Katie is sure that if she'd heard anything about her from Jamie, then she must at least have heard that.

But then, Jamie has said, they aren't big talkers in his family. It's one of the things that she chalks up to a kind of cultural difference, beyond the realm of examination or dispute.

Once Katie has told Karen what her job is there doesn't seem much else to say, save that the meal is delicious. It isn't bad, but Katie finds herself praising it to a degree that feels almost manic.

But then, anything might have felt manic in the static whiteness of that too-warm room.

Karen then gingerly asks how Katie's mum is – a question that feels genuine, but unanswerable. Katie mentally reaches into a drawer and fumbles around until she finds her habitual smile, which she quickly pastes on, then says, 'She's doing okay, thanks.'

She wants to move the conversation back on to something they can at least pretend sits between the three of them, rather than resting so squarely on her. She turns to smile at Jamie and says, 'This one's a huge help. He's been amazing.'

She's a little surprised to see the questioning look sit on Karen's face for a second, before smoothing itself out into blankness.

'He's always been a very dutiful boy,' Karen says.

She smiles at Jamie in a way that seems to pour out some kind of excess. 'Very conscientious. His work are so lucky to have him.'

'They're lucky to have anyone who'll join,' Jamie says. He stabs at his meat as if it's annoying him.

Katie's body is still nagging at her, reminding her that she's hungry. Something about the restless eagerness of Karen's eyes has made her feel that only the smallest portions of everything are appropriate. The hard knob of overcooked meat. The vinegary red wine. The ice-crystallized vanilla ice cream and flavourless chocolate cake that Karen digs out of the freezer for dessert.

'Anyone for tea?' she asks brightly after they've got up from the table. Katie offers to make it, but Karen shakes her head, frowning a little.

'No, no, you sit down.'

Katie sits on the sofa next to Jamie. Not the way they usually sit – close, like they're trying to press any air between them out of existence. Instead, she perches just on the edge of the low sofa. When Karen has receded into the kitchen, she leans over and puts her head on Jamie's shoulder. But he shrugs her off.

'Not now, Katie. Come on.'

'I was just going for a hug . . .' Katie does her best not to put on too wounded a voice. Her usual way of looking at Jamie seems to be having no effect on him.

'Yeah, I know. Not here, though. It's weird with my mum here. She's funny about that stuff.'

Karen returns from the kitchen with three mugs of tea on a

flowered plastic tray. The tea is more grey than brown. It sloshes close to the rim of the mug as she sets the tray down.

'What now?' she asks brightly. 'Bit of telly, maybe?'

'We need to get going, Mum,' Jamie says sharply. 'Need to get back to Katie's place.'

Karen's eyes widen briefly, then her lips pull upwards again. The same abstracted smile.

'Of course,' she says. 'But you've got time for your tea, don't you?'

'Not really.'

Jamie's hands are already reaching restlessly for his car keys, which sit in isolation on the neatness of the coffee table.

'We've got to head off.'

'Well, that's nice,' Karen says.

Her voice is so perfectly modulated that Katie does a slight double-take. If it wasn't for the blankness of her face, then Karen could have been reading a script for an advert for a happy family. She has no idea what it is. Every tiny muscle in Karen's face seems to suggest a smile, yet whatever warmth naturally exists in a smile is absent.

'It was lovely to meet you, Katie.'

Karen stands up, the three mugs clutched between her hands. She seems like she might be withholding a wince from the hot porcelain, but the lines of her body betray nothing as she walks back into the kitchen.

That night Katie watches Jamie while he sleeps. His long eyelashes are spread out over his cheeks, his mouth soft and newborn-like. She turns on to her side and nuzzles into his neck. He gives a little murmur, then turns over to slot his body next to hers. One arm clamps her into his stomach. The weight of it makes it a little hard to breathe, but she feels safe.

'Good night, Jamie.'

'Good night, beautiful.' He presses his face into her neck. 'I love you.'

She takes his hands in hers. Starts to move them over her skin. Lightly at first, as if she is finding her body anew with his fingertips. She keeps moving his hands until she isn't sure who is doing the moving. It is as if the two of them are locked in the contracted spell of a Ouija board. The impulsion exists somewhere between them; she can't say whether he is touching her arms, breasts, thighs, stomach because that is what she wants or what he wants. Her will seems to merge with his for whole moments at a time. Her breast is tight in his grip, her hips locked close to his, his breath soft and intentional in her ear.

Then – 'Not tonight, Katie.' He kisses her on the naked space beneath her ear. 'I think we'd better not tonight.'

20.

Now

They were standing in the corridor, for want of somewhere else to brief. Noah was tucked up in a little room where they usually took witness statements. Not an interrogation room. Whitworth didn't want Khan getting wind of an official interrogation. That would imply a suspect, which would imply a murder.

'You can lead,' he said to Brookes. 'I'll step in if it's going off track. It'll be less intimidating coming from a junior officer.'

'Are we questioning him, or not?'

'Not quite. Just leaning.'

They went into the room. Brookes was holding Noah's written statement in his hand.

'How's it going, Noah?' Whitworth said jovially. He must have overdone it a bit, because Noah looked alarmed.

'Shouldn't I get a lawyer?' Noah said uncertainly. 'If you're interrogating me?'

Whitworth felt slightly touched at Noah's faith in his own honesty.

'We aren't interrogating you, mate. Like we've said, this isn't a murder investigation.'

'But you think I did something,' Noah said miserably. 'I didn't. I was in Glasgow. I was hammered. I wasn't here.'

'The more you tell us the truth, the more we can help you,' Brookes said. He was standing above Noah. Whitworth could see the tableau of the interrogation as clearly as if it had been painted on to a canvas. Even the lighting was melodramatic – Brookes had turned off most of the main lights and kept on only the one directly above, casting his own face half in shadow and giving both men a devilish look. That was the idea, Whitworth supposed.

'Why didn't you report her missing, Noah? Eh? What was that all about?'

'I wasn't here.'

'And you don't usually talk to her when you're away?'

'She wasn't answering her phone.'

'So what?' Something changed just a little in Brookes's voice. 'So you don't make an effort to work out what's happened to her? You weren't worried? You didn't ring around? You didn't come back?'

Noah's head was bent. Whitworth heard the noises before they assembled themselves into words, understood from them only the overwhelming sense of defeat, of what it meant when even your words were broken.

'I thought she'd left me.'

'And you didn't find out for sure?'

'Katie was like that. She didn't do confrontation. She just closed down. You could see her working out where the exit was, but she never said anything.'

Whitworth felt a strange jolt. Perhaps it was just surprise at hearing what felt like something reasonably perceptive emerging from Noah's mouth; perhaps it was just the recognition of something that he'd seen before. Not in his own wife, nor even in his mother. It was something he'd known in himself, from long ago, before he'd become the man he was now.

His brother had lashed out once at his dad, hit him, and hadn't even been hit back. Whitworth would never forget the fury on Andrew's face when his dad had left the room, the gradual realization that the fist laid on his father hadn't made him feel a damn jot better.

But that had never been Whitworth's way. He'd never said anything. He'd pacified, acquiesced, taken any excuse he could find to simultaneously make himself useful and leave the room.

It was only now that he was starting to understand his father, to understand how readily available that endless spring of anger was to him, too. He had assumed that it must simply be mingled with the blood. That he was, whether he liked it or not, from one of *those* kinds of families. That all he could offer was the strength to shield his daughter from it. If there was that rage in him, then the spring of it was so far below underground, completely hidden from daylight, and he was determined to always keep it that way. That way, there was never the ugliness of that scene, of Dad standing over Mum with a fist that had been raised and would be raised again.

That was something. As a father, that was something.

'So you didn't find out where she was?'

Back in the room, Whitworth. Set a good example.

'If she wanted to go, then I'd want her to go, too. No sense in her staying where she didn't want to be.'

Whitworth saw that Brookes was throwing him a subtle glance, and he nodded. Time to deploy their one trick card.

'We've got reason to believe that Katie was living under a false identity.'

Noah looked prosaically baffled, as if he'd been given incorrect change in a shop.

'A false identity?' His voice was the voice of someone who'd never seen a lie through in his life, who wouldn't know how. 'I don't . . . I don't really know what you mean by that.'

'I mean her name, Noah.' Brookes leaned closer. 'Did she ever say anything to you about using a false name? Did you ever see any documentation under a different name? Anything at all?'

145

'No. No. It was real. She was real. You've made a mistake, I'm sure of it.' Noah looked up. His face was apologetic. 'Look, I'm really sorry, and I want to help. But I feel like maybe I ought to have a lawyer here, if you're going to keep asking me questions.'

Whitworth's inward swearing didn't match Brookes's when they returned to the corridor.

'Jesus fucking Christ.'

'All right, Brookes. You did a good job.'

'Could do plenty more with that one, if you'd let me. Before you let him cry for his lawyer.'

'Steady on.' No point in getting angry, Whitworth knew. But boundaries mattered. Rank mattered.

Brookes took a deep breath, and in a remarkably short time he seemed to have regained his composure.

Whitworth was impressed, truth be told. He knew Brookes well enough to know that this loss of cool wasn't a habit, but you had to expect it from time to time from a young guy who was hungry for his first big win.

'Look how shifty he was,' Brookes continued, his face intently focused. 'He thought she was going to leave him. He knew she was going to leave him all alone and he'd do anything to stop her. I bet you anything.'

Something about the scenario sounded convincing. The human drama. The breathtaking pettiness, maybe.

'What about the name, though?' Whitworth frowned, folding his arms. 'I believed him about the name, didn't you?'

'I did,' Brookes said, seeming to catch himself slightly. 'I . . . yeah, no, you're right. I did.' He shrugged. 'Maybe the name thing's a distraction. Maybe it's just a database error. Maybe that really was her name. We don't know.'

Whitworth thought of that world of names and faces which

existed in the ether of a computer. Could there have been a mistake? Why the hell not? He didn't trust all that stuff, anyway. The idea that anyone was just a few clicks away from being found and pinned down was supposed to be a boon to police officers, but the truth was that it made him shiver.

'Look. You may well be right. Could be that your instinct's sharper than mine and he is hiding something. Wouldn't be the first guy to kill his girlfriend. But . . . look.' Whitworth thought back to the CCTV from Amir's.

He thought of Khan. *Do I need to come in, DS Whitworth?*

He put his hand on Brookes's shoulder. 'Let's at least follow up the one solid lead we actually have. Before we go accusing a perfectly nice lad of murdering his girlfriend just because the statistics say there's a chance of it. People aren't numbers. It's more complicated than that.'

21.

The refuge's large garden was chilly in February. But, Sonia reminded herself, it was good for the boys to have somewhere to run around.

She was cold, even in her puffa coat. She scrunched herself into the corner of the grey wooden bench and let her shoulders cave in, screwing up her face as if she might trap a little bit of warmth into its creases.

'Mum. Watch us! *Mum!*'

The boys seemed to be everywhere at once: leaping off the mossy slide, trampling over what Val always optimistically referred to as the 'vegetable patch', churning what was left of the lawn deeper into the mud with their trainers.

Lewis and Danny had everything that she loved about David in them, all his dizzying qualities. Whatever it was that David had that could make Sonia – shy-girl Sonia, always at the edge of a party – dance around the kitchen, singing at the top of her lungs – they had it, too. In their faces she saw the same devotion as when he told her that he had never met another woman like her, that she was irreplaceable.

'I'll die if you don't marry me,' he said. That was how he proposed, and how Sonia recounted it for years, a broad smile on her lips at the memory.

I'll die if you leave me.

Sonia had repeated those words to Val on the day she arrived at the refuge.

Sonia had brought David home when she was eighteen and had been unable to suppress her proud grin. Her mum's voice, usually free of all restraint, had been so careful when she said she hoped Sonia would be happy. Her voice was the same when Sonia had produced those two caramel-coloured babies with their silky mess of black curls and their beautiful, crumpled little faces. She had touched these babies cautiously, with just the tips of her fingers. It wasn't that there was no love in her touch, just that there was something else as well.

David told her to take no notice of her mother. They visited less and less.

The boys were charmers; they could get away with anything. They had a silly side that was more than just being kids, the kind of joy in life that made you feel that all the colours were turned up.

They adored her just as much as their dad did, burying their faces into the front of her sweater the same way he did when he was asking forgiveness.

They even had the same quick little fists that would snap out and strike her in moments of frustration.

'*Watch* us!'

The deflated tennis ball hit Sonia right in the chest, on a rib that wore the memory of being cracked. She winced, but drew her face into a smile when she saw the ease drain out of Lewis's face.

'Here you go!' she called, throwing the ball back to him. Its arc through the air was distorted by its dented shape and it sliced away from him.

They started knocking it back and forth between them. *Thud. Thud. Thud.*

She watched as their faces relaxed and realized that she was tapping out the rhythmic thud of the broken ball on her own arm. Trying to convince her body to exist in perfect sympathy with theirs once again.

★

The detectives hadn't bothered interviewing her. Not properly, anyway. The younger one had sort of brushed against a few questions without seeming very interested in the answers. He hadn't wanted her analysis of Katie or what she had or hadn't been going through. That was – well, not fine, but not unexpected.

'One of the ladies mentioned something about seeing people hanging around,' the cop said casually. 'You don't know anything about that, do you?'

Sonia shrugged. 'Yeah, I've seen men,' she said. 'They're half the world's population, right?'

The detective laughed. 'Right, point taken.' But then he looked serious again. 'But nothing that's worried you?'

'No,' Sonia said firmly. She didn't have time for this, not in her life, and definitely not in her mind. There was no time to think about anything other than her boys, and there was certainly no time for chasing ghosts.

He'd played footie with the boys for a bit, though. She had seen the adoration blossoming on their faces but pushed back the feeling. Now wasn't then, and the cop wasn't David.

Her analysis, for what it was worth, was that it was all a hateful, fucking waste. That it had been Katie who'd walked towards them when she'd stood waiting at the pillar box with a small hand in each of hers and her throat turned to concrete. Katie who'd made her a cup of tea at the kitchen table, Katie who had seen the shine of her eyes and hurried the boys off to sit down in front of a DVD.

In that sense, she resented Katie for dying. God knows Sonia'd had the idea of killing herself, too, but the idea had never taken flight in her head; it was always tied down by reality. For a mother, suicide isn't on the roster of options.

She wasn't looking forward to finding a way of telling her boys that Katie was dead, a way of pre-digesting it for them like a mother bird so that she could spit it out into easy sense. Besides, she had started to realize, she always somehow ended up telling her boys the wrong thing.

She'd have to find a way to explain that in court, too, to make enough sense of it that the judge could gobble it all up without needing to chew too much.

'Why can't you both just say sorry to each other? It doesn't *matter* who started it.'

There was her boy, her little Lewis, wheeling out his best six-year-old morality. 'You need to try and see each other's side of the story.'

If time had slowed down to allow it, and if Sonia's mouth hadn't been too swollen to speak, she would have praised her boy. Because he was right, of course. There were things more important than being right, that was what she had tried to teach him. Things like being kind and gentle and honest and brave.

But she regretted teaching him about bravery. She regretted telling him that if he saw something that wasn't fair, he needed to stand up to it. Because now his small body was between Sonia and the fist. The fist continued towards Sonia, but the impact absorbed into the body of her boy.

Lewis didn't have her solidity. When David punched Sonia, her flesh would yield a little, absorb and accept the blow. She might be flung back, but she wouldn't be conquered by it.

But when David hit Lewis, his body was no match for the force that confronted it. He seemed to fly through the air.

There was a beat. A silence. A moment when no one moved.

Then Sonia flung herself at David in a way that she had never moved before, didn't even know that she was capable of moving. Her nails seemed to grow into talons as she scratched at his face. She didn't even recognize the noises that were coming out of her. It was what it meant to be human, mother, woman, to tear him to pieces.

If she could have killed him, she would have.

A neighbour called the police. They pulled her off him and held her down and ground her face into the floor and snatched her boys away, as if *she* were the monster.

Perhaps she was. Because, in that hanging moment when no one moved, Sonia had looked into the future and seen a life in which the boys carried bruises on their skin, and she smiled and lied and told them that Daddy loved them really.

And that was far too easy to believe.

'All right, Sonia?'

Sonia turned to see Val coming through the sliding doors in a flurry of fussy little movements. Sonia moved her mouth into a smile and slid over on the grubby wooden bench. She imagined the line of dark grime carving into the seat of her jeans.

'Lovely to see them enjoying themselves,' Val said, nodding towards the boys and plumping down heavily on the bench. Sonia could hear the pacification in Val's voice, and something else as well, something that had more of a systematic reek to it.

Lovely to see they're not broken beyond repair.

Sonia wanted to say something sarcastic, but she was so used to controlling the impulse, for the boys' sake, that it took little effort to squash it back.

'Yeah,' she said instead. 'Yeah, they're doing well.'

'Good.' Val settled back into herself, looking like she was casting around for a tactful way to change the subject. Then, 'Have the police interviewed you yet?'

Sonia frowned. 'Yeah, of course. Way back when he was arrested. Why, is there supposed to be another one? Nobody told me about . . .'

Val's cheeks reddened slightly. 'Oh, no, sorry, Sonia. I didn't mean about that. I mean . . .' She pointed one scarlet-tipped, pudgy finger towards the refuge. 'I mean *these* police. I mean about Katie.'

'Oh.' Sonia folded her arms and crossed her legs, knowing that the move made her look confrontational, even though she was only trying to stop her embarrassment and disappointment from leaking out of her and getting all over Val. 'Oh, yeah. For about two minutes.'

'Two minutes?'

Danny kicked the tennis ball hard towards them. It hit Val square in the shin, leaving a dusty brown mark on her black polyester trouser leg. 'Oh . . . ow!'

Her boy froze.

'Don't worry, Lewis,' Val added hastily. 'No harm done.' She gave a wide, wide smile. Sonia could see that it wasn't a real smile, but that wasn't the point. They both knew that.

Gradually, Danny's body defossilized.

'Sorry,' he said, his voice uncertain at first.

'Good boy,' Sonia said. 'Well done for saying sorry.'

'No harm done,' Val said again, and, finally relaxing, Danny's movements became fluid again and he sped off across the grass.

'Sorry, Sonia,' Val resumed. 'Did you say two minutes?'

'If that,' Sonia replied, thinking back to her talk with the younger detective.

He'd just asked her to confirm the last time she'd spoken to Katie. When she'd said she didn't remember for sure, but it hadn't been on the day Katie died, he hadn't really pushed the matter.

Sonia had been slightly surprised by that – in her head, she had been practising her soft, gentle voice and squaring up for a fight. She had felt sad for him. That the death of a young girl was clearly routine for him, young as he was.

She had said as much. He had smiled and said it was okay, but Sonia could see for herself that it wasn't.

The kindness, the caring, had been instinctive for her, a behaviour learned from years of broadening her shoulders in accordance with expectations. For a minute, in his plain clothes, he'd been just a boy, not a cop.

'Right.' Val heaved herself up, narrowly avoiding another assault from the squashed tennis ball, and began to stride back towards the house. 'I'll be having a word, then,' she said, to no one in particular.

Yeah. Take it out on a cop who's still barely more than a kid himself.

Sonia realized that her arms and legs were still crossed and let herself slacken. With the distraction of Val gone, the shard of panic lodged deep inside her was making its presence felt with a series of scrapes and scratches in her every movement.

Her court case was next Wednesday.

Family court. Custody. Access to the children. *Arrangements.*

All the hard, pragmatic words that had turned to ghosts in order to haunt her over the past few years.

Everything she'd feared. Now it was happening.

She looked back towards her boys, feasting on every little aspect of their movements like an animal storing up fat for winter. She tried not to imagine herself sitting in the same spot a week from now, when the empty pots might just be empty pots, and the tennis ball might lie undisturbed in the sparse, churned grass.

22.

There was a sharp knock at the door, a man's knock. The detectives must be back. Peony had toddled away, but Lynne clutched reflexively at the space where her daughter ought to be.

The door opened. It was the older detective. Kinder, Lynne thought. Maybe he reminded her of one of her uncles, though, probably, everyone had an uncle who looked a bit like him.

'Hello, Lynne.' He smiled at her, the kind of smile she had seen before on Katie's face. The I-don't-see-you-as-just-a-victim smile. 'Not sure if we've met before, but I'm DS Whitworth. I'm still trying to clear up a few things about the night Katie died.'

Lynne kept forgetting that Katie was dead. It was as if there wasn't enough room in her brain to permanently store that information. The detective sat down on the sofa.

'Would you be happy to have a quick chat with me?'

Lynne dragged the corners of her mouth into what she knew must look like a parody of a smile. Nodded. Stood up.

'We can stay in here,' the detective said. 'As long as you're not worried about your little girl being present?'

It hardly mattered where Peony was; Lynne was worried about her little girl being anywhere. Sometimes she wished she could usher her into the absolute safety of non-existence.

That was the post-natal depression talking. Even now, Lynne was waiting for the afterbirth.

Besides, Peony wouldn't understand. Her language level wasn't very high. That was Lynne's fault – she hadn't talked to her enough at the right stages of development.

'Could you tell me a bit about what happened on the evening

of the ninth of February?' The detective leaned back into the faded paisley sofa cushions. 'Anything you can remember.'

It sounded like an invitation rather than a threat. Lynne imagined him in a police drama. Imagined him lying to her, misleading her. Entrapment, that was the word. His kind face swam before her and she saw him crouched across the chintzy couch like a great spider.

Lynne selected at random a fact that she knew beyond all doubt to be true. That was a technique she'd learned from pacifying Frank – find a centre, a base of reality that she knew to be undeniable, and then cling to it for all she was worth.

The pool of things she knew for sure had dried up over the course of their marriage.

'She left early that night.'

The detective nodded.

'When did you last see Katie, Lynne?'

Lynne tried to remember, but it was like swimming backwards through wet cement.

She could remember so little from that day. The only image she recalled clearly was from the house meeting – dropping a few crumbs of biscuit on the floor and ducking under the table to see Katie's foot rammed into a fossilized angle, determinedly keeping herself stable.

She remembered that from her days in the City. The way the terror always seemed to sit in the small muscles of the jaw, the ankles, the balls of a fist.

Peony had given her terrible grief that day.

'I want my daddy.'

She had said it with calm malice. Hateful little creature.

Lynne knew that children tried to test their parents and she shouldn't be worried. It was just a button that Peony pushed to get a reaction.

But she looked so like Frank. She couldn't look at her daughter for too long without seeing the thing that had ripped her in half and then pinned her tattered pieces to the ground so she would never be able to move again.

Frank had put her back together. He always did.

Lynne realized she hadn't replied to the detective.

'I'm not sure exactly. Afternoon, early afternoon. She said she'd be back in the morning and she'd see me then.'

'Did she?'

The way the detective leapt on the information reminded Lynne of a cat.

'What exactly did she say? Did you get the impression she was really expecting to see you?'

'It was through a door,' Lynne replied. Frank did this kind of thing all the time, drilling into detail. 'I'm not sure. I think she said that.'

'Lynne.'

The detective looked deep at her.

'It's really important that you try to remember this.'

It was. Very important.

'I don't know,' Lynne said. 'It was through the door. Maybe she only said, "I'll see you tomorrow," because that's what people say.'

'What did you say?'

'I said I'd see her tomorrow. Maybe I said it first. Maybe it was the kind of thing that you just always say. I don't know if she meant anything by it.'

'I can see that you're scared.'

The detective laid a hand on hers. His right, her left, covering her wedding ring. She didn't jump, because you must never jump, or that would show you were guilty. He met her eyes and she felt herself harvested, plundered. A familiar feeling. Frank had protected her from that. Some of that.

157

'I'm not scared,' Lynne said, sounding like Peony when she put her to bed in the dark. She took a deep breath and set the mechanics of a smile into motion. She turned her head to look at her daughter, who was looking out of the window, waving.

Lynne's body turned to ice.

'There's a man outside,' she said.

Her throat was so tight she was amazed she managed to get the words out.

There was a shape. A presence. A man like a streak, cutting the world in half. Smiling at her daughter, as if he had the right.

Dark hair. Dark eyes.

Sent by Frank?

Sonia's David?

Angie's Charlie?

The detective frowned and stood up, jerking back the net curtains without fear and leaning forward to peer out.

Then he laughed.

'Don't you worry, love.'

He was waving, too, now.

'That's my trainee. That's Brookes. He's a good lad. Don't you worry.'

The young man raised a hand. Waved. Of course. Young. Too young for any of them.

His face was inquisitive, yes, but open.

Not all men were like *that*. She was seeing ghosts.

You stupid bitch.

Without warning, Peony abandoned the neon plastic shape she had been playing with and threw herself into Lynne's lap with all the urgency of love.

'Your little girl's got a lot of energy,' the detective said, settling back down in his chair. 'They're lovely at that age. Tiring, though.'

Too much energy for a girl, Lynne thought.

That wasn't sexist, that was just a fact. Little boys were wired differently; they needed different things. Peony couldn't sit still – at her nursery, they had said she might have a learning disability. She didn't sit and focus on things but tore around with the boys, screeching at the top of her voice.

It made Frank laugh.

There's nothing wrong with her, darling, apart from your overactive imagination.

'But that does remind me,' the detective said. 'One of the other ladies mentioned that you might have seen something a bit out of place. Someone hanging about?'

He was looking at her, encouraging her. Encouraging her to say something she might even believe. What was the right thing to say?

Lynne's chest closed up and she shook her head.

'I'm not sure,' she said. 'I thought I . . . but it was probably nothing. Just my overactive imagination.'

The detective nodded.

'Sometimes I don't like my daughter,' she had said to Katie, one of the last times they spoke. Katie hadn't blinked. She'd just nodded.

'That's okay.'

'No.' Lynne had said it wrong. 'Sometimes I *hate* my daughter.'

'Lynne . . .' Katie had looked a little helpless. 'What you're saying isn't as unusual as you might think. A lot of mothers in your position have difficult relationships with their children. He *made* you feel that way.'

'Nobody can *make* you feel anything,' one of the therapists had said. 'You feel something because, on some level, that's what you've chosen to feel.'

Lynne had chosen to hate her daughter.

Lynne could see Katie discreetly eyeing the shelves behind the desk where they kept all the pamphlets. Was there one for 'So you hate your own child?'

'I think it might be a good idea if I referred you for counselling,' Katie had said, jotting down a note on the pad on the desk. 'I think you need support to deal with what's happening. I promise you, Lynne, you won't always feel this way.'

This behaviour is out of control. I think you need to see someone.
For my sake. For the baby's. For yours.

Lynne had done it all. Cognitive behavioural therapy. Psychodynamic psychotherapy. Meditation. Exploring all the ways she was longing to self-destruct, the reasons why she needed to shift the blame on to other people. Pills were offered at every turn.

The first therapist had been the smallest, neatest man she had ever seen, folded up in his chair, his black suit like a dust covering. He had been very kind and very soft, and he had told her that she had drunk that glass of wine because she resented the baby inside her. The baby would mean she would have to be less selfish in the future. Yes, he used the word 'selfish', but he wanted to be clear that there was no judgement in that.

Lynne had gone home and cried and told Frank that she wasn't paying someone to call her a bad mother.

'But, darling,' he had replied mildly, 'you're not. *I'm* paying someone to call you a bad mother.'

Ritualized honesty was one of his little ways.

'You're a really good mum. I know you want what's best for Peony.'

That was the thing. Lynne knew she wasn't a really good mum. But she'd certainly settle for being good enough.

Then Katie had stood up. 'I think it's best if we have a check-in with each other every day for a little while, so we can talk about how you're feeling and how we can support you. Do you think that would be a good idea?'

Lynne had nodded. Then she had said softly, so softly that she wouldn't let the weakness seep out, 'I miss Frank.'

Katie had nodded.

'That's normal, Lynne.'

As if that was a useful thing to say.

Frank had fucked their au pair on their bed. Left the bed unmade and the used condom lying in their otherwise empty waste bin in plain sight.

Men are like that: they don't see the detail.

Lynne had seen it, and he had seen her see it.

Frank had never hit her. But when she confronted him about the au pair he had put his hands around her throat, almost as if he was just showing her that he could. The span of his hands was big, much bigger than her neck.

There was barely any grip. He couldn't have clenched them for more than five seconds.

Lynne hadn't moved. Hadn't breathed. If she could have made her own heart stop, then she would have done.

That was the reality of it. It's important to establish the facts.

She could feel herself stretching the facts like chewing gum as she picked up the phone and dialled her mother's number. She said, 'Frank strangled me.'

As soon as she said it, she felt the indignity of her exaggeration. It had been the clench of a moment, falling between one breath and the next.

Frank followed her to her mother's. He stood outside her dining-room window, waving at Peony through the glass before her mother drew the curtains. Then Peony cried and cried and had to be pacified with television.

It was always Frank at the centre of everything. You saw it even as he stood outside her mother's house, begging her to come home. Frank played the part of the repentant. He did it so beautifully. He hadn't shaved, and the suit he was wearing hung with contrasting neatness over a rumpled shirt, open at the neck. He stood in the street and bellowed like a new kind of troubadour. Lynne was wearing a roll-neck jumper. You'd never even know what was underneath it.

Lynne's mother was perennially making tea in those days. She didn't want Lynne and Peony going out. She would stand in the porch, arms folded across her chest and eyes narrowed at Frank's car.

'He must be missing a hell of a lot of work to hang about like this,' she'd muttered. That seemed to outrage her almost more than anything else.

Lynne's mother had always adored Frank. She had adored the idea of him long before they'd been introduced, and sided with him in any argument Lynne recounted to her.

It was always that Frank would have his own point of view, that Frank was a reasonable man, that Lynne was dramatic – that was the word she always used to describe what therapists referred to as her anxiety and depression.

'If you paid me fifty pounds an hour to tell you that you had anxiety and depression, then maybe I would,' her mother said.

It's the economy, stupid.

But now she said, 'It's that man outside, Lynne. He's the problem.'

It's the way I frame things that's the problem. It's all a question of perspective.

'You're not safe here, Lynne. Peony's not safe.'

'Frank would never hurt us,' Lynne murmured reflexively.

'Frank did hurt you.'

Her mother had done all the legwork. Called the helpline,

got the refuge referral. Even when the woman on the phone risk-assessed Lynne, she'd been listening on the extension. She vaguely remembered editing her answers, even then hoping that they'd fit with the kind of daughter she wanted to be.

So here Lynne was now, talking to a detective, a bit part in some sordid plot of death. Poor Katie.

Lynne did her best to focus. The detective's jovial look was fading away. He was raking his eyes over her in a way that made her feel manhandled.

She wrapped her arms around herself, smoothing down her sleeves.

'Did anyone leave the refuge after Katie left that night?' he asked.

'I think . . .' Lynne spoke without thinking, just longing for his eyes to let her go. 'I think I heard Jenny go somewhere.'

The detective's voice changed sharply. 'Who's Jenny, love?'

'She's . . .' Lynne didn't want to say, *she's the whore* – a word that surprised her with its ancient vehemence – so she gestured helplessly. 'She's . . . one of the residents. She's in the room next to ours.'

The detective was clearly trying not to look too interested, but he wasn't doing a particularly good job of it. Maybe his carefully arranged face would have worked to soothe most normal people, but Lynne was so used to parsing every pixel of Frank's face for signs of his mood that perhaps she was a tough audience.

'Right . . .' He tapped his pencil on to his notebook and made a few, seemingly cursory scribblings, before standing up. 'Well, Lynne . . . that's great.' He smiled at her broadly. 'That's super. Well done for remembering, Lynne.'

Lynne twitched into a little smile.

'Bye bye, poppet,' he said to Peony, before leaving and shutting the door behind him.

Lynne sank back into the too-soft sofa. Her body felt flimsy and insubstantial. Peony rushed over again and began to climb over her, and Lynne felt herself half expecting to be crushed by her three-year-old weight.

She had got Jenny in trouble, that much was obvious. Jenny would surely know it had been her who'd dropped the clue – who else would be so pliant to the detective's will? Who else would have heard her shadowy steps in the hall the night that Katie died?

Lynne imagined nights awake, staring at the door, waiting for the strip of light above the carpet to be blocked out by that wraith-like sentry. She imagined Jenny sliding something small and sharp into her – a fingernail filed to a point, perhaps, or a used needle.

She brushed absent-mindedly at her daughter's curly hair.

'Mummy,' Peony said, ramming her little palm into Lynne's face. '*Mummy* . . .'

Lynne stood, because she was tired of sitting – there had been too much sitting that day – and mechanically peered through the net curtains, Peony in her arms.

At first, she almost forgot to be frightened. She was still chastising herself for getting into a state at the sight of the detective.

But Peony's frantic waving, her gurgles of delight, made it real. There he was.

A man. Outside. Again. The streak of him dividing the world in two. Again. Not such a slim man, though his silhouette was refined by a well-cut suit. Not a young man with a veneer of police legitimacy this time. His brow arranged into uncertainty. Staring up at the refuge.

23.

Then

Katie is shrinking.

She notices it every time she steps out of the shower. How the flesh is gradually peeling from the bones, how the skin has started to pucker and cling, hinting at the structure beneath. When she inspects herself in the mirror, front or sideways, she no longer sees those little puffs and bumps, the excesses that made her feel she was spilling out of her shape. Now her ribs are articulated clearly; her hip bones rear up through her skin as if to break out.

Everyone says she looks good.

Jamie's helping. Jamie always helps.

'You feel *gorgeous*,' he often says, wrapping his arms around her waist and squeezing.

She's trying to think more about what she eats. He makes her think, makes thinking easier. Jamie goes to the gym. He wants her to go, too, but Katie can't imagine taking up rigorous exercise – she's always so tired these days.

The doctor says she's anaemic and gives her iron pills that she doesn't bother to take. She hasn't told Jamie about them, although it's hard to say exactly why.

The sun is out. Jamie has taken his shirt off. The pale skin, dappled in the sun, is stretched over his stomach muscles, which move fluidly, like fish under the surface of water. Katie's father always had scathing words for men who walk around shirtless in the summer. Katie glances at Jamie sideways and thinks the same words in her head, wondering if Jamie might understand them just from the look on her face.

He catches her eye and smiles.

'Checking me out, are we?'

She smiles back. She takes care to look at him always, or else he assumes she's looking elsewhere. Sometimes it's because she is; sometimes it's because other men simply cross her line of vision as she stares off into nothing.

But it hurts his feelings either way, so she has to make sure there's never any room for doubt.

He has a picnic in the carrier bag at his side. Another one. He seems to have got it into his head that that's what people in love do – they eat picnics by the riverbank in the sunshine.

That seems as good a way to pass the time as any. Katie has never wanted to think too much about how people in love are supposed to behave.

He always buys too much food, and always sits expectantly, waiting for Katie to eat it.

'Katie!'

She should have known. They were walking past the riverside pub, the one where she spent what now feels like so many long summer evenings. Laughing, she supposes, in retrospect. With friends – also in retrospect.

They all try not to see each other, she looking out towards the river, the girls – Lara, Lucy, Ellie – shuffling along the bench and leaning closer together. It is Jamie who says something, Jamie who smiles broadly and waves.

'Look, Katie, it's your friends!'

He takes her hand and pulls her over.

'They didn't invite me,' she says, but he pretends not to hear.

When they get to the table, Ellie smiles awkwardly up at her.

'It was just a spontaneous thing,' she says.

'Don't worry,' Katie says. 'It's totally fine. It's fine. Anyway, we were just on our way to something, so . . .'

'Oh, let's stay for one,' Jamie says breezily, and puts one leg over the wooden bench of the picnic table.

'Hang out with your mates, Katie.'

She hears them at the bar, on the other side of the oak pillar – Ellie and Lara. They get their drinks, but she knows they're staying there, and she knows why.

She's done it, after all – dropped little interludes of casual cruelty into evenings that everyone had agreed were 'lovely'.

'He's not any better this time.'

'Oh my God, I know. Last time I was thinking, like, *Blink twice if you need help.*'

A peal of laughter that settles into a glass-clinking quiet.

Then, 'Do you think we should say something?'

'No.'

Another wine-sip pause.

'Like . . . you've got to let people make their own mistakes, and sometimes when you're in a situation like that you don't want to hear it. And you never know.'

Another sip-pause.

'Maybe he's fine. Just a bit dull.'

'I mean, it's good to see her. She looks great.'

The soft glug of more wine poured out.

'She's lost a lot of weight.'

'I know. She looks amazing.'

'Probably worrying about her mum.'

'Yeah. That's probably it.'

'Maybe he's good for her.'

'Maybe he is. Seems reliable.'

'That's what matters sometimes.'

'Seems to know what to say to her.'

'More than you can say for me.'

They go away. Katie stays leaning on the bar.

They have sex that night – the sex has become usual so quickly. Katie can time to the minute what will happen when. Jamie has a hell of a sexual appetite. He doesn't use porn, he tells her, with an intensity that implies she'd asked. Never looks at other girls. Never even takes care of himself. It's only Katie.

It never varies, and always ends with Jamie labouring jerkily on top of her, his face more in concentration than ecstasy. He looks like a child fearful of passing an exam, so she wraps her arms and legs around him, burying her face in his shoulder so she doesn't have to see it any more. He doesn't seem to like it when she looks up at him, anyway.

Tonight, she crunches up a little and leans close to Jamie's ear.

'What can I do for you?' she says. Her voice feels seductive, but more in the sense that she is letting her desire seep out than that she is playing a part. But he leans away, and frowns.

'Nothing,' he says. Then he kisses her, putting all his weight on to her mouth, and says into the kiss, 'You're perfect.'

24.

Now

Lynne didn't put her jacket on, instead shrugging her arms around herself against the cold as she stepped out of the front door, crunched across the gravel to the line where the refuge turned into street.

'What're you doing here?' she said to Frank.

He didn't answer, instead looking up at the house, as if in accusation.

'What the hell kind of place is this, Lynne? Where's our daughter?'

'She's inside. She's fine. How did you find me?'

He gave a little laugh and held out his phone. A running app was open. He'd wanted her to get into running.

Good for her figure. Good for her mind.

'All your running routes led back here.'

All the nights she'd spent staring into the ceiling wondering how a bloated, fanged Frank, the Frank who was something called a 'perpetrator', would find her and take her baby away, and here he was. Giving her the same look he always gave her when he was implying she was useless at technology.

'I'm not asking for forgiveness,' he said. 'I'm not asking for anything. I just have to let you know how I feel.'

He reached out and took her arm as if he wanted to grip it hard, but seemed to think better of it at the last moment, instead letting his fingertips push the fabric of her sleeve over her skin.

'How I feel,' he said again.

Lynne was staring hard over his shoulder. Yet what harm could it do to really look him in the face? He was only a man, after all.

'I can't tell you how frantic I've been,' he said. 'With worry. About you. About our little girl.' A crack formed across his voice. 'If she's safe. But it's okay. I understand. I know it wasn't you who wanted to come here.'

It wasn't me. It never was.

'It was your mum, Lynne. I know that. I know she made you leave me.'

Maybe that was why she had never felt like she was really here. Why she had never felt the physical reality of leaving Frank.

'She doesn't understand us, Lynne. She never has. But we don't need anyone else, do we? It's just the three of us together.'

His hand moved from her arm to her hair, lightening the touch of his fingertips to nothing as if to marvel at its softness. For a moment she neither leaned into nor out of his touch.

'Look, maybe you're right. Maybe I'm no good. Maybe you're both better off without me. I had the most perfect family in the world, the most beautiful wife, and maybe I've screwed it all up.'

He raised his eyes to look at her.

'But I'll be damned if I let you go without you knowing just how much I love you.'

Lynne slid out of the refuge playroom, seeing on the opposite wall how her shadow's posture was distorted by Peony's weight on her hip. She mounted the stairs. They turned several times before reaching the second floor. On each little landing there was a different poster – on the dangers of charming men, a step-by-step guide on applying for benefits, mother-and-baby sessions at the local library.

Peony had seized a fistful of Lynne's hair and was in turn gently stroking it and yanking so hard Lynne thought she'd soon have a bald spot. She'd tried to detach Peony's hand, but it was like trying to pry an insect free from a Venus flytrap.

She went past Jenny's room. The two or three strides that carried her seemed a mile or more, and when she had unlocked the door to her own bedroom and re-locked it again behind her, her thumping heart let up slightly.

Yes, she was scared of Jenny. How could you not be scared of someone who made as little sense as that?

There was little of Lynne in the room – the bedside table held an eclectic range of cosmetics from the donation box. There were a few toys she'd deemed clean enough for Peony. Among these was a little pink Barbie rucksack. A hideous thing, but Peony had adored it on first sight and refused to be parted from it. Lynne set Peony down and started to gather together the few things that were definitively hers. Her bottle of perfume, her few nice jumpers, her hairbrush.

For a second she stood, peering out of the window at the silver four-by-four. *Their* car. Her car. Her husband.

She wanted life to be easier. Was that so wrong? The whole time she had been in the refuge she had felt as though she was slamming her hands against a plastic ceiling which kept her in a trap where everything was dirty and tiring, where there was no money and there would never be any money.

She thought of Peony. Of all the ways she had failed – was failing – as a mother. Did she really need to add this sense of material hopelessness to the sum of her daughter's suffering, all for the sake of being the right sort of woman? It seemed too much. Too cruel.

She held out the little pink rucksack to her daughter. 'Come on, darling. Let's get your toys together. We're going.'

25.

'I'm going to interview the old slapper first thing,' Whitworth said as they settled into the key work room again. Val had let them in without so much as a word, as if refusing to acknowledge them made their male presence just a little bit less offensive to her sensibilities.

'Want me to come in?' Brookes asked.

'Nah.' Whitworth stood up and stretched. 'I know what I'm doing with these types. Best if it's just one of us. You understand.'

'Right.'

'Oh . . .' Whitworth slapped his hand on the doorframe, as if reprimanding it for almost letting him forget. 'Anything on the joker who's sending . . . you know, who's twittering at Val?'

'Oh yeah.' Brookes twiddled his pen. 'Melissa's got the nerds on the case. Tracking his IP address or something. I don't know. They reckon it'll be another day or so.'

Whitworth nodded. Val had taken to shoving the print-outs under his nose whenever she spoke to him.

Fuck feminist whores. Feminism is cancer.

The bald accusation in her gaze made it a little hard for him to entirely disagree with the sentiments.

The woman waiting for him in the key-work room could have been one of any number Whitworth had run up against in his detective career.

She was clearly some sort of addict; heroin was his best guess, from her tallow-coloured skin and anchorless gaze.

Whitworth knew junkies – they weren't so much men or women as a pack of hungry foxes, with that loping gait and their eyes like busted headlamps.

This was where he was comfortable. This woman's wretchedness was chemical, not political; that gave her actions a sort of scientific certainty. She would do whatever, say whatever, be whatever. Chemistry overrides everything else.

She didn't reply to Whitworth's 'hello'.

'I understand your name's Jenny,' he said.

She gave a hooked sort of nod, her shoulders caved. *I can be whoever you want me to be*, the monotone of her posture seemed to say. *It's all the same to me.*

She wasn't a big, bawdy, blousey hooker, the kind they'd have sung songs about in the pub in olden times: she of the inviting eyes and generous thighs, with entire countries between her breasts. This woman was insubstantial. Tiny-thin. Her teeth weren't great either.

Whitworth couldn't for a minute imagine wanting to fuck her. But then, prostitutes could always surprise you.

'My daughter's a Jenny,' he said.

He said it to get her to look at him, even though the connection made him wince.

He had wanted the name partly because it sounded so little like the names of those crumbled remnants of women he'd seen on the streets. A name to be worn by a teacher or a nurse, or just someone who was loved and knew it. Jenny. Jennifer.

'Heartbreaker.'

The hooker's words seemed to have no context – they just fell out of her mouth like pebbles before an avalanche.

'What was that, love?'

'Jennifer. It's the Cornish form of Guinevere. She's the woman who broke King Arthur's heart. My mum told me that when I was little.'

'Yeah?' Just let her talk. Any talking will do. Don't expect any sense out of her. 'Mum from Cornwall?'

'Maybe. I think so.' Jenny blinked. Long. Slow. 'From by the sea, yeah. Cornish form of Guinevere. Also, enchantress. White lady.'

This woman was not so much white as colourless. Even her eyelashes. All the dyes had leached out of her, leaving only the pallid film of skin. She wore reddy-pink lipstick, incongruous in her flat face.

It was hideous.

'White lady. I always liked that. Cornish form of Guinevere,' she said.

Jennifer – his Jennifer – had sailed out the door the night before with her face painted much the same way. Dressed to kill.

'Going to a film,' she had claimed.

Bollocks going to a film. Going to a party.

Uniform had told him later they'd shut down the party where she was. He asked her about it. That was the kind of relationship they had.

'I told them who you were.'

'Oho?'

'And they said, "We'll let you off, you've got enough problems living with that bastard."'

She laughed in his face. The kind of laugh that made her look like she was still his little girl. It made her features splay across her face.

He'd laughed, too. Big, proper laugh.

'You look like a prostitute,' he told her automatically as she made for the front door.

She had looked nothing like. She had looked vibrant and lovely, as exposed as a mermaid flopping about on a rock. She had this look about her, as if she'd got a sense of her own power. Like the dictator of her own body, just waiting to take things too far and bring the world tumbling down.

She hadn't seemed offended at the comment. She hadn't needed to. It was his way of saying, *Yes, I can see you're growing up.* And her silence was her way of saying, *Yes, I know that you've noticed, and there's nothing you can do about it.*

It was surprising how much that hurt.

She hadn't gone to get changed. He had grumbled. It was what they expected of each other.

'She'll learn,' Maureen had said. 'She's just like I was when I was that age.'

That was in the script, too, the knowing look.

That seemed unfair to Whitworth. Perhaps that was the real reason why men craved sons – because there was something so secret, so unknowable, about daughters. That was what was so frustrating about all the fuck-me clothes and the fuck-you attitude. It made it seem like she was an open book, while his real daughter, the one that was small and neat enough to be known, smiled tauntingly as she walked away.

Perhaps the meaning had been hidden in her name like a stowaway all along. Heartbreaker.

It made sense.

'So.' Whitworth laced his fingers in front of him on the table, looking across at Jenny in a way he liked to think was part Bond and part bank manager. 'What did you make of Katie?'

Jenny shrugged.

'*Articulate*,' Whitworth mumbled, making a squiggle in his notebook.

This woman wasn't like all the others in this place. She knew how to play the game, and he needed to make sure he won.

'Jenny . . .' He folded his arms on top of his paunch, in the manner he knew would instantly mark him as a middle-ager, non-threatening. He presumed that Jenny knew something of the body language of men.

'We need a bit of help in this case. You could be really important to helping us solve it.'

That's one of the ways you could sometimes get people like Jenny on side.

Make them feel like they matter.

Still she didn't speak.

'Seen anything funny going on around here? Anything at all?'

Jenny shrugged. In a way, Whitworth wondered if there was any point in pushing it. A woman like Jenny was an uncalibrated instrument – she'd probably never learned that there was a difference between safety and danger. Whitworth wanted to shock her awake. He wanted to see her leap, like throwing a bucket of water over a cat. Maybe he needed to go nuclear, ask point-blank.

'Jenny, did you see anything on the night Katie died?'

She said nothing. She turned those statue eyes on to him, but it was an automatic movement, no yielding in it.

He went for the jugular. No need to worry too much about the truth. 'We know you did, Jenny. And if you lie to us, you'll make things worse for yourself.'

Jenny remained statue-like, the threat seeming to glance off her.

Worse than what?

'You're a smart girl, Jenny, I can tell,' Whitworth said. 'Smart as a whip.'

Her lip curled very slightly.

Whitworth knew women like Jenny. They had a kind of cunning that they wrapped around them like a heavy winter coat, but when that layer was taken away they were as gullible as children.

'You're smart enough to see that we're having some difficulty with this case. And you know just as well as I do that you can help us.'

Silence.

'I can protect you, Jenny. I promise.'

She didn't believe him. Neither did he.

So he said it again. He screwed up his eyes so that the frame of the woman in front of him blurred and forced himself to pretend he was talking to someone he loved.

'I can protect you, love.'

Then Jenny did something extraordinarily ugly. Her blank face seemed to divide itself as she furrowed her brow and screwed shut her eyes. It was as if she was thinking, and the sensation was painful to her.

'I . . .'

'Yes?'

'Say . . .' Her hand trailed through the air. Maybe to lead to somewhere. 'Say something was off. Say you saw a guy, and you got a feeling like you were being kicked, right?'

'Right.'

'I know that feeling. Really good at recognizing it. Used to get it all the time.' The crooked slash of a smile. 'Girls protect each other from those kind of blokes. Used to do it all the time. They did a big tough act, but they're nothing, really. They're just blokes. Got scared pretty quick when a few of us girls stuck together.'

'Okay, Jenny.'

'Like, once . . .' She got a far-off look on her face. Her eyes became even more unfocused. 'Once I was on the street with my friend and I saw this car slow down and I just got the feeling, you know? And I wasn't going anywhere near it, but my friend went up to him. She had a habit, you see. Bad habit.'

She sucked in her cheeks, shaking her head. Apparently, the irony didn't occur to her.

'She didn't care. And I said, no babe, no, don't go with him, you won't be coming back. And she didn't listen to me, and she didn't come back. You get what I'm saying?'

'I think I do, Jenny.' Whitworth leaned forward. Enough to show that he was interested but not so much that he risked scaring her off.

'He did it. Dunno if he killed her or she killed herself after he was finished with her. She turned up dead. Doesn't matter what happened.'

'It matters to the law, Jenny,' Whitworth said.

She shrugged. 'Like I said, doesn't matter.'

'What are you trying to tell me, Jenny?' Whitworth stopped the impatience from creeping into his voice. Finally, he was getting somewhere.

'There was a man.'

'Well, Jenny, there are a lot of men about.'

'I mean . . . there was something wrong. I know there was something wrong. With how he was acting.'

'Did you see him?'

'No.'

'Well, then, what exactly are you trying to . . .'

But it went no further. Brookes walked in, holding out his mobile phone as if it were a piece of vermin.

Jenny went very still at the interruption.

'There's a reporter from the *Echo* on the line.' Brookes held out the phone to Whitworth. 'She wants to talk to the person in charge of the investigation on Katie Straw.'

Whitworth winced.

The *Widringham Echo* was everything he loathed about small-scale local press. Staffed by a mix of bored old part-timers and young reporters bloodthirsty for a journalistic career; they were a mercenary bunch. Their job was to alchemize excitement and intrigue from Widringham's base metal.

Half out of irritation at the interruption and half in dread at the thought of returning the call, Whitworth made a swatting motion with his hand.

'Tell her I'll call her back.'

Brookes shrugged as if to say, *Suit yourself*, and retreated back through the doorway of the tiny room.

'Sorry about that, Jenny,' Whitworth said automatically.

Jenny mirrored the shrug Brookes had modelled moments before, but something about her face had changed, or at least deepened. That stony quality, that refusal to yield.

It could be withdrawal, Whitworth supposed. But a feeling deep in the pit of his stomach, a feeling he didn't yet dare give his full mind to, was glowing with victory.

Got her.

'So, Jenny . . .' he continued. 'You were saying . . .'

He did his best not to appear too much like a hound on the scent of blood, but something in Jenny's features shifted – almost imperceptibly, but he saw it. He could tell Jenny had the whore's eye to detect his secret desire.

'I want to talk to Val,' she said, in a quiet rush.

Fuck.

Clearly, the momentary distraction had given her the chance to gather her wits together.

Using all his willpower to remain nonchalant, Whitworth tried again. 'Oh, come on, Jenny, there's no need to . . .'

'I want Val in here with me,' Jenny said, louder this time. 'Look, I've had time to think. I've thought it all out. I'm a victim. I'm not a criminal. Val said so. I want to talk to Val.'

'Jenny,' he tried one more time, 'there's nothing to . . .'

'Let me talk to Val!'

Jenny was standing up now, and in the accentuated length of her painfully thin body Whitworth could see clearly the walking shadow from Amir's CCTV footage.

Tall. Slender. Sexless. Drained of colour. A witness who'd almost succeeded in making herself invisible.

Got you.

Though Jenny's face was still blank and collapsed, her voice was rising into a curdled panic. 'I'm not talking to you any more!'

Cursing inwardly, Whitworth stood up and placed a hand on Jenny's arm.

'Look, love,' he said softly, forcing himself to see his own Jennifer in this Jenny's eyes. 'I'm sorry. I can see I've frightened you.'

She didn't look at him. Her ossified face was lowered to the ground.

She said once again, this time controlled, 'Let me talk to Val.'

Whitworth sighed. He released Jenny's arm and let his hand drop to his side.

'I'll see what I can do.'

Jenny didn't sit back down as he left the room, but stood waiting, tension calligraphed into the lines of her body.

Whitworth closed the key-work room door behind him, leaned back on it and sighed. He'd fucked up there, he knew.

'Give her a minute to cool down. But don't let her go anywhere,' he muttered to Brookes, who was sitting at the desk which, he knew, had once been Katie's. Crossing the room, he held out his hand. 'Let's see about this reporter, then.'

Brookes handed him the phone, and Whitworth took a few breaths to steady himself. He loathed dealing with the *Echo*. He'd once had a few friends on staff, but they'd been picked off by the impact of reduced circulation numbers.

The *Echo* was now more or less a charity, propped up by a few of Widringham's wealthier and more righteous inhabitants. The stories consisted of petty-scale grievances – a 'spate' of uncleaned-up dog shits; the 'menace' of hooliganism (the local youth getting hold of a few cans of lager and making nuisances of themselves in the park). The anaemic content was always accompanied by a photograph of a squarish, reddened plaintiff pouting and pointing at whatever sign, turd or planning notice was offending them.

It was what those kind of publications needed to do to survive, of course, give fodder to the net-curtain twitchers.

And, Whitworth had to admit, the story of Katie Straw was irresistible. An unresolved suicide was almost as good as a murder.

'Right, then. So what was it that this reporter wanted to know?'

Brookes looked uncomfortable. 'Details of the case. Kept asking why we hadn't declared it a murder yet. She's a shit-stirrer, anyone could see that.'

Whitworth pinched the bridge of his nose and sat down in the chair opposite him.

'I'd better gird my loins, then,' he said.

'Makes me sick.' Brookes scowled at the papers in front of him. 'The way the press jumps on this kind of stuff to sell a few papers. Pretty young girl like that . . .' He gestured at the photograph of Katie Straw that lay on the desk in front of them. 'Bet they'd love it if she'd been murdered. Not just local press either. National press. Those bloody true-crime podcasts.'

'Can't blame them for trying to make a living,' Whitworth said wryly.

'Can't you? I think it's gross. You saw it all the time in London. National press finds out that some pretty young girl's been murdered, and that's a huge story. I know it sounds awful, saying that. But that's the way it is. Before you know it, you've got hacks swarming all over you with no sense of right and wrong, just desperate for whatever they can find that will sell a paper. Just because people want to read a *story*. It's exploitative.'

Whitworth stared at the waiting mobile screen. It turned his stomach, too, the way the world loved to sink its claws into the idea of a murdered girl.

And what would be the point in calling this journalist, after all? They still hadn't cleared up the question of Katie's real name. They still didn't exactly know who she was . . . When there was a blank, some journalist would find a way to fill it in, and they wouldn't be concerning themselves with the truth.

'By the way, sir, once you're done on the phone, DI Khan called. And Val wants to speak to you again, I think.'

'God save me from these people,' Whitworth half growled. Since when was he dancing to Val Redwood's tune? 'I suppose she wants us to look into . . . well . . . all men.'

'Thing is,' Brookes replied, 'she's not wrong. Women don't kill.' He rolled his eyes. 'Okay, so there's the odd telly thing about a woman who bashes a guy's head in, I know. But it's true. Women don't kill. Men kill.'

'You think women are better than men, then? You're one of Val Redwood's lot? Feminist.'

'Sure. Call me a feminist if you want.' Brookes shrugged. 'I don't care. I'm just telling you the numbers, and numbers don't lie. Women don't kill.'

Whitworth was starting to feel he had had enough of this conversation. He changed the subject.

'Anyway, I reckon we might have a lead with that one in there. I reckon it was her who followed Katie Straw to Amir's.'

Brookes didn't seem to mind the abrupt swerve in their conversation. Whitworth figured he'd successfully pulled rank. Brookes leaned forward sharply, but his tone was calm. 'A lead, eh?' he said. 'That's good.'

Trying to keep his cool, clearly. But the ambition was show-ing again.

''Tis good,' Whitworth admitted, even though it didn't feel much like good at the moment. 'It's very good. Problem is, she won't talk to me.'

Brookes's eyebrows raised a fraction. 'She won't talk?'

'You know what these hookers are like,' Whitworth said, standing up again. 'Reckon I came on too strong. Freaked her out a bit. Now she won't talk to me without Duchess Val.'

'Oh.' Brookes gave a little grimace. 'Well, Her Ladyship's somewhere around. Maybe outside.'

Whitworth waited for him to offer to go and fetch her then rolled his eyes. 'All right, lad. I suppose I'd better fetch her. Keep an eye on her.' He jabbed his eyes towards the key-work room. 'Will you?'

Brookes retreated behind a file. 'Yup.'

Whitworth went to open the door of the main office, and as he began to step out Brookes called, 'Oh, sir?'

'Yes?'

'What about this reporter?'

Whitworth paused for a moment then said, 'Leave it for now.'

She'll just have to hang on, he thought as he headed down the cramped corridor. *We'll have an answer soon, one way or the other. Then she won't have to guess what kind of story she's writing.*

26.

Then

They're walking down the street. She doesn't remember exactly where it is they're going, but she's sure Jamie must have told her. She simply forgot.

She looks down at her forearm, where he has laid his hand. He gives her a little pinch between his thumb and forefinger, pressing against the point where her pulse thuds. She's sure that it quickens under his touch.

'Be careful about getting *too* skinny,' he says. 'I don't want you looking like *that*.'

He jerks his head at a tall woman walking across the road. She doesn't look unhealthy, just like a member of a different species. Half woman, half birch tree.

'That's disgusting,' he says.

'I'm never going to look like that,' Katie says. She doesn't have the architecture of the creature across the road. Bones like javelins.

'You're getting too thin,' he says.

He holds her arm up. 'Look.'

Perhaps it's true. Her mother told her a few days ago that if someone had to guess, they'd probably think it was Katie who was the cancer patient. Then she'd let out a barking laugh.

'I was fat before, though,' Katie says.

He doesn't disagree. He just shrugs.

'I'm just giving you my opinion,' he says. 'You don't have to take it.'

They're out for dinner.

They still do that sometimes, although not as often as they used to. Jamie has a steak, Katie a salad. The waiter puts their plates down without asking who's having what.

'Eat,' Jamie says.

'I've eaten loads.'

Katie gestures at the expanse of empty plate. Before, it had held frills of lettuce. A little lemon juice squeezed over for flavour. Enough for the mechanics of eating.

She loves feeling so light, so insubstantial.

Jamie looks at her very closely. He breaks the eye contact to flag down a waitress and orders a side of chips.

When they arrive he pushes them towards her.

'All for you. Eat up.'

She knows that the chips are the end of everything. The end of controlling the shores of her self.

He grips her arm. It will bruise tomorrow, she can tell.

'Eat.'

In silence, one chip at a time, the food disappears into the black hole inside her. They're over-salted. The flavour is neither good nor bad, just too much.

Jamie is smiling. He orders her another portion.

'More. Go on. Eat.'

The lightness is gone. Katie feels her stomach spilling over the edge of her jeans like so much yeasted dough, vast and white and stretched like strands of gluten.

'I don't want any more,' Katie says. 'I'm full.'

Jamie picks up a chip between his thumb and forefinger. Tiny particles of salt and paprika seem magnified against his fingertips. With the other hand he takes her jaw, very gently, and presses on the place where it hinges with his thumb and forefinger, as if he's giving a cat a worming pill.

Her mouth opens. Perhaps by mechanics, perhaps surprise. He places the chip on her tongue then softly closes her mouth again.

'Are you going to eat the rest, or am I going to have to feed it to you myself?'

His voice is cool and flat.

Katie chews. Swallows.

'I'll eat,' she says.

She eats one more chip, then another.

And then another and another and another.

At some point she stops glancing at Jamie to see if his eyes are pushing her to eat more. She takes over the task.

Surely this was what she had wanted all along, really.

It's three portions of chips, in the end. She eats them in perfect silence.

He watches her, stacking the ramekins as she empties them. Then he grins at the waitress.

'Can we get the bill, please? I think we're finally both done.'

The waitress nods, gathering in the little dishes and giving Katie a comedy wink.

'Good for you, lovely,' she says.

Perhaps it *is* good for her.

Perhaps this is what proper nourishment is – the feeling of being so full, so overfull, that she can't separate herself from that sense of straining, of not being enough to contain the thing inside her.

It is a feeling she has denied herself for so long her stomach has shrunk into something hard and mean.

The waitress returns with the bill. Jamie glances at it, then pushes it towards Katie.

'I think that one's yours.'

He looks at her. Waits for a second, then adds, 'You had all those chips.'

Katie meets his eyes for a few seconds longer than she knows to be wise then nods and leans under the table to pick up her handbag, wincing at the tightness of her swollen belly.

Jamie leans across the table – she automatically presents her cheek.

'You look much better.'

The words echo in her ear.

'Let's go home. I want you.'

It takes her a while to get the word out, but she does say no.

The stabbing in her stomach increases in violence as she lies down on the bed. She can't – not tonight.

Her wretched belly feels like a stone. The rest of her is light, drained.

'I'm sorry,' she says, and begins to lay out her case. Too tired. Not feeling well. She won't be able to get wet. It won't be good for him.

He has lube, he points out. She can just lie there.

'I'll do all the work.'

It is impossible to say no to Jamie. He doesn't make it an option.

When would she even say it? There's no break between the trail of dry kisses he scatters down her neck, the cotton wrench of him pulling her knickers halfway down her thighs, the workmanlike motion of turning her on to her stomach.

27.

Now

Sonia crossed to the sliding doors and pulled them open, letting the stale cushion of refuge warmth hit her full in the face.

The sliding door led into the living room, the same room where Val had told them that Katie was dead. Sonia made to turn the television on but found that the remote control was gone. Lynne's Peony, she suspected. Quite the little klepto, that kid. Rich kids had no sense of what did and didn't belong to them.

She wondered if it was worth the fuss of going up to Lynne and accusing her daughter. She'd have to do it tactfully and try not to let her temper rise at the look of disdain that would inevitably take over Lynne's face.

Feeling oddly taut and shaky, Sonia went down the hallway and up the stairs to Lynne's room. She knocked on the door, but it gave way beneath her knuckles and swung open with a low creak.

Sonia had grown up knowing not to grass, not to do anything that might make her stand out. The voice she was trying to ignore as she stood outside the office door – already open a crack – was her mother's voice, yet again. *Don't get involved, you've got enough on your plate.*

But she couldn't help it. She thought of Peony – not a particularly nice kid, she had to admit, but just as blameless as her own two boys, protected from the world by a shelter as flimsy as that bloody Lynne.

She didn't let the rage grow, not yet, because then she wouldn't be able to get her words out, wouldn't be able to say what she needed to say to Val and those men.

Raised voices were coming from inside the office, and Sonia danced on the spot. Nothing changed with Val – you were always desperately trying to find a gap in her sentences to give you the chance to speak.

Val was talking to one of the detectives – the younger one. Her voice was tight and urgent.

'Detective Brookes, I'm not convinced that your investigation has exhausted all the options.'

Through the crack of the open door, Sonia saw the detective fold his arms, although from where she was standing she wasn't sure if it was a sign that he was listening or a sign that he wanted Val to shut up.

'Something doesn't sit right about Katie's death. Why would she want to drown herself?' Val shuddered, a movement that Sonia felt, too, in her own body. 'It's a terrible way to die.'

'Depression can do awful things, Mrs Redwood,' the young man began gently.

She could see that Val hated the boy – man – for being a man.

But Sonia couldn't hate him. She couldn't hate anyone who, the day before, had kicked a ball around with her boys and fallen to his knees on the muddy grass in celebration when Lewis scored a goal.

Val saw what she wanted to see.

'Ms.'

Trust Val. She never missed a chance to be offended.

'We have good reason to believe that Katie would have been suicidal, and no alternative theory,' the cop said.

Sonia wasn't overly fond of the police, not after everything that had happened. But even she had to admit that this one was doing a good job of keeping his shit together around Val.

Val opened her mouth.

'No *credible* alternative theory,' he added. Seemed like he could handle himself.

'Perhaps your lack of alternative theory is due to a lack of exploration, Detective,' Val snapped. 'I'm sure I don't need to tell you that absence of evidence is not evidence of absence.'

Her voice had that sing-song feel that it had sometimes, as if she were reciting the words to a song lyric that everyone knew.

'Nice line, Mrs Redwood,' the young detective replied, and his voice hardened. His cool was snapping. Val had that effect on people.

Something in his posture reminded Sonia of her boys when they'd been forced to sit still for too long.

'Here's another one for you. Occam's Razor. The simplest explanation is the most likely. Here's a girl with no marks on her, no signs of a struggle, no foreign DNA, no one in her life with the motive to kill her.

'But what we *do* have is a history of self-harm and mental illness. We *do* have her jumping off a bridge in a local suicide spot, and we *do* have a boyfriend who says she was acting oddly. Unless you know something you're not telling us . . .'

'I'm not sure what you're trying to imply.'

'I think I can hazard a guess at what you're trying to imply, though. That we're incompetent, right? I get it. You think she shouldn't have died. You think she had things to live for.' His hand was on Val's arm. Her body was tense. 'Well, maybe she did, I don't know. But sometimes women make their own choices – you're all about women making choices, right? – and you can't always find a way to pin it on a bloke.'

There was a long pause. Val tilted her head back a good way to look down her nose at Detective Brookes.

'This is exactly the sort of attitude I've come to expect from your profession, Detective,' she said.

In a swift motion, the older detective came out of the office and into the hall, placing himself between Val and his colleague.

'Well, Mrs Redwood,' he intervened, 'perhaps that's your prejudice talking. Detective Brookes' – he placed a large hand on his colleague's chest – 'is working extremely hard on Katie's case. Now' – he took on the stance of the playground diplomat, with those infuriating patting motions – 'I think it's probably for the best if everyone sets aside their preconceptions. I know it's hard. In your job, you start to see a pattern and it's hard to unsee it. But . . .' He held up a finger when Val Redwood opened her mouth. 'We're doing our work as professionals here, working very hard, and it's easier for us to get on with that work if we're not having to answer to criticisms from you.'

Sonia sneezed, and all three of them wheeled around. For a moment, Sonia forgot why she had been standing there. Then –

'Lynne's gone,' she said.

'Gone?' Val said, advancing on Sonia, as if forgetting the policemen. 'What do you mean, she's *gone*?'

'I went up to her room and . . .' Sonia jerked her head upwards, to indicate the floor above.

Go and see for yourself, she wanted to say, but she thought she might as well practise her soft act. 'Well, she's not there. All her stuff is gone. And her kid's stuff.'

Val said nothing, but pushed past Sonia, knocking her slightly off balance. Sonia remained hovering in the doorway while the two detectives stared at her blankly.

'Jesus,' the younger one said finally. 'Impossible to get anything done round here.'

The older detective heaved an outsized sigh, his face reddening. It wasn't hard to see that he was angry – humiliated, even – but he hid it behind a bluff smile.

'Wonder why she's gone?' he said, to no one in particular. 'What on earth do you think makes a woman go back to her rich husband?'

The younger detective had the grace to look a little embarrassed. 'All right, sir,' he said quietly. 'I think that's enough of that.' He nodded at Sonia. 'Thanks for letting us know,' he said, before crossing the room, smiling at her carefully and closing the door in her face.

Sonia remained standing there for a second, and her arms seemed to lift themselves and fold across her chest. *Practise,* she whispered to herself, and forced the corners of her mouth into a gentle smile, unknotting her arms from around her.

She turned and made to go back along the corridor, only to see Val moving down the stairs at a pace Sonia wouldn't have thought her capable of. She had a wild look about her.

'Sonia, where did Lynne go?' she said, her voice fruitier and more crushing than ever.

Sonia felt her mouth opening wide despite herself, the shard in her chest seeming to grow and expand. The words *How should I fucking know?* were already blossoming on her tongue, but Val and the detectives had run back upstairs and she was standing in the hall alone.

'All right, Jen?'

She didn't know why she was sounding so friendly. She never normally spoke to Jenny. Jenny's head snapped up as if she were frightened. It made Sonia want to frighten her.

'Don't suppose you've seen Lynne?' Sonia said it breezily, but there was nothing breezy about a disappeared woman. Not in the refuge. Not today. If anyone had bothered to care about her, then maybe she could have made herself care about Lynne, or about Jenny, about any of them. But there it was.

'Lynne?' Jenny snorted. 'Nah.'

Clearly, Jenny didn't have much time for Lynne. That was something they had in common, Sonia figured.

'Well, looks like she's cleared off. Val's in a flap about it.'

'Yeah?' Jenny stood up. It was always surprising how tall she was when she unfolded herself from a chair. 'Yeah? They're all het up about it?'

'Val is. So she's making it that detective's problem. They're all bashing about looking for her, but she's gone, I'm pretty sure.'

'Yeah?'

Before Sonia knew what was happening Jenny had slid past her like a vapour, and all at once was standing in the hall.

'Thanks, Sonia.'

Then she went down the hall, opened the front door and left, with a wave of chilly outdoor air behind her.

Nazia was sitting in the living room, a woolly beanie in the place where her headscarf used to be.

'Don't suppose you're going to do a runner, too?' Sonia said. For something to say.

'What?'

'Lynne. And now Jenny. They're all making a break for it, by the looks of it. Do they know something I don't?' Sonia laughed.

She hadn't actually been expecting Nazia to stand up sharply and dash past her, along the hall and out of the front door. Sonia thought about calling her back, but instead she just sat down on the sofa and let the exhaustion take her. The familiar theme music started to sound. *Morse* was on again.

28.

Then

She wakes the next morning at the feeling of a soft impression on the bed beside her. Jamie propped up on the pillows next to her with his legs stretched out over the covers, dressed, with a mug of tea in his hand. He's not really a tea-drinker, but he's learned how to make it. For her. It's always somehow a little scummy, a little grey.

She takes the mug.

'And' – he reaches over to the bedside table to pick up a plate – 'for the lady!'

A pain au chocolat, warm and flakey. A bunch of grapes, with little drops of water still clinging to them, giving them a still-life look on the blue ceramic plate. He must have been out already.

Katie pretends to be less awake than she really is so she can nuzzle closer, making soft little noises as he feeds her grapes and pieces of pain au chocolat. The bed starts to fill with crumbs.

'Drink your tea,' he says. 'It'll go cold.'

Katie takes a gulp. It's still hot enough that the taste isn't too noticeable.

'It's a beautiful day,' Jamie says, popping a grape into his mouth. Katie can hear the soft, wet burst of it cracking between his teeth.

'I was thinking . . .' He rolls over slightly so that his face is above hers and lays a hand on her cheek. The morning light softens his face, with its sharply drawn boundaries, into something open and golden. 'Picnic?'

It's a lovely day, in the end. For the most part. The kind of day she always imagined she would have when she was in a relationship.

They buy a baguette and cherry tomatoes and ham and cheese and crisps. They eat, or he eats, watching the pairs of ducks swim by. They talk little.

Katie keeps catching, in frames of a second or so, how pieces of her body look in her new sundress, how sleek and neat they are now. Jamie's hand drifts at her waist, brushing back and forth with the tips of his fingers. Every stroke seems to emphasize the disparity between waist and hip. Her stomach still aches from the excess of food last night, but it's a distant ache. She doesn't have to feel it if she doesn't want to.

They lie back on the blanket he brought and drift into a doze together, waking only when the air turns chilly.

Perhaps it's because she's feeling so calm, so normal, that she says it. It's only an idle comment, as they're in the car going home.

'I was thinking maybe I ought to learn to drive.'

Jamie doesn't look away from the road. 'I'm not sure that that's a good idea,' he says.

'Why not?'

She shifts, unsticking her sun-warmed skin from the leatherette seat. 'It would be good to be able to drive my mum to her chemo appointments.' She pauses for a second, glancing at him sideways. 'You know, instead of relying on you to do it.'

She shouldn't have said it. She knows that for certain, before she can begin to understand why. He pulls over so sharply the seat belt takes a strangling grip on her neck. He switches the engine off, one arm dangling casually off the edge of the driver-side window. His mouth has formed a little twist.

'Sorry,' she says.

'What's wrong with relying on me?' His voice is soft. 'Aren't I reliable enough for you?'

She gives a little laugh. Surely that's the best thing to do.

'Why are you smiling?'

'Just because it's so silly . . . of course I think you're . . .'

But the rest of the sentence is lost under the growl of the engine, switched on with the same brute abruptness with which it was switched off.

He swings away from the kerb, nearly cutting off the driver coming in the opposite direction. Katie can see a sign that specifies thirty miles per hour. He's doing fifty . . . sixty . . .

'Jamie . . .' Her voice is normal, neutral. She's good at that these days. The histrionics have been stripped away. 'Could you slow down a bit?' He doesn't seem to hear her.

She can see the rubbish truck coming around the corner. It's vast, bulky, its surface a labyrinth of jagged metal.

In those seconds she wonders if Jamie answers to some higher laws of mathematics and physics than those she understands, because she doesn't see how there's any way of them not smashing into the rubbish truck, their last impressions of grinding metal, that foul, gin-like smell.

Jamie swerves, the car snapping down the narrow vein of a side road which seems to have appeared from nowhere. Their speed is maintained as they career down a residential street, missing a cat and a set of dustbins by inches.

Then he slows the car. Switches off the engine. Turns to look at Katie. The twist in his mouth has been ironed out and his expression is calm now. Katie is trying to keep her breathing as quiet as possible.

'See?' He tilts his head casually. 'Could you have done that?'

It can't be more than a split second before she answers. She's dizzy with the deceleration.

'No . . .'

'I know you're clever in some ways. You've made that pretty clear.' His voice is taut. 'But you're not good at everything. Your reflexes are terrible.'

'You could have been caught speeding,' she says.

She knows there is an unspoken accusation there, deeper in her mind, but she can't get the words to form under the chill of Jamie's stare.

'No speed cameras. It's a dead zone round here.' He continues to look at her. 'I'm not fucking stupid, you know.'

'I know you're not.'

He turns the key in the ignition and the car springs back to life.

'So you still want to learn to drive?' he asks.

'No.'

29.

Now

'Jenny?'

Nazia had never called her by her name before, not out loud, but the name seemed to do its job anyway.

Jenny paused, and when she looked back she managed a smile. She'd eaten most of the pink lipstick off her mouth.

'All right, Naz? What you following me for?'

Nazia stopped short, realizing she wasn't yet sure of the answer herself. Instead, she countered with her own question. There were only questions here.

'Where're you going?'

'Off.' Jenny sniffed. She looked resolute, and her shoulder made an odd movement, as if she were hitching a bag higher on to it, but there was nothing there. 'Cops're distracted. Ruckus with Lynne. I don't know. Don't care. I'm off.'

'What for?'

'Got to go.' Jenny's teeth were working back and forth across her lips. 'Sometimes you've got to go. Rattling, you know?'

'I thought you said you'd got your methadone sorted?'

Nazia didn't mean it to sound accusing, but it seemed that way to her ears. It reminded her of the way Sabbir had sounded the first time she'd said she didn't want to play with him any more. Jenny was dancing a little on the spot, as if desperate to move, but at Nazia's words she became still.

'Sweet of you to remember that, Naz. Sweet of you to ask about me. You're a mate.'

'Yeah.'

Nazia didn't know why she felt like crying, but that didn't make any difference, because the tears were starting to come anyway.

'So why're you leaving?'

'Nothing for me here.'

'You've got me,' Nazia said. Why did her voice sound so strange to her ears, so full that it might burst?

Jenny didn't say anything to that. Maybe she didn't hear it.

'Not safe here,' Jenny said. 'Not for me, anyway. You'll be all right, though. I'm sure you'll be all right.'

'Why's it not safe?'

Jenny's cheeks sucked in.

'There's . . .' Whatever she was thinking seemed too vast to be able to get out of her mouth, so she shrugged, and started dancing in place again, looking anxiously back at the refuge. 'Look, I just know, all right.'

'But . . .' Nazia reached out a hand to take Jenny's. 'Whatever it is, we could work it out. Tell the police.'

Jenny just laughed.

But then she stopped and looked Nazia in the eye. Clearer than Nazia had ever seen her look at anything. Not just sober, but penetrating. Alive.

'I'm going to tell you something, Naz. Then I've got to go, okay?'

'What is it?'

Jenny put her hand on Nazia's arm to pull her closer. There was something in the gentleness of her grip that broke Nazia's heart.

'I'll tell you what really happened. But you've got to keep it safe, okay? Don't go blabbing. Not yet. We've got to pick our moment, Naz. Got to wait till it's the right time. Can you do that?'

Nazia nodded.

30.

Then

Her mother asks her what's wrong. She laughs.

'Oh, it's a silly thing, but Jamie drove a bit fast yesterday. Not too fast. Probably not over the speed limit – you know Jamie, he's very sensible.'

Her mother is frowning slightly – the shape of the frown is still there, although the eyebrows are not.

'And you know what young men are like. Boy racers. Ha ha.'

Her mother laughs and tells Katie that she's too much of a worrier and that she shouldn't worry about Jamie; he's a lovely young man. 'He'll look after you.'

Then Katie's mum hugs her. She doesn't do it much these days. It's as if she knows she's not doing Katie any favours by getting too close.

'He's nothing like your dad, Katie.'

'What?'

'I know you're scared of car accidents. You've always been a nervy girl, right from when you were tiny. But truly, you don't need to worry so much. He's nothing like your dad.'

She confronts him about it a couple of days later, if you can call it a confrontation. The feeling that she needs to say something has hatched inside her like a family of baby snakes; now, she can think of nothing else.

She tells herself that to talk to him about it is the healthy thing. It's the kind of thing, she thinks, that any of her friends would have parroted, if she'd felt able to call them.

'I don't speed,' he says, looking straight at her. 'Don't be stupid, Katie. I wouldn't risk my career like that.'

'You were doing fifty . . .'

'Fifty?' His laugh is as clear as a bell. 'Don't be ridiculous. It's a thirty zone. I was doing thirty-five, absolute tops.'

There must be something in her face that continues to ask questions, even though she's holding her tongue. Jamie laughs and pulls her close to him, nuzzling her hair.

'Don't worry, beautiful,' he says. 'I know you were scared, but I wasn't speeding. It just feels faster in a smaller car.'

She doesn't sleep. Sometimes she doesn't because he's not there; sometimes because she can't navigate the limited stretch of bed when he is there. So it's easier to say that she just doesn't sleep at all.

''Course you can't sleep when you've got no routine. It's the inconsistency,' he says. 'If I'm always there, you'll get used to it. If I'm never there, you'll get used to that, too. But it's all the changing. I could just go away,' he says, leaning in close, his eyes teasing. 'Do you want me to go away?'

Her mouth smiles, but her hands reach for him reflexively.

'No, don't go away,' she says, her eyes fixed not on him but on the jumble of her mother's pill bottles on the kitchen table. 'Don't go away. Don't go away.'

There is endless time to turn it over in her mind at her office desk. Her daily undertaking – transferring information from one spreadsheet to another – makes her mind flabby through lack of use. The only thing that can keep the muscle strong is the exercise of anxiety. She really needs to get one of those mindfulness apps, she thinks. Take control of her thoughts. Shift her perspective.

She knows in some distant way that the job is making her unhappy, that applying to be an administrative assistant in a City law firm was nothing more than a knee-jerk reaction to the terror of graduation. But when it comes to thinking about a new job, the first thing that she can think of is fitting in with Jamie.

'I'm not leaving London,' he'd told her when she first brought it up. 'No way. I'm doing well here.'

Besides, he had added, he didn't understand why she would want to be anywhere else. Her network of friends was there, and his. And her mother. The constant, dead weight of her mother.

She is deteriorating by the day, the sheen of waxed paper invading her skin. She's vague about her oncology appointments. She won't let Katie come with her. She mentions numbers – white blood count, that seems to be the number everyone's interested in – as if they are works of art that would be diminished by the indignity of interpretation. Perhaps it's her mother's philosophical side emerging, but she seems removed from the idea that anything about her treatment could be either good or bad. All these things, they just *are*.

Jamie drives her to and from her appointments. He, too, simply is.

But Katie feels herself straining at the leash, with all the subtlety of a frantic dog.

A new job – that seems like the thing to think about.

He finds her looking through a brochure one day. Graduate scheme with the UN.

'What's this?' He picks it up.

'Oh.' Katie makes to shove it away, but he has already grabbed it.

His voice is calm, velvety even.

'Are you thinking about working abroad?'

She isn't thinking about applying for the job in any serious sense. It's just an idea to play with, like a shadow puppet on a wall.

'Not really.'

She says it too quickly.

He looks at her for a moment then blinks and glances away so quickly that the mood switches to casual.

'I think it's kind of selfish, Katie,' he says.

There it is. One of Jamie's judgements, hard and smooth as a pebble.

'What about your mum?'

He's right. Of course he's right. What kind of daughter would think of leaving a mother who was so ill, whose baby-cloud of hair is barely clinging to her head in a chemo halo?

'I'm not thinking about it,' she says.

In her mind's eye, her mum's pale, dry lips curl up into a dead-saint smile.

'Good,' Jamie says.

With one quick motion he tears the brochure in two, then two again. The pieces in his hand, he glances up at Katie and smiles.

'Glad that's settled, then.'

That night Katie wakes up to feel Jamie inside her.

She forgives him before she even gives herself a chance to be angry. She lets him finish, lets him roll off her. Then she murmurs, very quietly, 'I'm awake, you know.'

She's sore.

He doesn't seem to hear her for a while. Maybe he didn't – he's still panting. Then he replies, quietly, as if it doesn't change anything – 'Oh.'

'Why didn't you wake me up?'

It isn't the question that Katie really needs to ask, the question that sits deep inside her, but it's the only one she's able to formulate.

Jamie sits up, switching the light on and glaring at her.

'Why? I couldn't sleep. I didn't want you to be tired tomorrow.'

'Okay.' Katie feels herself searching for the next reasonable thing to say, although reason seems hard to reach when they are lying there in the rumpled bed, their shapes distorted by the distant light of the street lamps.

There is no reason when it comes to love, after all. It isn't supposed to make sense.

Stop analysing it, Katie.

Maybe she said yes and just doesn't remember. It scares her how much she forgets things now. But that's not Jamie's fault.

She doesn't know what to say, so she gets up and goes to the toilet, as if it had been normal sex deserving normal rituals. He will expect her to stay there for a few moments, so that gives her time to think.

If he'd asked her, of course she would have said yes. There never feels like any option of saying no, because then he'd sulk and turn away from her and she would lie beside him feeling cast out.

And besides, she would have wanted it. She likes sex with him, craves it, initiates it.

'You're all I want,' he tells her, pressing a kiss into the top of her head when she lies back down beside him in the dark.

They go for a walk in the park the next day, sitting on a bench to watch a pair of stags rut violently in the carved hollow of a dried-up lake.

He keeps asking her what's wrong, and she keeps not knowing the words to say.

It would seem excessive to call what happened between them a violation. No violence, for one thing. No struggle. And if she had been awake, it would probably all have ended up the same way.

'You're worried about your mum,' he tells her. 'You're fixating on this because you feel like it's something that you can control.'

Perhaps it is true. It might as well be true. Katie starts to cry, and he hugs her.

'You look pretty,' he tells her, when she's calmed down a little. 'Even when you've been crying, you look pretty.'

She hates crying. It feels like crying relegates her to the children's table, and yet she finds it very hard to stop these days.

That night he does it again.

31.

Now

It was pretty clear that Lynne had gone because she'd decided to go. A glance at her room told them that. It had been done neatly. Whitworth half expected to see a thank-you note on the bed.

He didn't linger there long, though, once he heard the shout from downstairs. He dashed back to the office, to find Brookes enraged.

And Jenny gone.

Fuck.

It was obvious, Whitworth realized as he looked wildly round the tiny key work room, as if it had swallowed Jenny up somewhere in its fluorescent lighting and cheap carpet. So shamefully obvious that Jenny had known something. She had known it all along, she must have done. Whatever it was, it had to be why she had followed Katie that night, maybe even part of why Lynne and Peony were missing.

Nazia was sitting in the lounge, her face slightly dazed beneath a heavy woollen beanie.

'Have you seen Jenny?' Whitworth asked, trying to keep his voice calm. Nazia's head jerked and she flushed a little.

'She said goodbye,' she replied.

'What kind of goodbye?'

'Just . . . goodbye.'

'How long ago?'

Nazia shrugged, seemingly lost for words.

Whitworth felt something inside him sputter and stall and wheeled around, back down the corridor to where Val was still standing.

'Detective, you need to . . .'

But Whitworth was sick of hearing what it was he needed to do. 'Where's Jenny's room?' he asked brusquely.

'Jenny? But Lynne . . .'

'Jenny knew something about Katie's death.' Whitworth knew he was taking a gamble, but everything could happen more quickly if Val Redwood were in a more cooperative mood.

Val's forehead creased. She made a noise that would have been a laugh if she hadn't been such a humourless woman.

'Oh, Detective, I very much doubt that.'

'Well, Mrs Redwood, you're entitled to your opinion, and I'm entitled to mine. But as a police officer, I'm asking you again. Where is Jenny's room?'

Val Redwood eyed him for a few seconds. It occurred to Whitworth that she might be idiotic enough to demand a warrant. She sucked her puckered red mouth first to one side of her face, then to the other, before finally letting her hand drift to her pocket and withdrawing the heavy bunch of keys.

'Come on, then.'

Jenny's room was neat. Anally neat. The kind of neatness that can only come with emptiness.

Three little stubs of lipstick – red, pink, purple – were lined up like a row of soldiers on top of the chest of drawers. The bedspread was as flat and featureless as a blank page. There was nothing in it to indicate that Jenny either did or didn't plan to return. If Whitworth didn't know smackheads and how they worked, he might have been inclined to suggest that they should wait and see if she was coming back.

He hurried in, then stopped short, noticing the clumsiness, the gracelessness, of his own footsteps in that still, bloodless room. Brookes was hovering around in the hallway and Val stood at the door, leaning against the doorframe with her glasses in her hand. She had the oddest expression on her face, as if some internal scaffolding had collapsed and gravity was doing its work on her.

'What would Jenny take?'

'Hmm?' Val looked up at him. She spoke mildly, as if she had forgotten to be her usual, obdurate self. 'What do you mean?'

'What would be important to Jenny if she was doing a bunk? What would she take?'

'Oh, Detective . . .' Val put her glasses on and gave a strange little smile, which gave a kind of coherence to her face. 'Jenny doesn't have anything worth taking.'

She walked over to the window and looked down into the garden. The light was starting to fade. 'Women don't come here if they've got anything to lose.'

'Hmmm.' Whitworth picked up one of the lipsticks then cursed himself for disturbing the scene and put it down again.

'Now, if you'll let me get a word in edgeways, I thought you'd better know that we've had more threats.'

Val shoved another stack of print-outs under Whitworth's nose. He took them automatically. Her mouth sucked in and disappeared, her head snapping to look at Whitworth. 'Does this mean you're actually going to start taking the things I say seriously? Does this mean you're going to start seriously looking at this stalker?' She rummaged in the overcrowded pocket of her black slacks, producing a piece of crumpled paper. 'Here's a new one from today. Rape threats. Directed at me, thank you very much.'

Her hand was trembling as she passed the sheet to

Whitworth. If she'd been a little easier to like, then maybe he would have tried to comfort her, but instead he just took it.

How about i come over and fucking rape your fat whore cunt and maybe you'll see how fucking stupid you sound talking about so called rape culture you overprivileged bitch.

Whitworth handed the paper to Brookes.

'Look into this, will you? I'm sure Jenny didn't go walkabout because of some online loony,' he said. 'Imagine she's heard worse language than that. Profession like hers.'

'Detective . . .'

'Look, Val, you can make a report to the station and they can deal with this separately, but I don't need a keyboard warrior clogging up my inquiry.'

'And if it's connected?'

'It isn't,' Whitworth said with a finality he didn't feel and made a mental note to tell one of the computer whizzes to hurry up.

'Sir?' Brookes's head appeared around the door of Jenny's room. Val remained staring out of the window.

'Yes?' Whitworth wanted to get out of that bedroom, out of the refuge, out of the endless crushing intimacy of these female spaces. Yet he stood his ground, not wanting the younger man to read his discomfort. Brookes gestured sideways along the corridor, past Jenny's room.

'Does look like Lynne's gone. Should I call it in, sir?'

Why, Whitworth wondered with an ancient sort of weariness, *can these bloody women not look after themselves?*

'Well . . .' He shrugged. 'She's an adult, isn't she?'

'She's not well,' Val added, with a strange sort of excitement. 'She's been struggling for a while . . .'

'And how exactly is going back to her husband going to help her?'

209

'*Assuming* she's going back to her husband.'

'Assuming, of course, Mrs Redwood.' Whitworth took a breath. 'And if that's the case, then I don't see anything to worry about.'

'Assuming she went back to her husband.' Val took a deep breath, as if she were about to launch into a lecture in the middle of the bedroom. 'Assuming she went back, I don't suppose you're aware that the average battered woman returns to her abusive partner between five and seven times before she's finally able to leave for good.'

'Did he actually hit her?' Whitworth asked, and Val looked as if she could barely bring herself to spit out the syllable: 'No. But that's not the only –'

'In that case' – Whitworth was already turning away from Val – 'I see no reason to think she's in any immediate danger, and –'

'Even so . . .' Brookes said it abruptly, cutting Whitworth off. 'Just saying, sir . . . she seemed a bit vulnerable. And, of course, there's the kid. Could be a Child Protection issue . . .'

Child Protection. Yes. That little girl.

Whitworth noticed that Brookes's cheeks were burning and some of his swagger seemed to have dropped away. Brookes seemed to have a soft spot for little kids.

'We've got to find that kid, sir,' Brookes said. His voice was quiet, but there was a force of feeling behind it. 'She's just a baby. She can't make her own choices. She's helpless.'

Val's head snapped back behind her to look at Brookes. She looked irritated for a second, then said carefully, 'Well, yes, Detective. I think you might be right there.'

'Lynne seemed like a competent enough mother to me,' Whitworth said.

But he knew it was useless. Once the words 'Child Protection' had been uttered, they would curse the air they were breathed in. More so, of course, with Val Redwood as a witness. She wasn't the kind of person who would hesitate to accuse him of negligence.

Whitworth deliberately turned his back on Val Redwood.

'Fine, then. DC Brookes, I'd like you to lead the efforts to locate Lynne Ward. And her daughter, of course.'

He crossed back over to the threshold. 'I'm going to investigate Jenny's whereabouts.'

He saw Brookes's eyebrows raise a fraction and continued, with a self-justification he knew wasn't warranted in the face of a junior officer, 'I think she may be a key witness in this case.'

Whitworth wondered if Jenny even had the imagination to try to leave Widringham. But if she did, then the train station was the main artery out. She was very unlikely to have the money for a train ticket, but a snakish type like that would probably be able to wind herself around a kindly train conductor and squeeze every last drop of goodwill out of him.

Brookes was driving them faster than two police officers should strictly have been driving along the narrow roads. But if Whitworth didn't make the next train, then there was no chance of catching up with Jenny. Brookes was clearly still shaken, his knuckles white on the steering wheel.

'It'll be all right,' Whitworth told him firmly. 'We'll find them. We'll find them both.'

Brookes shook his head. 'If she's endangered that kid on our watch, sir . . .'

He left the sentence uncompleted. What was there to say?

'Wait. Stop.'

They were on the bridge. The bridge that would never be just a pretty tourist attraction to them again.

'Is that . . . is that *Noah*?'

The tall, scraggy figure standing looking down into the water was unmistakeable.

Whitworth's mind had been miles from Katie Straw, but the sight of Noah had brought him back to the reason for their mission with a jerk. He glanced at Brookes, who looked perplexed.

'Back at the scene of the crime?' Brookes said. His voice was doubtful, echoing the sense of *surely not* Whitworth felt in his own mind.

Noah's head was bowed, his shoulders shaking. Did this man *ever* stop crying?

'Or just mourning?' Whitworth said. It was half rhetorical. The jolt of seeing Noah had interrupted the flow of adrenalin in pursuing Jenny, but he realized that his heart was still racing. Brookes looked equally caught off guard. The car was idling.

'Should we . . .' Brookes made a gesture to get out of the car, but decisiveness tugged at Whitworth, urging him forward. He shook his head.

'There's no time. You've seen him there. I've seen him there. The thing now is to find Lynne and Jenny. Cut back here on your way to the police station and if he's still there, then see if you can get anything out of him. Else we'll get him in the station tomorrow.'

They arrived too late, and Whitworth missed the train. Served them right for hesitating. The process of tracking Jenny was slowed by the man in the ticket booth, who seemed to have no idea how to recall footage from the security camera. Whitworth found himself in the unusual position of feeling like the technology whizz in the situation. They eventually found her on the CCTV footage of the station platform, boarding the train to Manchester. She had a decent head-start.

It was too late, then. She would be swallowed into the metropolis and have disappeared.

Whitworth rang Brookes while he stood on the platform.

'Any luck with Lynne Ward?'

'Steady on, I've only been at HQ five minutes.'

Darkness was pooling in the creases of Widringham. Half an hour by train to Manchester, so Jenny wouldn't be that far ahead of him. But by the time he got into town, all her people would have come crawling out of their cracks, emboldened by nightfall.

'Look, can you alert the Manc police that we're looking for Jenny? Give them her description. She boarded the last train, so chances are, by the time I get there, she'll already be well away from the station. But I'm not interested in just chances. I'm going to follow her there, got it?'

'If you think that's best, sir.'

'I do,' Whitworth said, with an inexplicable sense of irritation. 'I do think it's best. Keep me updated on Lynne Ward.'

He tapped the end call button before he could get any reply from Brookes. Perhaps there was never going to be any reply, but he had an odd compulsion to have the last word.

The train pulled into the station and Whitworth got on.

32.

Then

The conversation starts innocuously enough. An invitation to Katie's cousin's wedding. They – *he* – they – rule out attending immediately. It would require overnight travel and they can't leave Katie's mother.

To distract him, Katie starts talking about the amount of credit-card debt the cousin's got into in order to put on an enormous wedding. She feels a little sanctimonious even as she's saying it, but Jamie seems to warm quickly to the theme of fiscal responsibility, so they keep the conversation up.

'I feel like it's more about the wedding than the marriage these days,' she says. 'It's not like getting married actually changes anything. I mean, my mum and dad were never married.'

She sees Jamie frown.

'Or . . .' She takes a mental step back. 'No? What do you think?'

'I'd want to get married,' Jamie says. It feels more baldly honest than Katie has understood the calibration of the conversation to be, but she nods.

'Yeah?'

'Yeah. I mean, wife . . . kids . . . aren't those what everyone wants?'

'I don't know.'

The idea of marriage was as alien to Katie as it was unfashionable. The only married people she knew of her age were either deeply religious or permanently damaged by a bubble-gum ideal of love, growing up as they had in the *Twilight* era.

'It's tough. Careers and everything.'

'You might as well have kids young.' Jamie was speaking fluently. Speechifying. 'Everyone knows that there's . . . like, a window for women. When it's better. When it makes more sense. All this idea of a career path – it doesn't take that into account, you know? It's different for women.'

'Right.'

'You know?'

'Yeah. But I like having a job.' When had the abstractions died? she wondered. This conversation had abruptly turned concrete.

'Come on, Katie. You spend the whole day texting me telling me how awful it is. How much your boss is scaring you. How you feel like you do everything wrong.'

'Yeah, but . . .' She cast around for something more solid than herself. 'There's money, right? Money to consider. You need a certain amount of stability, don't you?'

The conversations snake over a number of days. The parameters change – she doesn't notice how. But it's good that they're talking. It's good to talk.

'Look. Just quit. Focus on your mum. You don't need to worry about money. I don't make much, but it's not like we need to pay for accommodation.'

'But it's my mum's house.'

He didn't live there. Not officially. But what would *officially* look like? Changing his address at the bank? Registering to vote? All his things were at her mother's house. They'd accumulated so gradually she'd scarcely noticed.

'It'll be yours. Ours.'

She supposes that's true. It implies an end in sight. Because this can't continue. This limbo. This nothingness.

'What do you mean?'

He gives her that look. He's handsome in certain lights. It always catches her off guard.

'Let me take care of you,' he says.

It is tempting.

Things were falling apart at work, but then, why should they not?

Why should she have to keep photocopying, diary-inviting, memo-printing, when soon her mother would be dead and no one at the office would care about it any longer than the time it would take for them to sign a card from Clintons?

There would be something wrong with her if she was functioning normally. That was what her boss seemed to be implying in her appraisal meeting, doling out the calibrated amount of manufactured kindness.

'I think that maybe it would be good for you to talk to someone,' she said, her face fixed firmly on her notepad as Katie sat opposite, her hands clenched in her lap. 'We've got access to a talking helpline. If you need it.'

Katie nodded.

'Yeah. That might be good. Yeah.'

'Oh,' Jamie snorted when she told him later. 'My work has that, too. It's so they can kid themselves they're trying to look after you but, really, they don't give a fuck.'

He looked as if he had been caught off guard, seeing the look on her face, and backtracked. In tone, at least, if not in the substance of his words.

'I'm sorry, Katie, but it's true. They don't care. They want you well enough to function, sure, but they don't care if you're actually doing well. They want you well because it's better for their profits if you're well.'

He put an arm around her and pulled her close.

'It sucks,' he said. 'But it's the world of work.'

The feeling of constant terror just was. It rattled around her body like lightning, animating it with explosive, useless energy that channelled into a pounding heart, a bolt of terror every time her boss appeared.

She's standing outside the office and, if you were to look at her, you'd just see a young woman, and you wouldn't know that it was a young woman who knows she's going to die any second.

The buildings of the City are going to fall on top of her.

It's not based on any reasonable thought. So it can't be reasoned away.

She just sees the glass blocks of the City falling like dominoes. Converging on her.

She sees it. She feels her ribcage being crushed. No wonder she can't take a proper breath.

She's left her coat upstairs. It's so *cold* out.

Her handbag, too.

But her wallet is in her hand.

So she walks to Bank Tube station, her presence made illegitimate and foolish by the lack of coat.

The walk through Bank is as endless as Purgatory.

The Tube will never come.

But then it does. The faces around her seem to reprimand her, but the Tube starts to pull in with a remorseless roar.

She leans on to the ball of her front foot. It would be easy to jump. It wouldn't take much. The tracks are only a few feet below, and they look warm. She could curl up on them for a few moments. It wouldn't take long.

A single soot-stained mouse threads its way across, fleeing the oncoming train, down in this place where it's always night-time and the only version of daylight comes with the roar of metal.

She leans backwards.

Maybe she'll fall.

She doesn't.

The doors are open. The train is almost empty. It's the middle of the day.

It continues to be the middle of the day all the way home, though she can't check the precise time. She left her phone in the office.

She feels exhausted and crushed. She's alone, very alone, even more so when the Tube line makes its final dart into daylight and she understands with a shudder that this is what freedom feels like.

She stays on until the end of the line, long past her own stop. She sits in a bleak train-station café – none of the comfort of a train – and orders a cup of tea, then another, and then realizes she has no idea where she would go once the cups of tea stop.

She asks the man in the café to call her a taxi, and it costs her £50 to get home, but it would have cost her much more not to.

For a long time that night she sits on the sofa staring at her phone. Jamie had gone into the office to get it for her. She could call someone. The numbers are all there. Lara, Lucy.

Ellie.

The last text from her says, *hey babe haven't heard from you for a long time is everything okay? Call me if you need anything xxx*

At first, she hadn't replied because she didn't know what to do with the live, wriggling piece of kindness that had been handed to her. Then she didn't reply because she knew she had waited too long, and she was ashamed.

So she deletes the text.

In the end, Jamie writes her resignation letter for her. Because this can't continue. The anxiety. The depression.

It must be her job. It *must* be.

They'll find a way. They'll manage. Her mental health is more important. Sometimes, you need to alter your circumstances. Sometimes, it's not just a case of thinking more positively. You need to *change* something.

So she changed a comma or two and signed her name.

There. Easy.

33.

Now

The train to Manchester was by far the quickest route from Widringham. Though it wasn't a great distance as the crow flew, the road out of town made a narrow, winding progress through the hills. If you got stuck behind a coach or a bus, you were stuffed for the next twenty miles. Whitworth couldn't afford that, not with a junkie to trace.

Whitworth had taken that train more times than he cared to count. When he was a kid his dad had taken him into Manchester to watch the footie. It probably hadn't been more than two or three times, but those giddy train journeys shone so brightly in Whitworth's memory they felt like the main feature of his childhood. His life, even.

Then, as a younger man, he had taken Maureen on dates to see the groups playing at the Apollo – The Police, ELO, Dire Straits. They'd never been up his street, but he didn't mind admitting now that those had been some good shows.

The first time they'd ever gone he'd promised to take Maureen for dinner before the show. He'd made much of it, told her to put on her glad rags, ironed his shirt with care. But he hadn't known any restaurants in the area and the only places he could find laughed in the face of a policeman's salary. So they'd gone for egg and chips in a caf round the corner from the venue.

When they reminisced about those early days after a drink or two, Jennifer would laugh at how crap it all sounded, what a miser her dad had been.

'Couldn't just do a google in those days,' he'd told her indignantly, but she'd just laughed harder.

It hadn't felt so ridiculous at the time, but the shame had kicked in as soon as their daughter started to laugh. Perhaps Maureen remembered the whole thing rather differently than he did. She'd probably say so now.

He thought about calling her. Let her know she shouldn't expect him home that night. There was a time when he wouldn't have thought twice about it. Hearing her voice used to be the bright spot in a long evening at his desk or on the beat. An opportunity to remember that nothing could beat chatting to her as she scraped away the remnants of Jennifer's fish fingers and the two of them settled down in front of the telly with their feet just touching on the leatherette ottoman.

In the end he texted her.

Won't be home this evening. Working late. Love to Jen.

He imagined his wife picking up her phone, reading the text. Maybe she would consider replying, but most likely she wouldn't bother, not now that there was so little to say between them.

In such a long relationship there was passion and contempt and every emotion that could possibly exist in between. Though he'd never hit her, it would be a lie to say he hadn't felt like it once or twice.

His phone buzzed.

Okay see you in the morning x

There was a group of girls on the set of seats next to Whitworth, five of them cramming their narrow behinds into the space for four people. The spindly bodies still suggested childhood, though breasts and hips were forming almost before Whitworth's eyes, and their faces had been carved into the ageless, blank perfection all the girls seemed to have these days, courtesy of enormous quantities of makeup. They were talking, laughing loudly, looking around the way teenage girls did to make sure that they were making an impact. It was as if they had arranged themselves into a photograph, facing outwards into the train carriage, with only scraps of Lycra to stave off their adolescent nudity.

Off for a night out in Manchester, Whitworth thought. Younger than his daughter, he would have guessed. One of them seemed to catch Whitworth looking, picking up his gaze and holding it in a way that made the father in him twist and turn away. The girl had blue eyes that she had dirtied with some smudgy black stuff, and Whitworth couldn't work out if her look was a challenge or an invitation. He had half a mind to demand to see these girls' IDs, to point out their inevitable fakeness and send them back to whichever small, quiet town they'd come from, back to their parents, who could cover them up and keep them safe from the stares of men Whitworth's age.

That was what Jennifer didn't understand when he told her to change her clothes.

I should be able to wear whatever I want.

Of course you should, love, he thought. *You should be able to leave your drink unattended and dance the night away. You should be able to get into a minicab off the street, too. You should be able to get the night bus rather than the taxis I insist you get, which I'll go without anything for myself to pay for.*

He leaned his forehead against the grubby glass of the train window. *But the world isn't a* should. *If it was a* should, *then you'd waltz through life naked as the day you were born without a single filthy eye hooking into you.*

Whitworth knew you had to do all you could. You could never stop being diligent, never let your guard down, never gamble your life on an abstraction. Or if not your life, then something worse.

Whitworth had seen what women looked like after they were raped. Properly raped, that was, not when they had had a few too many and decided they regretted it afterwards.

The train pulled into Piccadilly.

Whitworth had an idea of the homeless and drug-dealing topography of Manchester. The problem was, that gave him plenty of places to start looking.

He made for Piccadilly Gardens, with the idea of moving towards the Northern Quarter, where he knew there were plenty of crevices for a creature like Jenny to pick up and to be picked up.

He seemed to see her around every corner, but perhaps that was because there were so many blank-looking homeless people scattered around the streets, like the bleached components of a skeleton.

He began to doubt he would even recognize her if he saw her. The photo they had of her in the police system was taken when she was much younger, when her features had been more defined, when the pigment hadn't evaporated from her and left only that oily mess of bones and eyes. When she had been more sharply drawn, perhaps less afraid.

But there was no Jenny like that left.

As far as he could see, Manchester was a city planned for wretchedness. The wretchedness of the majority, that is, for the comfort of a few.

The centre was dominated by the great hotels. The Midland, the Principal. The moulded intricacies of brown terracotta seemed to invite the weary to rest in the shelter of a doorway, only to be evicted by men dressed in stiff coats like Victorian footmen. All the red arches of the railway lines, the secret places to crawl, the network of canals, the bold sweep of potential bed space around Piccadilly Gardens were carpeted by swathes of cardboard that would never make the ground any softer.

There was one man lying face down and spreadeagled outside Superdrug. A pool of vomit, slackened by the rain, was starting to run away from his face and slide across the pavement. A security guard was looking down at him with weary disregard. Whitworth didn't envy whatever young PC would end up scraping the drunk off the floor and taking him back to the station to sober up.

To say that it was raining that night would have felt trivial. The rain battered. It violated. It deadened. It soaked those little cardboard homesteads and old sleeping bags which, on a lucky night, might have kept a person warm, or at least kept the idea of warmth alive. It was exactly the kind of place for someone like Jenny, which is what made someone like Jenny so impossible to find.

He asked a group of likely-looking smackheads, showing Jenny's photograph to several of the homeless around Piccadilly Gardens. He wasn't in uniform and most of them would have been too out of it to notice even if he had been, so they stayed still long enough to look blankly at the photo and shake their heads. He showed it to a local beat cop, who gave him a brotherly shrug and said with what was probably a smile, 'She could be anyone, mate. But I'll keep an eye out.'

The light was failing and Whitworth didn't have his glasses with him.

After an hour or so of drifting he caught something in the corner of his eye. He marched straight up to a woman sitting on the ground, convinced that it was Jenny.

But it was just someone who looked like her, who *was* like her.

The woman looked up in interest for a second. Thinking he might have wanted to buy . . . something . . . from her, but once that chemical rush of hope had cleared away she reverted to her unfocused expression, picking at the cardboard edge of the sign she was holding, which insisted that she wasn't on drugs, she just needed a bed for the night.

He tried to focus on the things that made Jenny resemble a person. He thought about those tubes of cheap lipstick on her dressing table, remembered the hideousness of her face when it split into deep thought. Tried to think his way into what a person like Jenny would do, as was his training, as was his instinct.

But his training and his instinct and the feeling of the rain on his skin pointed him towards just one thing, and that was heroin. And the problem was, that didn't point him in any particular direction.

Then his phone rang.

34.

Then

Katie is packing a bag.

For her mother.

Possibly the last bag her mother will ever need.

But you can't think about it like that.

Notions float through her head like stingrays. She has to repel them, watch their boneless motion as they drift away.

She finds one of her own sweaters in the dresser where her mother's clothes live. It's the sort of mistake that is often made in their home. They're not sticklers about that sort of thing.

Automatically, she packs it.

Soft wool. Bright blue. The colour is too bright. Siren-bright.

Her mother won't need it. She has a fever. That's the whole point.

She closes her eyes, but the colour stays, flashing.

Then she stands up and carries the overnight bag into the next room. The bag contains her mother's face cream, her mother's nightdress, her mother's pills.

But the sweater belongs to her.

She adds pairs of her own knickers, counting them. One two three four five six seven.

Enough for the week.

What week? Any week. Any lifetime starts with one week.

Knickers. Passport. Those are the things you really need.

She almost forgets to add her wallet. She doesn't carry it

much these days, and there's nothing in her current account, anyway. Hasn't been for a while, not since she left her job.

But there's money. Left by her father, in an account she labelled 'grown-up savings' when she set it up online, with vague ideations of mortgages. Maybe a mortgage with Jamie.

'Katie?'

A stinging bolt. He's calling her name.

She drops the bag and hurries down the stairs. She always hurries for him.

'Are you nearly ready with that bag?'

He's standing in the middle of the kitchen with his car keys in his hand, shrugging on his jacket. It's well cut across the shoulders, with the strong lines of an anchor.

'Nearly,' she says. 'Hang on a minute. I'm nearly ready.'

She glances over to the sofa, where her mother is sitting. She's holding a cup of tea they all know she won't drink, but Jamie made it, anyway, for something to do.

That's the brutal shame of it.

They're all just trying to do something. To change something. They don't even know what it is they're trying to change.

Katie walks up the stairs, the tempo of her steps slow. Steady. Predictable.

She takes out knickers. Passport. Wallet.

She takes out the sweater, too.

She carries the bag back into her mother's room and fills it with an armful of nighties. Her mother didn't use to wear nighties, but she does now. Slippers, too, and a dressing gown.

Another stingray thought drifts across her mind. She doesn't look at it.

She throws a book on top of the jumble, for optimism's sake. Zips the thing up and carries it downstairs.

Jamie is waiting for her at the bottom. He reaches up an

arm towards her, pulls her close. Kisses the top of her head. She leans into him for a second. For a moment, she can abdicate responsibility for holding herself upright.

'I know how hard this is for you,' he says.

He knows. He knows it all.

Jamie drives. Katie sits in the front, next to him. Her mother's in the back, her forehead pressed against the cool glass of the window. Her cheeks are flushed.

Katie doesn't say anything. She wonders how many times her parents sat side by side like this, alone but for the vast presence of their shared responsibility in the back seat. In those moments, she now understood, it didn't do to ask yourself any questions about love or fear.

35.

Now

Death?

Seen him. Loads of times.

Death's just a bloke.

Average height. Brownish hair. Couldn't tell you what colour his eyes are, but I can tell you he's nothing special to look at.

He doesn't look angry or sad or evil. Just . . . a bit bored.

But at the end of the day he's a guy with a job to do. So what he does is he comes up to you and he opens your mouth and he just pulls the life out of you.

Tell you what it's like. It's like a dentist pulling out a tooth.

Imagine that.

Then he turns around and he shrugs like he's saying *I don't make the rules* and he takes out his little machine he carries and logs the life into his system.

And then he walks off to the next job. And that's that.

He's been hanging about.

He's been trying to look in the windows. Leaving gates open.

Messing with cameras.

Left a note. I FOUND YOU.

But then *I* found *it*.

Didn't give it to anyone. Lay on it like a grenade.

Bang.

Rains all the fucking time here. Always has.

So I scrunch myself into the smallest space.

I think he's looking for me.

I know the fucker's looking for me.

Just stay still Jenny.

Just keep your head

Down.

Yeah, I talk to myself. Keeps people away. Makes me a risk no one's willing to take.

I haven't picked up yet, which you wouldn't think, but you should be able to tell cos I'm rattling like you wouldn't believe, but I tell you what, it's true, swear to God.

What a good little junkie.

I'm saving it. Saving up the best feeling in the world because, once you've spent it, it's gone.

I'm not waiting for business. I'm not waiting to be wanted. I'm just saving the feeling up like a kid with their last sweet.

It's starting to rain.

So I fly away. Above the rain to where it's warm and dry.

I learned to fly when I was small in the Home. I learned to look down on myself from a safe height.

Best thing I ever learned.

Fuck knows no one believes me when I say shit like this, but I'm telling you I saw Death getting out of his car and going up to Katie and taking her in his arms and making her disappear.

You can call it what you want and blame whoever, but when Death comes calling there's nothing you can do.

She caught my eye just for a second, Katie did, and I tried to be brave and smile for her because, at the end of the day, it's just a guy and he's going to do what he's going to do, same as the rest of them.

I did think about it for a second when the detective was talking to me.

Honest to God, I thought to myself I could be the kind of person who talks to the coppers and tells them what's what. I could be the little helping hand to bring the whole bastard thing crashing down.

I could tell that cop what happened, and how it happened, and why.

He'd get nasty, of course.

But maybe then he'd believe me, in the end, when everything else is washed away.

But Death gets everywhere.

I want to say that was when I knew I couldn't do it. But maybe I already knew it. Knew it from the start. I was never going to do it, never going to come through for Katie, never going to be that brave.

Never going to be that stupid.

Death speaks to me. He says Now Jenny, I just want to talk.

And I say I've heard that one before mate.

He says Jenny, what did you see? and I want to say get my name out of your filthy mouth, but I don't.

Too smart for a thing like that, me.

What did you see, Jenny? he says again and I say I saw Death, because Death's not stupid, he knows if you're lying to him.

Supposed to be a fucking refuge. But he got inside.

I look him right in his fucking dead frog eyes and for a good few seconds the brave in me comes back and I think *I've got you mate, I see you, you're nothing, and you want to be something and you thought you'd feel like a big old something if you did what you did to that girl.*

It was only a tiny splash.

Been in refuges before. Been in hospitals before. Been in hostels before. Been in Homes before.

Most of the rooms I've slept in have had someone just like me behind the wall to my left. Someone just like me behind the wall to my right.

You take it in turns to cry at night. Can't all fall apart at the same time.

I'm good at that institutional shit. Got to learn to play the game. Got to learn to dance to the creaking and the crying and the tap-tap-tapping, got to learn that there's more to a refuge than four walls and a front door, got to learn that as long as you toe the line and stay off the gear – ha! – and put the milk back in the fridge and don't argue about the telly and say yes please no thank you . . .

Then you're safe. No one comes into your room at night.

Got to learn that.

Until the fucking police show up, that is.

Until a girl turns up dead.

Until you're the only one who understands why she's dead and there's no one there who understands the world like you do.

That's when those four walls come down – crash crash crash crash. Now there's nothing left but you and that big sky.

That's when you've got to open that front door and walk down that old cracked path and down the road to the station and get on the train and get as far away from the wreckage as you can, far enough away that you can't hear the crumbling sound any more, can't hear Katie asking why why why am I dead?

Because you know why. And you really don't want to be the one to tell her.

I kissed Nazia before I left because I could tell she'd never been kissed and I felt sorry for her. It's nice to give presents when you haven't got anything left to give.

I could tell she wanted more but I told her no. Not with me.

What're you going to do? she said and I shrugged and said Same as always. What about you?

Don't know. Her eyes got this charged look and she said Maybe I'll do what you do.

I kissed her again. Light. But that's the best kind of kiss.

Don't do that, I said. Fucking hard to stop once you've started.

She didn't look like she believed me. But I know.

Then I said another thing that I knew she wouldn't believe me about, because you might as well keep talking when people have given up on you. Makes no difference to them.

I said Katie didn't kill herself. Not like you think.

I told her what I saw. There aren't many people who've clocked it like me, who can see it so clearly. I tried to tell her the truth that started at the beginning of time and ended with this poor sad dead girl.

I don't know if she got it. She just said Okay Jenny.

And I told her other things and she didn't look like she believed them either.

That's okay.

At the end of the day I did my job. I passed it on, the little seed.

I didn't tell Val about Katie.

Who's left to care, anyway? Not me.

When I was stood on the platform waiting for the train to Manchester I could see her looking at me with that Val expression of hers and saying Well then Jenny, if you don't care what happens then why are you running away?

And I say Mind your own business you daft cow and she rolls her eyes and shrugs but I can see she's giving me that little smile.

I love Val. In a funny way. There aren't many people that I love, but I love that woman. When you do business you

233

have to judge people quick – you've got like four seconds to decide if you're going to take a job or not. I took Val, and I love her.

I've loved her ever since she turned up on the corner of our street with a plastic bag full of condoms and chocolate and sandwiches and big soft jumpers.

She sat down next to me on the wall and I pretended not to see her until I realized she wasn't going anywhere.

She sat up all night with me, talking on that bloody wall. Nobody sent her, nobody knew she was there, and if she hadn't gone home that night, then nobody would have known. It's true it was mostly shite she talked, and she knew I thought so, but she still came back the next night, and the next night.

And when the punters pulled over, she let me go and do what I had to do. I knew it was hard for her to give up on me and then take me back over and over again, but she kept doing it.

Maybe she'll get nasty, too, in the end, but she hasn't yet.

She'll do it again. She always takes people back. Can't help herself.

I'm going to be honest with you now, like dead honest (*dead honest!*). This is the stone-cold truth, and everyone always says Don't listen to Jenny she's a fucking liar but for fuck's sake what've I got to lie about?

To be honest with you, I followed Katie home that night. First to the meeting. Sat outside the church and wondered about God. Then after. Followed her after.

Not all the way home because she didn't get all the way home before it happened.

But I did it because I wanted to tell her that I could see she was like me, and I thought if I said it, it might make her feel better.

Fuck knows why I thought that.

I saw it.

I saw *something*.

Val would call it one thing, and that copper would call it another. And Katie would say What the fuck does it matter?

I'm dead either way.

36.

Then

Jamie has taken her to a funfair on the nearby green for her birthday. She hates funfairs. Or at least, she used to. She's more open-minded now.

She doesn't remember deciding to go, but she's so forgetful these days.

They walk through the fairground with clouds of candy-floss. A firework display. Smashes of beauty against the night. A gloved hand in hers, the sharpening feeling of a wind-nipped cheek.

These are the things, she knows, that relationships are made of. Memories to fold away and store up in tissue paper and mothballs and keep for the bad times to come, near and far. To be kind and to love. To not be alone, to not have solitude silhouetted against that craze of stars. To be with Jamie, to weather his storms, to see that gunpowder look in his eyes and know that it's for her.

Because soon, cancer could eat away any organ; soon, some fold of steel might circumvent one of those stab vests he now wears every day and stop Jamie from existing.

The very idea makes her feel like someone has plucked a string deep inside her.

She's so swayed by the sensation she hardly notices the way he's looking at her.

Then he says it.

She frowns. She can't hear him.

So many sounds clamouring for attention.

Whatever it is, he says it again.

'Katie Bradley, will you marry me?'

There are people all around, smiling. Cooing like a jury of pigeons.

Jamie is still kneeling down, his hands spread out in supplication, a great smile carved on to his face. He looks wonderful in the golden light of the fairground.

'I can't, Jamie.'

The syllables don't sound to her like words, but like the crack you hear when a bone is breaking.

Jamie's face is a theatre of surprise.

'But I want to be with you,' he says.

It's a child's logic.

She wants to tell him yes.

She can see their wedding now, her mother still well enough, perhaps even in a miracle of remission. She sees herself, an indistinct shape bleached bone-white. Jamie looking handsome in a suit or a formal uniform and smiling – oh, *smiling* – the kind of smiling that seems like there couldn't ever be otherwise, because he loves her and needs her and that means she deserves to be loved and needed.

He is standing up again now.

She isn't ready for the moment that his eyes draw level with hers.

Everything is smashed now. There is something trickling down the side of her face – maybe a tear?

She is pretty sure he's gone out.

It's never certain, because Jamie always moves so quietly. But she hasn't heard anything from downstairs for a long time since the door slammed.

Before that, on the drive home, the silence ached with his hurt.

She said she had a headache. So they didn't have to talk.

She calls her mother. She doesn't think, she just calls. She tells herself she'll let it ring five times then hang up. Any more would be unfair on the rest of the ward.

Her mother won't be awake, she tells herself. Even if she is, she probably won't be up to talking.

She answers on the sixth ring.

'Katie.'

She has somehow lost the ability to intonate her words, even though the things she says are the same things she always says.

'Hi, Mum.'

'What's the matter?'

'Nothing.'

Surely her mother can't hear how her voice is shaking. Not with so many dimming drugs in her bloodstream.

'I just wanted to call for a chat.'

'Chat away, lovely.'

A soft, rustling sound. Settling back into blankets.

'I'm listening.'

'We went to the fair today,' Katie says. The phone makes a noise that is probably a laugh.

'Since when did you like fairs?'

'I like fairs.'

'Okay.'

'And I've got some . . . well, it's not exactly news . . .'

'News?'

'Not exactly news.'

'You've got some not-news?'

'Jamie asked me to marry him.'

There is a long pause. Long enough to read anything into it you want. Joy. Anger. Morphine.

'Well, that sounds like news to me.'

'But . . . I don't know. I think maybe he's being a bit . . . eager? I'm too young to get married.'

Another gentle rustle.

'Oh, Katie . . .'

'What?' She says it loudly and sharply, loud enough that she can imagine her mother wincing.

'Sorry . . . I mean . . . what do you want to say?'

'I just think . . . with you young girls these days . . .' Her mother gives the softest little chuckle. 'You've got so many choices. You expect so much out of one person.'

'I don't expect too much,' Katie says, more out of habit of contradiction than because she really believes it's true.

'And I think . . . although what would I know . . .' Her mother gives a dry little laugh. 'But for whatever it's worth, I think . . . I think the most you can really ask for is someone who'll be kind to you.'

'And Jamie *is* kind.'

'Jamie's kind.' A breath in. A breath out. 'And you're not as young as you think you are.'

'Right.'

'Oh . . .' An intake of breath that would have been sharp once. 'No, Katie. I didn't mean it like that. I meant . . .' Another long breath. 'I meant you've been through so much. And I'm very glad you've found someone who takes good care of you.'

'Yeah?'

'Yeah.' A little laugh. 'That's what I've learned, if nothing else.'

'You mean it?'

Katie knows she should get off the phone. That it isn't fair to make her mother use up whatever strength she has on repeating herself.

She wants to say, *Just stay on the phone with me.* But that isn't the kind of thing they ever say to each other. Instead, she says, 'You really mean it?'

'I really do.'

'Okay, then, I'll let you go.'

'Oh, no . . .' She could hear her mother trying her best to insist. 'Oh, no, you're all right.'

'I'll let you sleep now, Mum.'

'Are you sure?'

Just a blurry collection of rasps from a thirsty tongue. Are. You. Sure.

'Yes. Sleep well, Mum.'

'You, too, my darling.'

'Have you got some water, Mum?'

'Yes, darling.'

'Have some water, okay?'

'I will.'

'Now?'

'Good night, Katie.'

Katie puts down the phone and looks towards the door. There has been no noise, but some section of the light is blocked away. Enough for two feet standing outside. She can hear sharp, contained breaths but she doesn't know if they're coming from Jamie or herself.

She crosses to the threshold and opens their bedroom door to see him standing on the landing, motionless. A glass of water in one hand, the other cupped.

'Brought you some aspirin.'

He puts down the glass. Holds out his hand.

'Here you go.'

She doesn't really register taking the pills, but suddenly they're gone and he's sitting next to her on the bed.

'Who were you talking to?' he says.

'My mum.'

She knows it's always the most sensible thing to tell him the truth. He shrugs slightly.

'You shouldn't be bothering her,' he says. 'She's ill.'

'I know,' Katie says.

He nods.

But she says it again, not knowing why.

'I know that, Jamie. She's my mum.'

'I'm just telling you.'

'But I already know. I *know*.'

She lies in bed. She's never felt so tired in her whole life. Every part of her aches, not just her head, to the point that her body has become one unified ache.

Jamie has left the room. After he kissed her forehead and told her to go to sleep. After she muttered, 'But I already know, I *know*.'

37.

Whitworth put the phone down.

He stood, frozen for a good thirty seconds, in the middle of Piccadilly Gardens. People swerved around him – office workers, girls like those on the train, heading out for their share of sin.

The rain was churning into the mud. Whitworth found himself able to focus on nothing but the slick, distorted glaze it cast over the ground.

Then he wheeled around – sharply, trying to gather his bearings – and cursed himself for not having come by car.

As it turned out, they didn't need to find Lynne Ward.

The first responders had contacted Brookes almost as soon as he had made inquiries at the Wards' address. They were already there, they said.

Frank Ward had called the police at three minutes past nine. In a controlled voice, he'd told them that they needed to send an ambulance. When the paramedics arrived, Frank was sitting on the front wall of his garden, a calm, drained look on his face and a flower of blood blooming across his shirt.

Inside, they had found Lynne's tiny, slender body stretched out on the sofa, as if she were posing for an editorial photoshoot. Her daughter was standing next to her, her little hand on her mother's cheek, like in a Victorian painting.

As the paramedics entered and the child was scooped away from the body in reflexive horror, she murmured, 'My daddy cut my mummy.'

38.

Then

A door slams, thudding through a larger silence.

Did Katie dream the noise, or did the noise take her from her dreams?

She half wakes, smelling smoke. Her sleep is thick and chemical.

She sees, illuminated by the light of the street lamps, the little curls of smoke entering around the edges of the door. In the spaces between those drowsy seconds it seems that they are supposed to be there. Phantom fingers seem to wrap around her hair and gently pull her head back towards the pillow; a soft hiss that might come from within or without tells her that there is nothing to worry about.

Jamie is there. This is the exact sort of situation that makes her love him so. The moments when he takes control.

Her eyes close again.

A car alarm jolts her awake. She is coughing, coughing.

There is no chance of catching her breath.

Smoke is pouring frantically under the door with the urgency of waves on a beach in a storm. She can hear fire – the vengeance and bloodlust of its low, crackling bellow.

She can hear all the things they have put together, Jamie and she, ravaging and turning to ash.

She can't breathe.

Her lungs won't fill.

It would have been panic if the smoke hadn't made her mind too dull for panic. Rather, she knows, and distantly understands, that she is going to die.

39.

Now

Nobody had moved the body, even though Whitworth didn't arrive at the Ward family home until nearly midnight.

Forensics were still snapping photographs from every angle, the sweep of blonde hair spread out on the sofa catching the light from the cameras' flashes. Patches of her powder-blue cashmere jumper still peeped out between heavy, wet bloodstains.

Her face was untouched, her outlined eyes closed. Whitworth wondered if Frank Ward had closed them himself – the effect was so picturesque he was sure it was the work of some theatrical hand.

'You all right?' Whitworth sat down heavily next to Brookes on the low stone wall of the Wards' front garden. He looked shaken. Probably never seen a homicide before, Whitworth thought.

'Fine.'

It wasn't true. There were tear-tracks down Brookes's face. But Whitworth felt he owed it to someone – maybe to himself – to pretend not to see them.

'I know it's a bit of a shock when you see stuff like that.'

'I'm not shocked.' Brookes's voice was tight and flat. 'What's there to be shocked about? Wife-beaters. No self-control. It's pathetic.'

Whitworth had to disagree. It seemed to him that Frank Ward had shown remarkable self-control. The bruises the ambulance team had found were almost too many to count, as it was difficult to ascertain where one trauma ended and the other began. Yet her hands, neck and face were untouched. Nothing an elegant crewneck couldn't cover.

'I've seen enough of that, you know?' Brookes said. 'On the beat. Not murders, but all the stuff that happens around murders.' He stretched his legs out in front of him, crossing one ankle in front of the other. 'The stuff that becomes murders. It makes you realize, that stuff. Some people just aren't like you and me.'

Whitworth didn't know what to say, but it seemed he should let Brookes talk. He probably needed it.

'There's something missing in them. Call it whatever you want. Maybe their mummy didn't love them enough. Whatever it is, I don't care. That kid's never going to grow up normal, and it's all the parents' fault.'

Whitworth let the silence rest for a few seconds.

'Do you think anyone's capable of murder?'

His voice in the darkness sounded shaky, unsure. Whitworth knew it was the kind of question that Brookes should be asking and he should be answering. He was the more experienced officer, after all.

Maybe it really was time to retire.

Brookes didn't hesitate. 'I think anyone's capable of having their buttons pushed.'

Frank Ward had been very helpful when they took his confession.

He had explained that Lynne had come back with Peony. There had been a row of some kind. Lynne had flown at him in a rage, he said. He had the scratch marks on his face to prove it. She had grabbed a knife from the kitchen and had threatened to kill both him and Peony.

Then a struggle, and he'd got the knife off her.

And stabbed and stabbed and stabbed.

He had blacked out, he said.

There was no reason not to believe what he said was true. The doctor who examined Peony had found bruises on her body. A row of some kind. It was impossible to say what had really happened in these situations.

Valerie Redwood would be incensed, of course, Whitworth thought. She would want Lynne to have had the kind of death that suited her purposes, a martyr's death. Some steely piece of reality would slip between her theory and the reality like a penknife picking a lock. The door had swung open to reveal – nothing at all.

The front door of the house opened and the gurney carrying Lynne Ward's body – bagged, labelled, thingified – rattled down the garden path, its spindly wheels skipping over the gravel.

'Nothing more we can do for her tonight,' Whitworth said.

Brookes gave a sharp sort of nod, like a military cadet who was learning to receive orders, and stood up. They walked towards the car.

All the lights in the house were still on, the front room lit invitingly behind heavy velvet curtains.

'She thought he was following her. I could tell. When I talked to her,' Whitworth said.

'How?'

'She was scared. Convinced that any bloke on the street had come to spy on her.'

'Maybe she was always scared. Just her personality. Even a stopped clock, and all that.'

'You'd never think it of a guy like that, would you?' Whitworth looked over to the police car Frank Ward was sitting in. Someone had wrapped a blanket around his shoulders and, from the way his hands were clasped together, you wouldn't know that they were cuffed.

He could hear Peony wailing. *Daddy Daddy Daddy*. It tore at Whitworth's own breath.

'He wanted his kid back,' Brookes said. 'He wanted his life back.'

'Maybe. Either way, sounds like we know who the bloke hanging about was.'

'That'll make Val happy.'

'Val's never happy. But it clears it up.'

'Doesn't help with the Katie Straw case.'

'Do you think Val Redwood's right?' Whitworth said. 'Do you think some men just hate women?'

Brookes frowned a little then took a bottle of water out of his coat pocket and unscrewed the cap meditatively.

'Nope,' he said, after a gulp. 'I don't. Look. It doesn't make any sense for men to hate women. Biologically. It doesn't work. Look at Lynne Ward.' He gestured back towards the house with the water bottle.

'We don't know what she did. For all we know, she spent every day dragging her husband through the dirt while she lived off his money. You saw that house. You saw all the things he gave her. And what did she do in return?'

He gestured at the police car in which the social worker was sitting with Peony Ward. 'She took his kid away. She stopped him seeing his own kid. When you think about it like that – I mean, I don't know the full story – but you've got to understand why people can snap. It's not right, but you can understand it. Doesn't make it any less pathetic, but it makes sense.

'It's just individuals,' he said. 'Humans. It's not this big ideological thing, like everyone makes out.'

Whitworth had always made a point of not trying too hard to understand criminals.

It was so easy to go native, to slip into their systems of logic, their ways of thinking, and then the next thing you knew you were understanding them, and then the next thing, you were forgiving them. Then the next thing, you were letting them get away with it.

But sometimes, the questions nagged.

Whitworth believed that women and men were equal. Different, but equal, and the problem these days was that people tried to get rid of the different part to make the equal part easier.

Did that mean that women were more able to accept the wounds that men dealt them? He thought perhaps they were.

Frank Ward had gone too far, of course. He wasn't justifying the behaviour of men like Frank Ward.

'Bye, sweetheart.'

Brookes was crouched in front of the little girl. Every angle of his body was bent towards her. He looked like he wanted to say something important – maybe give this little girl a key to navigate what promised to be a fucked-up life.

'Take care,' he said, in the end.

Whitworth wanted to shake his head. That wasn't the point. The little girl would learn to take care of herself, sure she would. That wasn't the point.

They drove, back through the winding hills, the fifty minutes to Widringham. It wasn't the kind of road that was important enough to be lit at night, and Whitworth felt a childish wariness of whatever it was that lay beyond the circle of the car's head-lamps, though he knew it was only the heathery rocks, the sheep fields, the smattering of woods he'd grown up among.

'One of the nice things about moving to the country,' Brookes said, after a good twenty-five minutes of silence, 'is that you can see all the stars.'

Whitworth wasn't sure what to say, so he just grunted.

Brookes dropped him outside his house.

It was nearly two in the morning, and all the lights were off. Whitworth went to the fridge, wondering if Maureen might have kept back a plate for him, but there was nothing apart from a carton of eggs and a few onions. He thought briefly about making himself an omelette, then shut the fridge door and put a couple of pieces of bread into the toaster.

He'd get Brookes to ask Frank Ward about it in the morning. How long he'd stalked his wife. Could you stalk your own wife? Was there such a thing?

Surely there was only such a thing as a father who wanted his daughter back, who wanted his wife back, who wanted someone to attend to the wound, to acknowledge what he'd lost.

40.

Then

The neighbour across the road had called the fire brigade. He had seen the flames when he had gone outside to switch off his car alarm. He had saved her life, all the emergency services are at pains to point out.

The fire started because she left her curling iron on. That is pretty clear.

I hope you understand you could have died, young lady.

It might be true. She remembers so little at the moment. She needs to sleep.

She is sinking in and out of consciousness. She isn't a young lady. She is either a child or an old woman, but she can't quite say which.

She is in pain, but she doesn't understand this kind of pain. It's a pain of the lungs, of the skin.

The pain is dimming, like music fading out. She doesn't have the chance to miss it before she falls into a state like sleep.

She's awake. Properly awake this time. She feels the way she always does when she's slept for too long. There is a heaviness in her, and an absence, the feeling that she ought to be feeling something – either pleasure or pain. But at the moment there is nothing.

The nothing will surely go away soon.

Jamie is here. Jamie is always here.

'How could you do this, Katie?'

But Jamie hasn't been . . .

Did he not come to bed?

Her fingers grasp at squeaky cotton sheets. This isn't her bed. This isn't home. The lights are too bright.

'Never mind how could you do this to me – how could you do this to your mum?'

His voice is right in her ear. Everything else is distant.

It had been so quiet. Quiet apart from the door. Apart from the car alarm.

There should have been something else.

Her mum is there. Mum is always so sick, so tired of being so sick.

Her father's there, too. He is standing behind the glass as well, with his arm around her mother, kissing her face and pinching at her shrunken breasts and laughing, always laughing. Nothing is ever too serious for him.

Maybe her mother will watch her die. Then she won't have to watch her mother die.

'Why did you leave the curling iron on?'

His voice is so loud it rings and clatters in Katie's every cell. 'This is why I can't trust you to look after yourself.'

'I didn't curl my hair.'

Jamie seizes a fistful of it, yanking it around in front of her face. The ends fall into corkscrew curls. 'What's this, then?'

'I don't know.'

She is so tired. Too tired for lying.

'You did it,' she says.

Jamie draws in his breath. She wonders if he is preparing to scream at her. Finally. She has been waiting for this for so long. Always dangled in front of her. Never realized.

But the scream doesn't come.

A nurse has walked in.

'Just taking your blood pressure, my darling.'

Jamie smiles.

'Thanks so much,' he says. 'You're doing a wonderful job.'

'I want him to leave,' Katie says, her voice cracking. Her throat is so dry.

Jamie laughs. 'She's been making jokes all morning,' he says. 'I think it's a sign she's on the mend.'

The nurse laughs too.

'He's going to kill me.'

'I should think he might be a bit cross, yeah.'

The nurse is now taking her temperature, pushing the gun-like thermometer uncomfortably far into her ear. 'That's all his things that got burned up, too.'

'She always worries too much,' Jamie intercedes.

Then he sits on the bed with her as if they are an old couple, in it together. He wraps his arm around her shoulders. The breath quickens in her scorched lungs.

'As if I'd be angry. I'm just so relieved she's safe.'

The nurse smiles.

'He's a keeper, this one,' she says, nodding at Jamie.

Yes. Jamie. He always keeps.

The nurse's face shifts into a knowing smile. 'I can see you already think that.' She is looking down at Katie's left hand, where a little silver ring sits against her red, swollen fingers.

'Let's hope that bump on the head didn't change her mind,' Jamie says, laughing again.

To say it is like a bad dream would be a lie. It is all the worst things about being awake, seeing that ring on her finger.

It sits like the one visible link in a chain that goes on for ever. It is a lovely ring, she has to admit. Bright and delicate and strong as the silk of a spider web.

Jamie has good taste.

★

'Oh, good!'

It's another nurse now, one who barely glances down at the bed as she makes her way through the curtains.

'You're awake,' she says. She looks down at the bandaged arm then frowns slightly. 'Wouldn't recommend that you wear any jewellery on the burnt areas for the time being.'

Jamie smiles. 'She didn't want to be without it,' he says.

The nurse has already gone back to her clipboard.

'Okay. Well, that's up to you. Anyway, since you're awake . . . just got a few standard questions. Could you confirm your full name for me?'

She draws in a breath, but before she can get any sound out the empty space in the air has already been filled.

'Katie Eleanor Bradley,' Jamie says.

The nurse writes something on her clipboard.

'Right. Date of birth?'

Jamie supplies it smoothly.

'Do you happen to know your blood type?'

Katie turns to Jamie, frowning slightly.

'A-negative,' he says.

'And last but not least . . .' The nurse turns to Jamie and jerks her chin a little. 'Can I assume this gentleman is your next of kin? Husband?'

'Fiancé,' Jamie replies. At the same time, Katie says, 'No.'

The nurse ignores Jamie and raises her eyebrows inquiringly.

'No?' she says.

'She's a bit confused . . .'

The nurse ignores him. 'Who's your next of kin, my love? It's really important that our records are correct.'

The pain in her arm starts to flare up again.

'There's my mum . . .'

'Where's your mum, Katie?'

254

'She's also in the hospital,' Jamie interjects. 'Over on the oncology ward.'

A small crease appears between the nurse's brows as she raises her eyebrows.

'Oh, I see . . .'

'She's forgotten. Or she's confused,' Jamie continues.

He is doing his authority voice, the voice they once practised together for his job interviews, the voice that summarizes the situation and squashes it into a neat little ball.

'She's . . . well, technically, her mother's her next of kin. But she's sedated a lot, you see. I'm thinking in practical terms, in terms of who can actually make decisions with regard to Katie's care . . .' He picks up the left hand with the ring on it, very gently, and holds it up for the nurse to see. 'It looks like, really, I'm your guy.'

The nurse's nod, which was as rhythmic as a metronome, is conspicuously absent.

She takes a pair of glasses from around her neck to look at Jamie before returning her gaze towards Katie in a way that somehow seems to exclude anyone else.

'So. Katie. The doctor's asked me to come and have a chat with you. Most of your burns are pretty superficial, but there's some fairly serious damage to your left arm which could result in a bit of scarring. Now . . .' She looks up from the clipboard. Her long black braids make a slight rustle as she tilts her head to one side. 'Now, one option is to have some surgery on that arm, where we'd clean up the wound. It's not essential, but it could reduce some scarring that you may want to avoid.'

Surely Jamie wouldn't want any scars on her? He is always talking about how much he loves the smoothness of her skin. He looks back at her and his eyes seem blank. Then he switches to an abrupt warmth, like a gas fire springing into life, as he turns to look back at the nurse.

'I think we'd better have a talk about it,' he says to the nurse.

She frowns again. 'Well, it's not so much for you to talk about. It's really up to Katie whether she wants to have the surgery or not –'

'She likes to have me as a sounding board,' he says. 'She'd tell you so herself but, as you can probably see, she's a bit knocked out from all those drugs you keep giving her.'

The nurse nods.

She seems to spend a longer time than usual making notes on her clipboard, which she then doesn't return to the place at the end of the bed but tucks under her arm.

'Well, Katie, the consultant will be over later. Maybe you can have a think about the surgery until then.'

Then she steps back outside of the blue curtains, but instead of drawing them shut behind her she pulls them a little more ajar, leaving a larger crack between the bed and the outside world.

'It's a nice sunny day,' she says, tidying the curtains and opening the window slightly. 'Bit of a shame if you don't get to see it.'

Then she disappears.

Jamie is still wearing a taut smile.

He stands up, stretching his arms above his head and rocking on to the balls of his feet before loping into the middle of the ward.

He casts his face around, looking into the other beds, then, apparently satisfied, he walks back towards the bed.

He sits down on the stool next to her and draws her left hand into his.

In the morphine fog, his hands feel too warm; they're the only things that keep her from floating away into a smooth, pleasant nothing. Then he leans into her ear, his breath close enough to brush the baby hairs on her face, and says, in his softest, gentlest tone, 'Now you listen to me, for once in your fucking life.'

The words don't stick.

'You're not getting any fucking surgery to pretty up your skin. You're going to wear those scars on your whore body for the rest of your life, and you're going to remember what you did to me. Got it?'

She nods.

Because, for the first time in a long time, she realizes that she does get it.

'Good,' Jamie says. He raises her left hand to his lips and kisses it.

'Now go to sleep,' he says.

And she does.

41.

Now

Angie stood on the bridge. She had thought it might make her feel close to Katie, but all it made her feel was alone.

Katie had been a young girl. Her whole life ahead of her. *Should have been* ahead of her. Angie was . . . whatever Angie was. A project that Charlie had started.

She could finish it.

Thing is, Charlie would hate it if she died. Because then she'd be gone for ever. He wanted her back; he kept saying so.

A new sensation bloomed up in her. Vindictiveness.

'Well, sod you, I'm not coming back,' she said. To the night, to the river, to the bridge. To the last place Katie had been alive.

'You got away. It's taken all this time, but you've done it. Can't you see what that means, Angie?'

Angie sat in the room where she and Katie used to talk together and nodded into the darkness. Yes, she thought. Perhaps she is starting to see it.

She could turn the lights on, but sometimes it was easier to understand things in the dark.

She lightly touched her wedding ring. She'd thought to take it off, but the knuckle had swollen too much. Arthritis, made worse by fingers that had been broken and had never properly set.

You could go to the jeweller's and get the thing taken off with a tiny saw. Lynne had told her.

She'd do it. When she got round to it.

Not yet.

Where should she begin?

Angie had lost all sense of beginnings. Things just went on for ever and ever. There was no possibility of change.

'How long have you been married, Angie?'

'Forty-nine years,' Angie had said. She had done what she automatically did – the wry smile, the slight roll of the eyes. The look that said, *Oh, well, you know, we put up with each other.*

Usually, people laughed. Or said, 'Ah, isn't that lovely?'

Sometimes they asked her what the secret was.

Katie hadn't done any of that. In fact, she'd done nothing at all. She had looked at Angie with an expression Angie hadn't seen for a long time.

It was curiosity.

'Well?'

Usually, nobody wanted to know.

When you got old, your skin had a different way of bruising. Young bruised skin can still be peach-pretty, the gathering of blood below the surface proof of life.

It changes when you're old. The skin resigns itself; there seems little point in pretending at real repair. Old bruised skin gathers in its collapse like a flock of wet newspapers grinding themselves into the pavement.

It seems unkind to say that nobody cares – it's just that nobody notices.

'And how often do you claim these beatings took place?' the defence barrister had asked.

'I suppose something like twice a week. It's been a great many years, I'm not quite sure. Perhaps twice a week. Always on a Sunday.'

'Twice a week for forty-nine years, Mrs Woods?'

'I . . . I think so. Yes. That's probably right.'

'Probably?'

'I . . .'

'Well?'

'Yes . . .'

'Louder, Mrs Woods, please.'

'Yes.'

'That's five thousand and ninety-six separate beatings,' the defence barrister had announced.

The judge had taken off his glasses and polished them on his robes. With his rheumy eyes and mottled pate, he was a dead spit of Charlie.

'Five thousand and ninety-six beatings, Mrs Woods. And why is it that you have only chosen to leave now?'

Charlie had stood in the dock with his tie neatly knotted, his saggy man-breast body held in by a pale yellow polyester shirt, his eyes swimming with tears which the light of the courtroom alchemized from self-pity into dignity.

What people didn't realize about an old man like Charlie, Angie had thought as she looked up at him, is that whatever was rotten inside him has had that much longer to rot. It had become dense and tarry-black and sticky as sin, spilling out from his eyes and mouth.

Katie squeezed Angie's hand.

'He's always pulling that one,' Angie whispered. 'The crying.'

'It's manipulation, Angie. Control.'

'Doesn't matter,' Angie muttered. 'The jury don't know him like I do.'

'Maybe they'll see through him.'

Katie didn't sound like she believed it herself.

'Maybe they won't.'

In his testimony, Charlie placed in Angie the ability to be in two places at once. To be simultaneously at the stove cooking his dinner and out on the town, the last forty years fallen away to let the silly, sexy girl she once was walk the night. To have power over all men, the power that, somehow, she held over him.

He told the court that she was a witch or a cat or a snake. Not a dumpy woman of nearly seventy with a caved-in face from all the fists that had fallen on it. Something beyond language, something with the ability to shrink and grow his cock at will and to distort his mind and lie, lie, lie to him, to make him believe that she loved him when she didn't.

Maybe there was some truth in the claim of her magic. Angie had known that she was invisible for a long time; she could enter a room and the great oil-painting bruises across her face would attract barely a second glance. Or those who did look would leave their mouths suspended like trap doors, waiting for her to reassure them.

She could always go above the pain and say the words in her mother's voice.

'Oh, just a little fall. Don't worry about me, love.'

They thought it might be dementia. Or that was one of the tacks the lawyers tried, in any case.

'They'll never go for that,' Katie had whispered.

He was acquitted.

'Tell me about Charlie.'

Charlie was all the things she'd loved when they'd married forty-nine years ago.

Heartbreaker. Jack the lad. Always dressed to kill, though God only knows where he got the money from.

'The best-looking young man in the village.'

'So he was charming?'

'I fancied him since school.'

They'd walked together, Charlie and she. Paraded, really, admiring the sculptures of light their two shadows cast, joined by the hand that enclosed her still-neat waist. She'd been terribly young then, younger even than this young girl, Katie, with the wide brown eyes and the unfeeling set of forms and the hand that kept twitching as if to reach out and take Angie's.

'And then you got married?'

She had held a bouquet of violets in the church and said her vows in a voice that sounded so much surer than her own. She had got the dressmaker to alter the collar of her dress, to show off her slender throat.

But it had ended up a little too tight, and when Charlie, her new husband Charlie, had tilted back her chin to kiss her as his wife, the sheath of lace pulled tight across her windpipe. That moment was frozen in a black-and-white photograph that sat on their mantlepiece for forty-nine years, until the frame was smashed.

She, so slim then, so pretty. Legs to here, eyes like a deer getting ready to flee. His big hand gathering in the neatness of her waist.

When he cried, he looked like how their babies had looked in the moments she'd first glimpsed them over the midwife's shoulder, when they were still wet with Angie's blood. Pre-human, agonized.

Charlie had lain down on the floor like a toddler having a tantrum when they took him away. A big man, Charlie – it had taken three policemen to get him up and into the car. He had wailed the whole time.

Angie had rolled her eyes at the police. *Men, eh? What're they like?*

That had counted against her later, in court.

★

Who did you fuck? Tell me

You

Old

Bitch

'He whipped me with his belt.'

Katie hadn't looked away. She'd nodded.

'Thought I was going to die. Hoped I was going to die.'

The moment when the belt was raised was even worse than the moment when it slammed down, on to torn flesh, on to flesh that had lost its integrity and unity.

'But you got away.'

She had told him that she didn't love him. It was a terrible risk, but it worked. Charlie howled like a dog that had been abandoned by its master and turned away, slamming his own head against the wall.

Angie used the moment to seize the cordless landline, dial 999 and throw the phone under the sofa, where Charlie would not be able to hear it over the roaring tide of blood sliding into his eyes. Even if he saw it, he wouldn't be able to reach it. His back was too bad.

Then he beat her more.

Look what you made me do, you old cunt.

In court, Angie had found out that the space between her calling the emergency services and the angel-sound of that calm, measured knock on the door had been eleven minutes. Eleven minutes of screaming, which she realized the police must have heard and recorded. Eleven minutes of calling herself a liar, promising she did love him, there was only him, there had only ever been him.

'I'm useless,' Angie said aloud. She didn't mean much by it beyond the basic statement of fact.

'You shouldn't feel that way,' Katie said.

But I do, Angie thought, and a piece of loneliness seemed

to crash into her and pin her against the floor so that she could no longer breathe. Katie reached over to take her hand, seeming to see her distress, but the hand didn't feel like anything at all.

They went for a meal for their wedding anniversary, Charlie and Angie Woods. Angie's bruises were still the colour of crushed violets, and the gash on Charlie's forehead was still blackish and scabby, a streak of humanity across his still-handsome face. Angie put on the purple silk scarf he'd given her for their ruby-wedding anniversary.

They just went to the Harvester, nothing fancy. A quiet meal, a little elegy to the life they sometimes agreed to pretend they had.

He had been silent, then sorry, and then they had shared a slice of chocolate fudge cake and he'd made her laugh and she had reminded him that he shouldn't have cake with his cholesterol levels.

He had laughed, patted her on her thigh and told her she was a bossy old cow.

The prosecutors were furious when they found out. You can't just see him whenever you fancy it, they said. It destroys the case for harassment.

He had sent her over three thousand texts since she had arrived in the refuge. Yes, her Charlie had learned to text.

'You hold down this button . . . and this button . . .' Katie held the phone in her hands like a ticking bomb. The screen flickered for just a moment. 'And that takes a picture of it.'

'Wouldn't have thought I'd have to put my own evidence together,' Angie said, without thinking. Then she looked up at Katie and smiled. 'Ever so good for me. Gets me into the modern world.'

They held a smile between them like a tightrope, then Katie looked back down at Angie's phone and frowned.

'You've still got your location on. You need to . . .' A few intricate swipes, the screen dancing under her fingers. 'There you go.' She handed the phone back to Angie. 'Now he can't use it to track you down. You never know.'

She did feel silly being in the refuge, but he'd been so damn persistent, following her to her sister's and posting nasty things through the letter box; in the end, Angie had relented.

When she'd entered the refuge Katie had asked her if she was frightened of Charlie – it seemed to be on one of her lists of set questions. It took her a long time to answer. She wasn't frightened of Charlie – he wasn't a frightening man, just a baby and a coward.

Who?

Who is it?

Who the fuck is it?

'I just have to let you know how I feel,' he had told her over the phone. He had gone to a phone box and slid in his chunks of silver because the phone had been cut off, everything had been cut off. He had stayed in that dark, dank place. She had no idea what he ate – her Charlie couldn't boil an egg.

She had put the phone down after hearing his voice start to shake because, somehow, when she heard it, she saw the old man with the rheumy eyes and the shaking hands. She'd felt herself fill with love – the kind of bone-deep love that meant you'd chosen *your* person – the person who'd swear blind at the gates of heaven that you'd existed. That there had been a woman called Angie and that Charlie had loved her like hell, that he'd never stop loving her.

Whatever it was he felt, he couldn't tell her. There was nothing available in him to tell.

Did you fuck that bloke George Fielding?

Did you fuck him?

Oh, bless you, love. He's forty-one. I'm a used-up old woman. You should know, you were the one that did the using.

The names he spat at her were like a roll call, or a prayer, or a volley of pistol shots in the dark. A boot in the ribs, each kick curving like a question mark.

Tell me tell me tell me

Not knowing is always the worst thing.

Oh, Charlie. Bless your fool heart. You think I'd be with all those men? I'm tired. All I want is to be away from men. From you. We're like Adam and Eve, after it all went wrong and they were thrown out of that lovely garden and left to scrabble around in the dirt.

42.

Then

He sits with her until visiting hours end, at eight. He is evicted by a large, solid-looking nurse. Jamie kisses Katie on the forehead and tells her to sleep well. She feels certain that, for a second, she saw the nurse frown. She isn't sure why that would be – she doesn't wince when he kisses her. She's trained herself never to do that.

It seems obvious to her that she needs to get out.

Perhaps if they'd had a night apart over the last eighteen months, it would have been obvious to her then, but the fantastical intimations of taking her things, leaving, are always blocked by the fact of his body.

If she tries to leave him, he will kill her.

He has said so, and she believes him.

Katie plucks the tubes out of her arm like daisies, one by one.

She has to have clothes around here somewhere – an overnight bag?

There's nothing. She isn't even wearing underwear.

Katie stands at the entrance to the ward. She doesn't remember how she got there.

There, in the space that isn't supposed to be a car park, Jamie's car dawdles. Perhaps her gowned figure has caught the moonlight more than she realized, but his head turns.

He doesn't smile, doesn't wave, doesn't look at her.

But he saw her, she knows. Perhaps more than she's ever seen herself.

She goes back into the hospital foyer, retreating to where Jamie's headlights can't follow her.

The nurse from earlier is watching her.

'Do you need any help, darling?' she says.

Katie shakes her head and feels like she would have cried if the fire hadn't evaporated the tears from her. The nurse's long black braids swing around her, but everything else about her has a stillness that makes something in Katie slacken and rest.

'I've been thinking,' Katie says. 'Sorry, I might have got a bit confused. I've been a bit out of it. Did you ask me about surgery earlier?'

The nurse nods. 'Yes, lovely, that's right.'

'I do want it,' Katie says, very, very quietly. 'Or maybe . . . maybe not. I don't know.'

'The consultant'll come round and talk to you about it properly. I know it seems intimidating.'

'I'd rather he didn't.'

'She. Why not?'

'It's just . . . it's just for the best.'

'If you think so, darling. But wouldn't you like to speak to the consultant, anyway? It'd all be confidential.'

'It's not confidential,' Katie says, feeling her voice thickening. 'The thing is . . . he won't let me. Jamie . . . makes choices for me. It's . . . it's not in a bad way. He loves me. He's got a clearer head than me, especially right now. I'm indecisive. I always have been.'

For a moment, the nurse looks as though she's deciding which claim to reply to, but then, instead, she takes in a sharp breath and tilts her head to one side.

'Jamie's your boyfriend?'

'Yes.'

'Are you afraid of him?'

'Yes.'

Katie doesn't know where the answer even came from.

It seems to slip out before she had the chance to slam the gates of her mind shut. Her heart gives a strange leap as she says the word. There is an old feeling there, under all the haze of the drugs and the fear.

The feeling of living in the sun.

The nurse is still looking at her steadily, as if nothing could surprise her. Maybe nothing could.

'I thought you might be,' she says. 'That's why I left the curtains open earlier. To keep an eye on you.'

Katie's eyes narrow slightly. She hadn't been expecting that. Now that she has acknowledged her fear, it seems to live separately from her, as undeniable as any fully formed being.

But this nurse is saying that she saw it earlier, when it was still unborn.

How is that even possible?

'I'm being stupid,' she says. 'There's nothing to be scared of.'

'Nothing?' The nurse is looking at her as if she's failing to pick up on something obvious. Katie has dreaded that look her whole life, has fled before it.

'You're in hospital, darling.'

'But that's my own fault.'

'Is it?'

Katie's heart has never pounded so fast before. It seems to speed up the sluggish tempo of her thoughts, dragging her back towards something she knows to be true.

'The smoke alarms were working. The smoke alarms *were* working. I know they were. Someone disabled them.'

'Why's that?'

'Because he wanted to kill me.'

'You just said he wasn't dangerous.'

Katie goes blank inside.

'I want to help you, darling, but you've got to be completely honest with me. Do you think he's dangerous?'

Katie doesn't answer, and the nurse sighs.

'It's all right. I know it's a shock. I'm not going to ask you anything more. I'm going to tell you that a man who disables a smoke alarm and sets a place on fire – or even a man who *might* have done those things – is not the sort of person I want a patient of mine around.'

'Jamie takes care of me.'

Katie can feel herself dissolving.

'Do you want to get away from him?'

'No.'

'Why not?'

'Because he's going to kill me.'

'Then that's why you need to get away from him, my love.'

'You can't call the police.'

'Why not, pet?'

'Because it's Jamie. He'd know. He'd find out.'

Someone calls a car.

Katie has no idea who it was, or who the driver is, or where they're going. But it doesn't matter. There's a car, and the nurse is talking on the phone in a low, urgent voice.

'No, the back exit, where the ambulances come. Yes, it's sensitive. We need to get someone out discreetly.'

'Don't worry, sweetheart,' she says. 'How could he possibly find out? Look . . .' The nurse zips her hooded sweatshirt higher up over her scrubs and gives an exhausted smile. 'It's the end of my shift. Why don't I come with you and make sure you get sorted?'

Katie knows she ought to insist: no. God knows how long the woman has been working. But instead, she flops back on to the seat of the car and nods.

As they drive past the main gates of the hospital she can see Jamie's car still sitting in the small bay outside the ward.

'What if he's not in the car?' Katie says. 'What if he's somewhere else? What if he knows?'

'How could he possibly know?' the nurse says. 'We're the only two who know anything about it. Just you and me.'

'Where are we going?'

'We're going to get you into another hospital a bit away from here. And we're not going to use your real name, because we don't want him checking up on you. What name shall we put you under?'

For a second, she thinks she sees her mother's face in the harsh light of the street lamps.

She blinks. There's nothing.

'Katie Straw,' she says.

43.

Now

'Mrs Woods?'

'Yes?' Angie supposed that was still who she was.

'I'm afraid I have some bad news about your husband, Charles.'

Angie put the phone down.

She took a breath.

There was something different about it, although she couldn't quite say what.

Died in his sleep, they said on the phone. *More than he deserved*, Angie thought, but all she said was, 'Oh,' and then, 'Thank you for letting me know.'

Angie passed the empty room where Lynne and Peony used to sleep. A cold seemed to emanate from the room, ramming hard against the stale heat hanging over the rest of the refuge.

Lynne was dead. There would be a funeral, the police had said, but not for a while.

The police were supposed to stop these things, but they were just people. One had reminded Angie of her brother, the other of her son.

Just men. What were they supposed to do?

Angie didn't think she'd go to the funeral. She'd had enough. Lynne wouldn't have minded. She didn't like fuss.

Angie slid open the door to the garden and stepped outside. It was cool, probably too cold for her, yet she didn't feel it. It was as if, for the first time in forty-nine years, she wasn't imprisoned by what she felt in her body. Her nerve endings were free and, instead, she could hear – hear the sound of the rain in gentle collision with the salty, fresh-scented flower-beds. She raised her eyes to the stars and understood for the first time why it was that people carved them into shapes and told stories about them.

'Hi, Angie.'

Angie jumped. Her throat closed up and her knees gave a spasm, reminding her that she was too weak to flee.

There was a shape and the glowing tip of a cigarette over by the bench.

'Hello, Val.'

There was a slight grunt as the other woman moved over, and Angie went to sit beside her. She could see back into the living room through the window. Nazia's and Sonia's faces were illuminated by the glow of the TV.

'Bit of peace and quiet?' Angie said, waving away the cigarette Val was offering her. In the dark, the shape shook its head.

'A bit of a think. About Katie, mostly.'

'Poor girl.'

'The thing is, Angie.' Val's voice seemed perfectly steady, so steady Angie was sure it had to be masking something. 'You get tough, doing this work. Too tough. And you forget sometimes . . . you have to be kind, too. It turns me into a cli-ché of a feminist, this job.' She laughed. 'But then again, what's more of a cliché than men beating up women?'

'You were kind to Katie.'

'Not kind enough.' Val flicked the butt of her cigarette away. Its sparks vaulted through the darkness of the garden, skittered and died on the damp paving stones. She lit another, the set line of her mouth lit for a moment by the flare of the lighter. 'She didn't have the training, Angie. She was good, she had instincts and she understood domestic violence. But you need the training, too. To hold it all together. To hold yourself together. I would have given it to her. But with what time? With what money?'

'It wasn't your fault, Val.'

'Perhaps it wasn't.' The smoke slipping out of Val's mouth was illuminated by the lights of the house, as if her soul were sliding out of her. 'But someone ought to feel the guilt. It might as well be me.'

Then, after a long silence, Angie said, 'So Jenny's gone.'

'Yes, she has.'

'Will she be all right?'

Val laughed. It turned into a cough.

'Jenny's always all right, Angie. If I'd been through half her life, I'd be dead by now. She's made of steel, that girl. Toughest woman I know. I do what I can for her, even though it's not really in the rules.' She shrugged. 'Sod the rules.'

'That's good, then,' Angie said. She was speaking so softly her voice dragged in her throat.

'They want to close us down.'

'Because of Katie?'

And Lynne, Angie thought, but she didn't say it. It was too soon to think about Lynne. It would always be too soon.

'Not because of Katie. Or Lynne. Although they're useful excuses.' Val tapped the ash off her cigarette. 'No – they've never wanted us around. We make council budgets look untidy.' She made a little breathy sucking sound. Paused. Blew out some smoke. 'The only reason we exist is because the law doesn't work. Nobody's terribly keen on the idea that there are dangerous men walking around and no one's doing anything about it. Like this bloke who's been sending us threats online. We got another one this morning, by the way. It's not Lynne's husband sending them.'

Angie let it hang there in the air between them. Didn't try

274

to argue or say, as she so often wanted to say, *Oh, I'm sure they don't mean it like that.* Instead, she said, 'Well, is the refuge closing, then?'

Val gave a big, bell-like laugh. 'Oh, Angie. If this refuge was run on goodwill from the authorities, we'd have shut down long ago. No.' She sucked on her cigarette. 'We'll keep muddling on. Don't you worry. I founded this place back in the eighties. It was a squat. Nobody gave us anything; we had to take it for ourselves. I'm still getting referrals, Angie.'

She took a drag.

'Did you realize that? I got a call today. Woman's only twenty-three, but she's already had four kids. Fifth on the way. He's kept her pregnant because he thinks that'll stop her from trying to get away. They do that, you know.'

Angie said nothing.

'Every day, a hundred and fifty women in this country are turned away from refuges. Two hundred children, too.'

Angie nodded.

'I know I shouldn't have to spout numbers. I don't. Not at you. It's just force of habit. But if I don't take in this woman, then I've got to live with that.'

'That's a lot to live with.'

'She's going to try and come, this woman. She's getting the train tomorrow. I sent her the money.'

'Okay.'

'It's going to be busy with all those kids around.'

'I don't mind.'

Val looked at Angie and smiled.

'We've got to keep going,' Angie said.

'That's right,' Val said. Her smile melted away and was replaced with something sterner. 'We've got no choice. I don't mind being a pain in the arse in this town, for as long as I need to be. They don't have to like me.'

'I always wanted Charlie to like me,' Angie said, because it was the first time she'd ever thought of it. 'Even when he was hitting me. I always thought, *How can I get him to think I'm wonderful, like he used to?*'

'He never liked you, Angie.'

'Well, I know that now. Took me a while, though.'

'It often does.'

'Well. Anyway.' Angie took a deep, full, beautiful breath. Was this what breathing was always going to be like now? 'I just had a phone call. He's dead. Charlie, I mean. His heart went.' Her voice sounded light, lighter than anything she'd ever felt before.

'I would have killed him myself, you know,' she continued. Her voice was so matter-of-fact. She'd never spoken like this before. 'I know I would. And I feel guilty about that, but not as guilty as I should. I don't mind that he's dead, I really don't. But I mind that he got to go so easily. I mind that a lot.'

Val reached over and patted Angie's hand. 'Are you all right?'

Angie laughed. 'That seems like a funny sort of question to ask.'

'Well, what are you?' There was something in Val's voice that reminded Angie of all the times she'd had to comfort her kids after a row. *Are you all right, Mummy?* Angie had a pet theory that every woman carried in her exactly the right amount of strength to summon up a smile and say, *Yes, Mummy's all right.* No more, no less.

'I'm something. And most of my life I've felt like nothing, so that'll do me well enough.'

44.

Whitworth got into the station at ten the next morning after only a few hours' sleep, and was already squared for a fight with anyone who might dare to challenge his lateness. He didn't bother speaking to Jennifer in the car, so there was no row.

His phone buzzed again, ringing. Could it be Maureen again? Calling him? Did she want to talk?

But the name on the screen dashed the idea before he could work out whether he was feeling hope or despair at the idea of talking to his wife.

'Sarge. Got an update.' Melissa sounded pleased with herself; the phone line seemed to crackle with it. Whitworth realized he was leaning forward in his chair.

'A lead?'

'Oh . . . well . . . not exactly. It's just . . . I thought you'd want to know that . . .'

'What?'

'Well, it's come through from the Glasgow police that . . .'

'What?'

'It wasn't Noah.' She seemed to let it fall out in a blur. 'Definitely not.'

Whitworth's elbow jerked and he had to lunge to avoid spilling his coffee.

'What?'

'Noah's out of the frame.'

'How do we know?'

'I didn't . . . like, *officially* check the alibis. But I thought it was worth doing a ring around. Anyway. One of his mates got in trouble with the Glasgow police that night. Well, sounds like they all did. Anyway, we've got CCTV of Noah in the Stewart Street police station in Glasgow, smack in the middle of the time frame.'

'Right.'

'So there's no way he could have got back.'

'Right. Why didn't he tell us that at the time, though?'

Stupid fucking boy.

Whitworth felt the annoyance twist inside him, but he wasn't sure if it was directed towards Noah, for his incompetence, or himself, for almost falling for the ideological rantings of Val Redwood.

Of course Noah hadn't killed Katie. He had loved her. That was obvious.

'He was pretty pissed up. Sounds like he might not have remembered. Or not remembered what night it was. You know.'

'I do.'

'I just thought you'd want to know.'

'I did want to know.'

'Thanks, sir. Sorry it's not . . . you know . . .'

'All right.'

'There's still this Twitter troll.'

Twitter troll. For fuck's sake.

Maybe this was how things were now. Maybe this was a modern kind of murder. Maybe he needed to take a step back. Maybe they now did live in a world where people killed each other over the internet, or else where people killed themselves over a few unkind words read on a screen.

It was so stupid it could just be true. It wasn't as if anyone's motives for murder had ever been very good.

'Yep,' Whitworth said. 'Keep on it. On the . . . troll.'

'Of course. Bye, sir.'

'Bye.'

Whitworth touched the red phone symbol on the screen and flung the phone down on the table. He didn't know if he was pleased or not. It meant they could stop leaning on the grieving boy, which seemed like a good thing. But then – and maybe it was just the atmosphere of the refuge seeping into him – he had been thinking that it *might* just have been the boyfriend.

Well, what did it matter now?

45.

Then

The new ward is just the same as the last one. Except that instead of sitting in the chair by the bed, Jamie occupies the shape of every hanging dressing gown, every orderly, every set of footsteps.

But – not these footsteps coming down the ward. They're squeaky, heavy, comfortable.

A cosily spread-out, well-upholstered-looking blonde woman is making her way down the ward, bent over slightly with the weight of her enormous handbag. She sits down by Katie's bed and, although she says everything in a whisper, her voice seems to fill the room with its bell-like warmth.

'Hello, Katie.'

The woman looks as if she wants to touch her somehow, but eyes her various burns and bruises with a professionalized caution. She ends up just giving the bedspread a little compensatory squeeze.

'My name's Shellie.'

She looks as if she's leaving space for a reply.

'Are you another nurse?'

'I'm not.'

Shellie is speaking very clearly, as if she's used to talking to people who don't speak English.

'I'm what's called an independent domestic violence advocate. Or an IDVA. That's a bit less of a mouthful. I'm based here in the hospital.'

'No, no.'

The air seems heavy, fuzzy.

'Sorry. You must have been told the wrong thing. My boyfriend – he's not violent.'

'No?' Shellie's face creases. 'I was told in your referral that you thought he might have committed arson.'

'Well – no, I . . . He never hit me or anything.' She blinks hard, opens her eyes as wide as she can. 'I don't think I qualify. I don't want to waste your time.'

Shellie laughs, pours herself a glass of water from the jug on the bedside table.

'You'd be very surprised if you heard how many of the ladies I work with say that to me.'

Katie calls him after she comes round from the surgery and finds herself alone.

Just once. She has no idea why she does it. She can only explain it by saying that the world feels so drab. That the ward is too hot. That the bedsheets are scratchy and there's sweat pooling in the creases of her skin and she wants to shake something off, even if she can't explain what it is.

When he answers, he doesn't let her speak at first.

He says he's so glad she's called. That he's been worried sick about her, that all she needs to do is tell him where she is now and it will all be over. That they can forget about it. That they can move on. That they can get married.

'I'll find you,' he says, and she doesn't know which script these words fit into. 'I swear, I'll always find you.'

'I know you will.'

'I love you, Katie,' he says, and his voice cracks like a whip. He's crying.

He's crying for her.

And she's crying, too.

Because he's the only person left who would cry for her.

'I love you, too,' she says, because how could she not?

Katie takes the phone away from her ear, slowly, painfully, with the last strength she has in her.

Then she leans over and drops her phone into the jug of water on her bedside table. She imagines Jamie's voice choking, bubbling, then going quiet.

She goes back to sleep.

46.

Now

The phone on his desk was ringing. When he answered, there was little to understand on the other end through the mess of sobs, which in themselves should have given him the clue that the caller was Noah.

Whitworth managed to get the words out of him eventually.

Noah had found a note. A note from Katie.

Where was it?

Under a pile of stuff. Laundry. In the bedroom.

That chaotic jigsaw of a bedroom. So there it was.

Noah was sitting in the exact place where Whitworth had last seen him when they had searched the house, off to the side of the sofa, with his body leaning to accommodate a ghost.

A sheet of paper was laid out in the centre of the coffee table.

I'm sorry. I've been unhappy for a long time, and I can't do it any more.

Goodbye.
Katie.

'It was under a pile of laundry on the bed,' Noah said.

He was still sniffing.

Whitworth wanted to punch him, grab him, threaten him, demand to know how come a fucking suicide note was only showing up now. He wanted to do that even though a hand-writing expert had already seen it and said that it was virtually certain Katie had written the thing.

Whitworth didn't care. He suspected that Noah was just the sort of man that other men wanted to punch.

Noah looked up, tears and snot coating his face, and Whit-worth had to turn away.

'What were you doing on the bridge yesterday, Noah?' Brookes asked. It was as if he were able to cut through the tears somehow, as if they didn't stick to him. Whitworth felt ashamed but didn't know why.

'I just . . . I just wanted to understand her a bit. I dunno.'

'You didn't understand her?'

'I didn't know. I didn't know those things about her. I didn't know about the . . . the false-identity thing. She lied to me.'

'Maybe she lied. We don't know for sure.'

'Yeah.' Noah sniffed. 'Maybe. I guess she had her reasons. She always did. I just never really understood what they were. There was always a part of her I was never going to really see. That was the deal with us.' Noah turned his gaze flatly towards Whitworth. 'There are so many things I don't understand.'

Whitworth called DI Khan. On the phone. That felt like a small victory.

'Whitworth?' Her voice was ratty on the other end. 'Haven't we got a conference call scheduled in for three?'

'Just thought you'd want an update now, ma'am,' Whit-worth said. He was trying not to sound too breezy. 'We've recovered a suicide note which seems to have been written by Katie Straw. Waiting to hear back from the lab, but at the moment it looks authentic.'

'A note?' He could hear a harsh, relentless typing in the

background, distorted by the phone line, but unmistakeable. 'Why didn't we find this earlier?'

Whitworth gripped the arm of his chair and said the usual things about limited resources and the lack of an available forensics team. He thought he might as well throw in an extra jab and pointed out that rural forces had – shall we say? – challenges around access to resources.

'I hear what you're saying, Sergeant.' A pause. More keyboard tapping. 'Look, it's noted. It's all noted.' He could hear her slurping on her coffee. 'And I take it the question of the victim's identity has been cleared up?'

For half a second, Whitworth thought about lying and saying yes, just to get off the phone with the damn woman.

Then – 'No.'

'Right.' A whistling noise down the phone as DI Khan pushed out her breath between her teeth. 'Look, do I need to come in?'

'No.' He shoved the word out quickly, hardly letting himself think about the question. 'Not at all. We're closing in. We're almost there.'

'I'm working on it,' Brookes muttered when Whitworth walked out of the office, doing his best not to slam the door too loudly. And he really did seem to be working on it. There were piles of print-outs stacked all over his desk. Print-outs of social media accounts, highlighted lists from electoral registers, photocopies of death certificates.

'Hmm,' Whitworth said, but in his head something reminded him to *have some bloody faith in the lad, will you?*

Then Melissa dashed towards him. Her hair was dishevelled, her face triumphant.

'I found him. I mean . . . we found him.'

'Who?'

'The troll.'

'Troll?' Whitworth stared at her blankly.

'The guy. Who's been harassing Val Redwood. And guess what.'

'What?'

'You've met him before.'

Whitworth was expecting to see some blunt-nosed, blank-eyed hulk of a man but, instead, it took him only a moment to recognize the face in the photograph. The young man looked almost girlish – rail-thin, with large, trapped-looking eyes and hair cropped close to his head. He looked like some defence-less baby animal. Yes, Whitworth had seen the boy before.

'He was at the community engagement event. I drove him home.' He saw the twist of confusion on Melissa's face, her open mouth stuck still.

'He made a bit of a scene. Wouldn't call it – what did you say? – trolling. But he was upsetting people. Not as much as he was upsetting himself, mind. I was heading off, anyway, so I dropped him off. Vulnerable, you know.'

Brookes was driving. Whitworth sat in the passenger seat.

It was about a twenty-minute drive, which meant Whitworth had plenty of time to bring up something he'd been putting off, even accounting for a few minutes' procrastination.

He did his best to introduce it subtly, though he knew Brookes was enough of a detective that he was sure not to be fooled.

'Did a good job, tracking this bloke down, Melissa.'

'Hmmm?' Brookes looked at him from the road, his expression polite and uninterested in equal parts. 'Melissa? Yeah.'

'Nice girl,' Whitworth said.

'Yeah. Good colleague.'

His words were chosen carefully. If Whitworth wasn't cautious, he'd end up looking like a dirty old man himself.

'Just – just remember to keep things platonic, all right? I've seen you looking at her a few times and . . .'

He trailed off before the meandering phrase could turn into an accusation.

'Hmm?' An expression of something that might have been disdain or embarrassment slid over Brookes's face, but it cleared away so swiftly Whitworth couldn't be sure. 'I mean, yeah, she's really cool and everything. But I'm already interested in someone. Nothing to do with work.'

'Right. Good.'

'It's nothing personal about Melissa. I just think it's best to keep that stuff separate. Work and life. You know.'

'Sure.'

They diligently resumed their silence for a few minutes. Then it was Brookes's turn to abruptly break it.

'I don't know how we're going to do it, you know. In the future,' he said. It came out of nowhere, but there was still another ten minutes to drive, so Whitworth took the bait.

'Do what?'

'Police the internet.'

Whitworth laughed. 'Not my problem. I'm one foot out of the door. Glad I'm not starting my career now, though, I've got to admit. Everyone seems to turn into a nutter as soon as they're behind a keyboard. I don't understand it myself.'

'Yeah,' Brookes said. 'That's how you get the Val Redwoods of the world, right? They're obsessed with the internet,' he said to the road.

'Who?'

'Feminists. You know. The nutty ones.' He heaved a sigh, as if in despair at the world. 'I s'pose it's easy to find stuff to prove their point on the internet.'

'Easy to find anything on the internet. Can't be bothered with all that social media stuff.'

'Lucky you. If you're my age, you don't get the option of ignoring this stuff. Everyone thinks that what the world needs is their statement on Brexit or the Middle East or whatever, and the hardcore feminists are some of the most annoying. Look, I'm all for equality and everything, but . . . Jesus.' He shrugged. His voice was exploratory, contemplative. 'They get slapped down now and then and they expect us to police it. But what they really want is for us to police people's opinions. Look at Val Redwood. She thinks she's got the keys to the universe.'

'Don't we all, in our way?'

Brookes gave a slight scowl, braking abruptly to stop the car.

'*I* don't,' he said, getting out and slamming the car door behind him.

They were buzzed into the eerily silent apartment building by a voice that could have belonged to anyone, its distinctiveness smudged away by the crackle of the intercom.

'Doesn't sound like a troll to me,' Whitworth said, half joking, as they got into the lift.

'Why? What were you expecting? Audible drooling?' Brookes rolled his eyes good-naturedly, his expression punctuated by the knell of the lift as it announced, 'Fourth floor.'

Whitworth wanted to laugh, but the truth was that there was still something nagging at him, even now, after the suicide note.

Maybe it was just the thought of a young woman *choosing* to drown. As Val Redwood had said, it was a terrible way to die.

Could there have been something else? Something foul and sinister that came out of nowhere and snatched Katie out of life?

The door to flat 46 was answered by a young man. A surprisingly young man. His youth had seemed incongruous at the community meeting, too, among all the old biddies. In his mid-twenties, at most. He was of shorter stature, slim. His dark eyebrows were drawn together in an expression that was appealing by default.

He asked to see their credentials immediately, and beyond that showed no resistance to the idea of their presence.

'I knew you'd come,' he said simply, stepping aside to let them in. He nodded shyly at Whitworth, seemingly in acknowledgement of their previous meeting.

He led them into his flat. The new-build apartment was well fitted out but dusty. There was absolutely nothing there that didn't need to be.

The living room was taken up mostly by a large desk with three screens and a bulky ergonomic keyboard. The sofa and TV were crammed around it, as if they were doing their best to sidle out.

'I was working,' the boy said, nodding at the lines of coloured text on black background scattered over the computer screen. 'But now my concentration's broken.'

'Sorry,' Whitworth said. The boy looked at him blankly, so he continued, too cheerfully, 'What's a young techie like you doing, living in a washed-up town like this?'

'I work remotely. My mother left me money to buy a place. But she's dead now.' The boy sounded very much as if he was trying not to care.

'You could sell up and leave. Property prices aren't bad round here.'

The young man turned around. There was a look of naked horror on his face. 'Oh, no,' he breathed softly. 'I could never do that.'

He looked more like a little boy than a man, really. Girl-size, Whitworth thought. You wouldn't be sure who would win in a fight between this man – boy, child – and a girl like Nazia. The word 'troll' could hardly have seemed less apt.

'I take it you know why we're here,' Whitworth said.

'Of course I do.'

'We're looking into . . .'

'Yes. I know. I'm surprised it's taken you this long. Free speech is dying, but we shouldn't be surprised. The legal system's very gynocentric.'

Whitworth blinked.

'Gyno—. Sorry?'

'Exactly,' the boy continued. 'We don't even have the vocabulary to describe what's happening. But that's not your fault.' He wasn't looking Whitworth in the eye.

The feminist lobby is incredibly powerful and will block anything that doesn't fit their agenda.

'Why are you bothering Valerie Redwood?' Whitworth asked, as gently as he could. It was hard not to be gentle when someone looked so fragile. 'Bright guy like you, good job, future ahead. You're not one of those people.'

'Typical feminist,' the boy said to his knees. 'Conflating accountability with harassment.'

Accountability? What was this boy's idea of holding a woman to account?

'You did say she deserved to be raped, though . . .'

'That was a thought experiment.' The boy waved the idea away. 'A comment on the feminist straw man of so-called "rape culture". Not a proper threat. She just wants unchecked power. That's all she wants. That's what they all want. It's nothing to do with equality.'

'Yeah,' Whitworth said. There was clearly something not quite normal about the boy. 'Look, I'm sure you're not some kind of woman-hater –'

'I don't hate women.' The boy had interrupted but didn't seem to realize that he had. 'I love women. I miss my mother every day.' He twisted his hands. 'It's the degrading of masculinity I can't stand. By people like Valerie Redwood. And that degrades women, too. Women like my mother, who did nothing but care for me.'

women are unbelievably coddled by the modern world even though men are committing suicide in droves it seems these feminists don't care at all.

'I can understand that, mate,' Whitworth said, not bothering to think too much about whether he really could. 'But you've got to lay off Women's Aid. The girl who worked there killed herself, you know.'

The boy sat down sharply. Stared at his hands.

'When?'

'Just after that meeting.'

'And you think it was because of me.'

'We didn't say . . .'

'I didn't make her do it. You can't make people do things they don't want to do. Media portrayals of people driven to suicide by harassment are vastly overstated. There are a host of factors at play.'

He didn't look like he believed this at all.

'We're not saying you did.' Whitworth wasn't sure if he entirely meant that. 'She had a lot of problems. A lot going on. I don't know if the hate mail was helping, but it wasn't the main cause. She had been unhappy for a long time.'

'I don't hate them.' The boy sounded desperate. 'I mean, I hate what they stand for – you know, female supremacy – but I know they're just people. I don't hate them because of that.'

Whitworth realized he had been scratching, scrunching, pulling at the wad of papers in his hand. All the boy's comments and threats. Printed out, they seemed laughably analog; old-fashioned, good old poison-pen.

How about i come over and fucking rape

Whitworth imagined this boy trying to scale the mountain

that was Val Redwood. The differential between them made him want to laugh.

But Katie . . . Katie had been fragile.

'I should give you an official warning,' he said gently. He wasn't sure whether that was exactly accurate – it was hard to remember what the guidelines on internet shenanigans were supposed to be. 'But I can see you've had a hard time. I don't want to cause trouble for you.'

The boy lifted up his face. Tear-stained.

your
fat
whore
cunt

'I don't know what to do,' the boy said. There was something painful about the admission. The lack of caveats. The imploring look.

and maybe you'll see how fucking stupid you sound

Whitworth felt his chest tighten and said, 'Look, don't do it again. All right?'

He stood up and patted the boy on the shoulder. The bone felt like it might collapse under the force of his hand.

talking about
so called
rape culture
you
overprivileged
bitch

They sat in the police car for a few moments. Brookes looked a little shaken.

'All right?' Whitworth said. He did his best to make it sound casual. Things had been piling up over the last day. It would make sense that it was starting to get to Brookes.

'Yeah,' Brookes said quietly. 'Yeah. I just feel sorry for the guy. It's so sad. And he thinks it's all his fault, you can tell.'

'Well, you've got to take some responsibility for your actions, I suppose,' Whitworth said. He knew that everyone claimed it was worse, being bullied on the internet. Having seen what had happened to Lynne Ward, he thought that was a bit hysterical.

'He doesn't really believe all that stuff,' Brookes said. 'You can tell.'

'No,' Whitworth agreed. 'No, I don't think he does. I think he's just unhappy.'

The word felt so heavy, even though the feeling was so unremarkable, so commonplace. Whitworth needed to lift things up and make them lighter, back into the world of work.

'So you don't think he killed her, then?' he said.

'What do you mean?' Brookes said. 'She killed herself. You saw that note.'

'I know. I'm just having a bit of a hard time getting my head around it, I s'pose. And I did wonder if there might have been something else going on.'

'Not a chance. You could write that guy off on the strength differential alone, before you even get into the psychology of it. Plus, if we're figuring that she went into the water on her way home from the meeting, then he had an alibi at that time.' Brookes turned the key in the ignition. 'You.'

'Couldn't he have come back?' Whitworth queried. But even as he said the words he felt the weight of their implausibility. How would this boy even have got Katie into the water? She would have been half a head taller and a good stone heavier than him. It made no sense.

'You're right,' he said flatly. 'We're no closer. It was just a . . . a troll.'

Just background noise. Internet chatter. Nothing to do with real life.

47.

Then

When Katie wakes up, Shellie is sitting next to her with a laptop open in her lap, peering into the water jug. Katie can see the distorted outline of the phone through the fogged plastic.

'Some kind of fish?'

'I got scared,' Katie says.

'What of?'

'That he'd . . . that he'd find me . . . that he'd trace my phone call.'

Shellie laughs. 'I doubt he's got that kind of equipment lying around.' She rolls up her sleeve slightly and fishes the phone out of the jug between her thumb and forefinger, then lays it out on a piece of coarse blue tissue like a little drowned corpse.

'Well, it's one way to stop him calling you.' She giggles. 'Bit expensive, though. Wouldn't do it as a long-term solution.'

Katie is still staring at the phone. She reaches out her index finger and touches it lightly.

'I don't know his number,' she says.

Shellie gives a little shrug, holding eye contact the whole time.

'Couldn't call him if you wanted to, then.'

Katie chooses Manchester. It's just a place on a list of names, read out to her by Shellie in the same modulated, warm tone she uses for everything. Chester. Sheffield. Brighton. Bristol. Manchester.

Anywhere out of what they call her 'danger zone'.

They buy her a bus ticket. Whoever 'they' is – whatever organization it is that Shellie works for.

'We would do a train for you, but they're so bloody expensive these days, eh?'

Shellie doesn't seem to let anything interfere with her professional brightness.

Katie wonders whether, when Shellie gets home, she lets her face drop and allows the sadness and hopelessness that gets pushed back in the crush of the day seep out of every pore. She wonders whether she can let herself sit in it, or whether she can sluice it off in the shower or burn it away with the sting of swallowed alcohol.

But Shellie just smiles again, and her face stays blank.

'Right. So when you get to the bus station in Manchester someone will meet you and take you to the refuge. That all right?'

It might as well be all right. Katie's going to need a new working definition of what *all right* looks like.

So she nods.

All the time she's on the bus she stares out of the window. The vast bulk of the coach feels fatal, as if the vehicle might take a turn too sharply and rock over on to its side. When they go under bridges she looks up and is almost surprised when they don't collapse. When it starts to rain, she waits for the bus to skid and overturn.

It's late at night by the time she gets to the bus station. She stands there by herself as the rest of the passengers drain away. After a few minutes the only people left in the terminal are Katie and another young woman, lounging on her suitcase with her headphones in, her eyes half closed.

'Katie?'

A woman in her late thirties or early forties, her hijab tucked untidily over a bulky jumper and ill-fitting trousers, is smiling broadly at her. Katie nods.

'Great. So lovely to see you've made it here safely. The car's just round the corner.'

Katie wasn't expecting the Manchester accent to sound quite so foreign to her ears. Each vowel delineates a hundred miles' distance between herself and Jamie, between herself and home. She follows the woman, who introduces herself as Yara, to a tinny-looking Ford Escort and gets in.

'Good journey?' Yara asks as she reverses out of the car park. Katie just nods.

They drive for twenty minutes or so, out of the city and into a suburb with lots of tree-lined roads and red-brick Victorian houses.

'Nice area,' Katie says.

'Lots of students live round here, so some of the houses are a bit run-down. However' – Yara indicates and turns the car left with a decisive jerk of the wheel – 'some of the streets are a bit better kept up than others.'

They pull up to a large Victorian house, no different to the rest of the street, aside from a few small CCTV cameras outside and a slightly higher chain-link fence around the back garden.

'It's not what I expected,' Katie says. She has imagined a hostel, a halfway house, with a drab manned reception area and beige walls, maybe with bars on the windows and a dreary canteen. Yara laughs.

'Well, we don't want to be anywhere dodgy, do we?' She lowers her voice to a whisper, though there is no one around. 'Not with the nasty pieces of work our women are getting away from.'

Up a gravel drive past a neat row of wheelie bins to a very solid-looking front door. Yara keys a code into a metal keypad and a buzz ushers them both inside.

'I know it's a bit warm.' Yara inserts a finger between the fabric of her hijab and her chin and puffs her cheeks out dramatically, fanning herself. 'The women are always turning the heat right up,' she says.

She leads Katie through a cramped hallway and up a flight of stairs, which turns tightly up two storeys before coming out on to a narrow landing. She takes a bunch of keys out of her pocket to unlock a white door with a number 6 on it and steps inside to switch on the light. She pivots slightly to let Katie into the room then stands in the centre of the floor, smiling. It's a kind smile, a boundaried smile.

'I'll let you get settled,' she says. 'I'll be down in the kitchen. Ground floor, on the left. I'll do us both a cup of tea.'

She smiles.

'Might even be able to find some chocolate biscuits. We've usually got some on the go here.'

She steps back from the threshold, and the smile leaves her face to make room for another look; her messy, jolly features rearrange themselves into a steel-clad promise: 'You're safe here, Katie.'

Katie is looking round the room, at the sloping ceiling, which has been painted neatly, if not too recently, at the single pillow and the polyester bedsheets, at the small pile of packaged items on the bed. Tampons. Body lotion. Mascara. Razors.

She looks back at Yara and nods.

48.

Now

'Sarge.'

Whitworth turned to see Brookes hurrying after him, a piece of paper in his hand. He was grinning. 'Mystery solved.'

Whitworth raised an eyebrow. That was the kind of thing you said in a film, not in a police station. 'What is it?'

'It's Katie Straw. Or rather, Katie Bradley.' Brookes thrust a photocopy of a birth certificate into Whitworth's hand, then stepped back and folded his arms as if he'd just put the finishing touches on a sculpture.

'Nothing fishy about it, as it turns out. Her parents were Eleanor Straw and Martin Bradley. Bradley left the family when Katie was fifteen, then died in a car accident a few years later. Drink-driving. Little to no contact with Katie. Eleanor Straw died of cervical cancer a couple of years ago. Looks like Katie was hacked off with her dad and decided to start using her mum's name after she died. To keep it going or whatever. It wasn't hard to find her.'

'Did she change it by deed poll? Why didn't we find a record of it?'

Brookes shook his head. 'Nope, just started using it. No record. Nice of her to make our job so much harder for us.' He rolled his eyes. 'Some feminist thing, I guess. Anyway' – he grinned – 'it gave us a bit of fun for a while, eh? Made it look like we had a proper mystery on our hands.'

'No mystery, then.' Whitworth's voice was dull and soft. He felt blunted. 'Just admin.'

'Just good old-fashioned detective work.'

Whitworth was still studying the birth certificate as if it held some deeper answer than name. Age. Date. Parentage. Place of birth. As if it gave him some real measure of this girl.

49.

Then

She chooses Widringham because of the postcards. And the jigsaw puzzles. And the fudge boxes. Yara suggests it – the cost of living is cheap. After six months in the refuge, just the idea of independent living seems to call out to her.

She has searched for Jamie's opposite and found it here, in this town laced with bleak, watery light and surrounded by heathery hills. The sky is big – big enough to keep at bay that permanent sense of claustrophobia.

Sometimes Katie feels too exposed, but she accepts that this is the way it may always be.

She maps Jamie everywhere. Large as a colossus, small as a heartbeat. She sees him in the body of every blameless man caught in the corner of her eye. She learns to greet these ghosts, and they learn to disappear when she waves at them.

It grows gradually. Not so much a feeling of safety as an exquisite sense of space around her eyes.

She learns to name the demon. To understand that, just as cities can fall without a shot being fired, a woman can relinquish herself, piece by piece.

There are still days when it doesn't make sense to her, when blaming herself becomes the easier option. Something in her DNA must have malfunctioned to make her stay with a man like Jamie.

Working at the refuge sometimes feels like catching a whiff of some half-forgotten smell. All those women, crammed together. It's like being back at her all-girls school. Not bitchy, which was always the complaint that came pre-levelled against large groups of females. It's something heavier than that – the weight of requirement to always be the best, the kindest, sweetest and least troublesome person in the room. Surrounded by women who have lived the last few years (and, in Angie's case, decades) under siege in their own skin, the effect is amplified yet remains unmistakeably the same.

In her bones, Katie longs for the women to explode, to hurt the world instead of relentlessly and insistently continuing to hurt themselves. They move like mice around each other, continually apologizing for a stream of imaginary offences.

Even though she knows that words are no good to any of them, she still wants to hear their stories. Perhaps that's nothing more than a ghoulish greed she isn't decent enough to shake off.

She always thought Jamie was bigger than life. Bigger than her life, anyway. But she is starting to wonder if, after all, he might have been smaller. If everything he had said and done, everything he had made her feel, had been nothing more than the inability to see beyond himself, to understand that he didn't have to act the way a man was 'meant' to act. He certainly didn't understand anything about women.

Maybe it was true, but it was too simple to be a good story.

Nobody has a good answer. Not Katie herself, not Yara, nor later Val, and certainly not the psychologists and sociologists whose works she googles endlessly in the months after she comes to Widringham.

She finds herself smacking up endlessly against the crash barriers of language. She can only guess at what lies beyond, and whether it would make her feel any better to articulate herself. It's an article of faith that it would but, really, she isn't sure.

Her story with Jamie was written in sensations rather than words, so maybe words will never be of any use to her.

It's that search, that mapping of her own psyche, which has led her to Widringham Women's Aid. She applies for the job shaking, and shakes all the way through the interview. Val is pleased by this – she takes it as a sign of dedication.

There are a dozen daily moments of terror. It seemed so easy at the time to change her name but little threadlike roots reach towards her from her old life to remind her of a person called Katie Bradley. A person who inherited her mother's money. A person with a P45 and a national insurance number. A person waiting at the other end of a background check. That person calls her back every day.

She hasn't caught up. Not yet.

She doesn't ask herself whether she feels less alive now, because she doesn't want to know the answer.

She missed her mother's death.

She got the news on the day she moved out of the refuge, two years ago now. According to the nurses, there wasn't much to miss; her mother spent her final six months in a morphine haze. She didn't dare go to the funeral. Typical of her parents is the way she has to say goodbye to them. Her father, scattering himself, asserting his presence. Her mother buried, melding with and decaying into the earth. Permanent yet absent.

Being in Widringham helps. People look you in the eye; you don't know if it's out of hostility or curiosity, but you always know it's out of something.

It had been so easy to go unseen in London.

There are days when she reminds herself again and again of the note she left him, until her whole consciousness seems limited to the edges of those sentences.

I'm sorry. I've been unhappy for a long time, and I can't do it any more.

Goodbye.
Katie.

It wasn't quite true. She knew that, even lying in the hospital after the operation, in the half-light of drugged sleep. She could have kept doing it. She could have disappeared, said yes, assimilated herself into Jamie's name.

But she didn't want to.

50.

Now

Katie's body still lay on the slab in the morgue, with a label around her big toe like a lot in an auction house.

Whitworth looked into Katie's face. He imagined her standing before him, tears rolling down those marble cheeks like a Madonna. Or maybe she hadn't been the crying type. He hadn't known her, after all.

Why am I dead?

He had no idea what her voice had been like in life, but he imagined it sounding a little like Jenny's. Both Jennys.

'Because you killed yourself, my darling,' he said aloud.

They could release her body now. To who? Noah?

Katie Straw deserved better, but there were no legal grounds for giving better to her. What was Whitworth to do – organize the funeral himself?

The death certificate was completed for Katie Bradley, with the cause of death listed as suicide by drowning. One of the few bits of documentation the poor girl had.

Bad luck. Case closed.

They hadn't managed to get hold of Jenny, but that didn't matter much any more. She was like a rat, disappearing into the bowels of the city to live in the damp and shame. She didn't know any different; maybe it was better for her in the end. She'd turn up, most likely dead from an overdose.

Though nobody would dare to say it, there was some sense in the idea that people like Jenny were better off dead. You wouldn't make a dog suffer through the kind of life she had. Besides, you had to draw a line somewhere, you had to make people take responsibility for themselves somewhere along the line. Else there was nothing.

Peony Ward had been taken in by her mother's mother. She was back in nursery, and her grandmother was insisting that she wouldn't remember what she'd seen. Her grandmother was clear that the kid didn't need any therapy. What she needed, the old woman insisted, was to be treated like a normal little girl.

She drew pictures sometimes, with the red crayon.

The case had received some attention in the *Echo*, though it wasn't quite big enough and the victim wasn't quite young enough or pretty enough for national news. Lynne Ward's sweet face gazing out. Husband kills wife. Dog bites man.

The way they reported it was that Lynne had been preventing her husband from seeing his daughter, which had driven him into a rage. When she had returned, Frank Ward had been unable to control himself. That was why he had stabbed her so many times.

The only thing Frank Ward had insisted on, over and over, was that he hadn't been the one hanging around the refuge.

He said he had no idea who it was. If he'd known where Lynne was, he said, he'd have talked to her. Pleaded with her.

Maybe he was saying that because it fitted better with his story, Whitworth thought.

You had to look at the facts. A man, hanging around a refuge.

A woman, turning up dead.

Or maybe, just maybe, it was a goddamn coincidence. Maybe the man was just a man. You couldn't place suspicion on every man walking down the street.

Frank Ward had pleaded guilty to manslaughter on the

grounds of diminished responsibility and received a six-year sentence. Temporary loss of control caused by years of stress. High-powered job. The strain of looking after a mentally ill woman all those years. Fear for his daughter.

He had cried in court. The judge had taken his remorse into account with the sentencing.

Six years. He'd be out in three with good behaviour.

51.

Here's the job.

Let me show you how I do it.

It's okay. Don't be shy. I've seen it all. People like some fucked-up stuff, but I know how to handle them.

Tell me what it is you want. Don't worry, I won't tell anyone. I don't care if it was because your daddy touched you or because you hate women and you want to see me on my knees or because it's the time of day or the direction of the wind.

I don't care what it is.

Honest.

Okay. Here we go.

Where are we?

Bridge. Pretty here, in the daytime, but fucking cold tonight, and I know cold.

They can't see me. You shouldn't be surprised. Lots of people can't.

I can see the two of them, here on the bridge. Him and her. Any him and her.

Let's watch them, you and me. Just let it happen. Don't think about it too much, okay? They don't know you're looking.

Tears running down her face, in that pretty way men like.

It's so fucking ugly.

They're saying things, but there's nothing to hear over the noise of the river, so the words don't matter. He's the only one who has them now and he can change them and he can forget them and then it'll be like there were never any words at all and it won't matter that I didn't hear them.

Oh and he's got her in his arms and you can't tell if he's trying to hold her back from herself or steal her away and who cares, all looks the same to me.

But what do you want? You can tell Jenny.

She jumped.

She was pushed.

Who cares?

The truth is whatever makes you come.

Feels good, eh?

52.

Then

Katie settles into the strained plastic of one of the cheap chairs, laid out in horseshoe formation in a small section of the church hall. You get to know the faces at these meetings. The artist in her fifties who's decided she's going to bring silk-screen printing to the at-risk youth of Widringham, whether they like it or not. The social workers, always seeming on the crest of the wave of their latest hangovers. The octogenarian widows who come to everything posted outside the church hall, who ask such long questions you wonder if they hope they might be allowed to never stop talking.

'Hullo!'

The room falls sharply to hush. A pink-cheeked bald man, perhaps in his fifties, steps into the centre of the horseshoe. Though he is in plain clothes, his bearing is PC Plod, with his arms folded on top of his gut. He grins round at the room and raises an eyebrow at the nearest pensioner.

'Rowdy lot tonight, eh?'

The old woman laughs dutifully. Katie wonders how long she's been laughing dutifully for.

The police officer smirks and the pink in his cheeks seems to deepen, like a berry being crushed. Clearly, this is his crowd.

'Good to be out here tonight,' he says. *Hello, Wembley*, Katie thinks.

'Some familiar faces, some new, which is what we like.' He chuckles, as though he thought he'd made a joke.

'For those of you who don't know me, my name's Detective Sergeant Daniel Whitworth. For those of you who do know me, my name's That bloody busybody detective.'

He waits again. Katie laughs with the rest.

'Now, the reason you're here tonight is because you've heard about the Police and Crime Commissioner's community-engagement priorities. Now, unfortunately I shall shortly have to dash off to take my lady wife away for our anniversary. Twenty-five years.'

A smattering of applause, and he bows his head slightly.

'Thanks very much. She's a very tolerant lady. Anyway, I'm going to ramble on for a few minutes, but I'm going to leave the detail to the capable hands of my new DC.'

He keeps talking for a little while. Katie is getting bored.

Boredom is a new luxury, one she's only started to become acquainted with since she developed the sense of space around her eyes, since the savage, raw skin of the burn on her fourth finger healed and became only a vague shininess. She runs her left thumb over that smooth place now, as is her habit.

A single hand shoots up and, before the police officer can so much as nod, a skinny young man stands up.

'Yes. I'd just like to say that I've read the funding allocations for this Police and Crime Commissioner's priorities and I have some grave concerns' – he glances down at what appears to be a set of cue cards – 'about the gender bias of the PCC, which has clearly been directed behind the scenes by a radical feminist agenda.'

The concerted attempt at polite interest on DS Whitworth's face makes Katie want to giggle.

'Those who have read the funding priorities will have noticed that page sixty-seven makes reference to a forty-thousand-pound budget for the provision of refuge accommodation for women fleeing domestic violence.'

The man – boy, whatever he was – looked up from his cue cards. The dramatic pause that follows seems to suggest careful study of the timing of public speeches, but with none of whatever it was that brought humanity to language.

'Women. So my question today, for the PCC and the wider community, is this: where are the men fleeing domestic violence in Widringham supposed to go?'

'Er . . . Melissa?' The police officer glances at a young woman sitting next to him with a fat file of papers in her lap.

The woman blinks then anxiously clears her throat. 'It's based on a needs assessment,' she says, opening her folder and flipping compulsively through it. 'If you read the crime statistics on intimate-partner violence –'

'We can all see for ourselves how profoundly politically biased these decisions are,' the young man interrupts. Even his snort seems pre-planned. 'And those in this community are well aware of the manipulation carried out by one Valerie Redwood.'

One of the older women turns her head serenely.

'Oh, *Val*,' she begins, but the man carries on.

This is why Val has always told Katie not to mention where she works at community events. Because of things like this. So she scrunches down in her chair. Waits for it to be over. Tries not to laugh at the idea of Val having shadowy control over anything.

'Encouraging women to leave the men who love them, who need them. Manipulating the court system to deprive loving fathers of contact with their children. Criminalizing the actions of men acting on hard-wired instinct, fighting for their families. So today, I say to Valerie Redwood, and to all those radical feminists influencing the agenda . . .' He's waving his finger around as if he wishes it were a flick knife. 'You have no *compassion*. No *compassion*. This is why male suicide is sky-high.

This is why male mental health is plummeting. This is why feminism has moved beyond equality to mean dominance over and discrediting of men. *Shame* on you.'

He sits down.

'Thanks . . . for that,' DS Whitworth says. He's flushed and shiny and looks off balance, as if the bulk of his belly might tip him over any second. 'We'll . . . actually, we were intending to take questions at the end, but if we just circle back to the priorities for a minute . . .'

And just like that, they're back to normal. The man is still sitting in the front row, his hands folded in his lap, his breathing heavy.

Even as she is staring intently at the back of his head, her body tensed to get out if need be, Katie's mind starts to drift. To Noah, to the house that will be empty without him when she gets home that night.

She met Noah on the apps. One of them. She can't remember which one. She just decided that she wanted to meet men – any men, not necessarily *the* man – and the universe batted Noah over to her. She is surprised to find they have made a life together, but they have.

Noah gives things a rhythm she can write herself on to, one he does little to interrupt. It is always the same: a bowl of overcooked pasta, a blob of own-brand pesto, a weakish cup of tea. Things that hold a kind of comfort, and comfort is what she needs after a long day with Val at her shoulder, or with an internalized version of Val in her head.

Noah is sandy and lanky, with an unexpected pot-belly and light blue eyes. His body has none of the precision of Jamie's.

There was a vocabulary – a language she and Jamie shared, which all couples share – into which everything needed translating. The vocabulary of a thousand little unspoken understandings and inferences of what he said – or didn't say.

There's an impulse in her to call that language intimacy, and perhaps it is. She has no such shared lexicon of tiny looks or gestures with Noah, only the lingua franca of what they both know love is supposed to be like. But she can fall asleep beside him, and that matters more.

Noah is inexperienced at sex. The idea of humiliating her doesn't seem to turn him on.

'And without further ado, let me hand you over to our new detective constable – James Brookes!'

A slim, wiry young man unfolds himself from the chair at the curve of the horseshoe where he's been sitting, just out of Katie's line of sight, and strides to where DS Whitworth is standing.

The blueprint of him is so familiar it takes a beat to notice the lightning rattling through her.

Her first thought, before she stops being able to think, is that of course it's Jamie. That it could hardly have been otherwise.

53.

Now

They went for a drink, he and Brookes.

Brookes seemed elated. He cracked jokes with Whitworth, with the barman, with anyone within the radius of his grin. It was good, after his disdain for the goings-on in Widringham, to see him getting some kind of satisfaction out of the closing of the case. Whitworth had to admit it was good police work, and he was starting to like the younger man.

Was he an arrogant sod? Yes, of course. But weren't all the good coppers?

'I'll be letting DI Khan know about your contribution,' Whitworth said. This was probably the best way, he was coming to realize. Give the younger generation some credit, let them get on with it, take a step back yourself. 'Got to admit, you got the measure of this case straight away. Great instinct.'

'Thanks, sir.' Brookes was holding his gaze in a way that made it hard for Whitworth to look away. 'And I don't want to embarrass you or anything, but it's great to have a boss like you. With all your experience.' He took a long gulp of his pint. 'I've learned a lot on this case.'

'Not all good,' Whitworth said softly, thinking of Peony Ward.

'No,' Brookes agreed, and his eyes clouded over. Clearly, he was thinking about the same thing.

'Always more to learn,' Whitworth said.

They stood in silence at the bar for the first third of pint one and the beginning of pint two, staring into space. It was always like this at the end of an investigation into a death. A celebration of bleakness, or at least bleakness tidied away. A libation to the two women who were gone, and who'd helped their crime-solve statistics.

'You saw her, you know,' he said absently to Brookes. It had been playing on his mind, what had happened that final night.

'What?'

'At the community-engagement event. You know, when that bloke was making a scene. She was there. Trying to keep a low profile, I should imagine.' He gave Brookes a little shove on the arm. Perhaps they'd broken the barrier into matiness now. 'Come on, lad, it wasn't such a big crowd. Don't you remember her?'

Brookes squinted for a second, then shrugged. 'Oh, yeah. Vaguely.'

'Notice anything funny about her?'

Funny? What the hell did he mean by that? *Anything that made her look like she might be about to kill herself?*

Brookes gave him the wide-eyed look, the palms-up gesture, the I-can't-explain-the-world-away attitude that Whitworth directed to other people on what felt these days like a daily basis.

'Nothing. She was just a normal girl.' He twisted his lip slightly; his eyes went blank. 'She was just a girl. And she died.'

'Yeah. She said she'd been unhappy for a long time, right?'

'Right.' Brookes's jaw tensed just a fraction. That humanity seeping through again. That ability would serve him well as a copper, as long as he used it properly.

'Still beggars belief that Noah didn't find that bloody note,' Whitworth said. 'But I suppose . . . we missed it too. When we searched her room.'

'We did.' Brookes cut him off a little curtly. It was only fractions of body language that showed his defensiveness – a furrowing of the brow, a little shift in posture. You saw those things if you were a detective. Brookes had searched that room, and he'd missed the note. Probably wasted them some man hours and money, but these things happened. It was a bad miss, but it happened to everyone early in their career.

'I'm not blaming you,' Whitworth said quietly. 'I know it's your first case like this. We all make mistakes.'

'Yeah.' Brookes seemed to relax a degree or two. 'We do.' His fingertips tapped distractedly at his glass. 'It's hard, though. To deal with that.'

'You learn.'

'Yeah.'

Brookes drained his pint glass and pushed away from the bar. 'Can't stay much longer, sir. Got a date.'

'A date?' Whitworth grinned, knowing this would be the time to rib the younger man about his love life. It was a welcome break in the tension. In times past, he would have skimmed over the feeling with a quick *give her one from me, will you?* But he kept his mouth shut. He was learning from his mistakes too.

'Good for you,' he said instead. 'It's easy to end up with no personal life at all when you're in this job.'

'Nah, sir, not me,' Brookes said. 'I'm good at keeping a balance, if I do say so myself.'

They said their goodbyes at the bridge where Katie Bradley had killed herself.

It was impossible to stand there for any length of time without teasing yourself with the idea of what it would be like to drown. That wasn't the kind of thought Whitworth usually indulged in, but there was something about tonight. He said it, half to himself.

'If she'd wanted to live, she could have swum to the bank, I reckon,' Whitworth said. 'I know that there's shock and the cold and everything to account for, but I think we all have a strong instinct for self-preservation. It's not a wide river. She could have made it. If that was what she decided she wanted.'

'Maybe,' Brookes said.

'If she'd decided . . .' But Whitworth didn't finish the thought. What was the point?

'Night, sir.'

Brookes gave a sort of flourish and then, seemingly only a few seconds later, was receding into the darkness.

Whitworth was feeling a little blurry, a little warm. The stone wall came up to just under his hips. He tilted his centre of gravity forward, just a little. Was that how she had done it?

Did she jump? Take a run-up and propel herself into nothing? Did she lean in, as you do into a daydream, or the idea of love?

He walked home. Wouldn't do for a cop like him to get caught drink-driving and, besides, the night air felt good. Just cool enough.

He opened the front door – he didn't think it was too loud, but he knew Maureen would moan at him in the morning that he'd woken her up coming in. The television was on, and when Whitworth went over to switch it off he saw Jennifer asleep on the sofa, her hair fanned across the cushion, looking as clean and sweet as she'd been as a kid.

He went to fetch the spare blanket from the chest and drew it over her. He bent down to kiss her on the cheek.

'You love your old dad, really, don't you?' he said softly.

She said nothing.

54.

Then

Jamie looks almost the same, with an atomic density to him no memory could possibly convey. He isn't wearing a police uniform, but his clothes have the same silhouette, somehow.

He looks normal. Human. Kind. More than all that, he looks *harmless.*

She looks at the door, but the door no longer means anything to her.

She can only imagine the laughter around her if she tries to get up and run. Running from this man?

He's no clawed demon. He's just a young man in a shirt and blazer from Marks and Spencer's. She can feel the sympathy for him in the room.

He's *nervous,* speaking to all these people. She can tell, because she knows him. She still knows him.

He talks.

It could be for any length of time at all short of infinity; it doesn't matter to Katie. His voice is like rain on a riverbed that has long dried out.

She doesn't know what he is talking about, because all that matters is that he is talking, again. And she is silent. Again.

So there it is. Jamie followed her. Jamie found her. Jamie stalked her. Stalked every woman in that refuge so that she'd be caught in the net.

Through the sludge of fear, she feels some keen searchlight reawaken inside her. Something that asks, reaching deep into each word and phrase he utters, to dissect this man for the sake of the question, or the plea – why did I stay with him? What possible sense could it have made?

She has told herself in the nights when she lay awake in the blue-cold light and laid one hand on the cooled sweat of Noah's back that some migraine-like blindness must have come over her eyes then lifted again. Yes, something hormonal, even medical, or so ancient it can only be explained by a creation myth of what men and women really are.

But now she isn't sure. Jamie has always made it impossible to be sure about things. Those long rationalizations, composed to the ceiling in the hours without sleep, fade to white noise, and the only beat is the pulse of Jamie's jaw opening and closing as he speaks to the room.

She could get up and move. Run away again.

Where would running take her?

He's just a man. She parses the lines of his body to see where the danger lives and finds only her own stupidity.

He hasn't looked at her yet. He seems to be making eye contact with everyone in the room except her.

He is wrapping up. She can tell by his cadence, if not his words, which don't matter at all. The words could have belonged to anyone, but what matters is that the voice belongs to him.

Everyone is filtering away now. She lingers. God knows why. He doesn't seem to have seen her. Does that mean she's stopped existing?

It's just the two of them left in the hall. He's packing away his papers. Then he pauses and looks up. Looks her in the eye.

'Have a good night,' he says.

And the voice belongs to him.

55.

Now

I'll tell you what happened. But you've got to keep it safe, okay?
  Don't go blabbing.
  Not yet, Nazia.
  We've got to pick our moment.
  Got to wait till it's the right time.
  Can you do that?
It was such a little splash, like the river's asking what all the fuss was about and nobody knows the answer.

Death's still standing there, watching her. He knows exactly what he's done. And now I know, too.

I stood there and stood there and I thought now it's too late no now it's too late no now it's too late and even now she's still screaming along silently in the current of that river and any hand – my hand – could have been enough to pull her out.

She's still under there, she's still waiting, and I'm still not brave enough. Maybe one day though.

I still can't feel anything, not even a hand.

Maybe I've got a truth inside me. Probably I've got a truth inside me, and all you need to do is strip everything that's covering me away and there it'll be, small and pink and naked.

I gave that little seed of truth to Nazia when I told her what I saw, and the two of us can plant it in a pot and let it grow until it covers the sky and we can shelter underneath it. Maybe others too. Katie, or a girl like Katie.

Till this fucking rain stops.

Author's Note

One of the biggest shifts in my understanding of the world over the past few years has been the realization that, far from being occasional, outlying behaviour, violence against women and girls, is stitched into the fabric of our society. These issues are, unfortunately, very real and widespread, and they are all connected. This drove me to write *Keeper*.

Perhaps you have been affected by one or more of the issues depicted in this novel, or you know someone who is. The organizations listed below can help you:

- The **National Domestic Violence Helpline** is run by **Refuge** and their lines are open 24/7 – call **0808 200 0247**
- There are extensive resources and a **Survivor's Handbook** on the **Women's Aid** website: https://www.womensaid.org.uk/the-survivors-handbook/
- You can find your nearest **Rape Crisis Centre** and information about sexual violence at https://rapecrisis.org.uk
- **Karma Nirvana** supports **victims of forced marriage and so-called 'honour-based' violence**. You can call their helpline at **0800 599 9247** (lines open Monday – Friday, 9 a. m.–5 p.m.)
- **Paladin** offers **support and advice to victims of stalking** on **020 3866 4107** (open weekdays, 9 a.m.–3 p.m., except on Wednesdays, 11 a.m.–7 p.m.)
- **Shelter** offers urgent **housing advice** on **0808 800 4444**, or for less urgent enquiries you can speak to one of their advisors online

Several of the people who have read this book have told me that it made them feel angry and that they needed to do something. There are many organizations – too many to list – that are doing incredible work to support women. All are doing important work and none have enough money, so below are just a few suggestions for where you might like to donate:

- Southall Black Sisters: https://southallblacksisters.org.uk
- Imkaan: https://www.imkaan.org.uk
- Centre for Women's Justice: https://www.centrefor womensjustice.org.uk
- Beyond the Streets: https://beyondthestreets.org.uk
- Level Up: https://www.welevelup.org

If you're a man reading this, then I urge you to take the White Ribbon pledge to 'never commit, excuse or remain silent about male violence against women' at https://www.white ribbon.org.uk.

There is no quick fix to this epidemic of violence, but we can demand that our local and national governments take it seriously. If you want to make your voice heard then please do write to your MP, engage with your local women's charities and hold your local councils accountable for their provision of services for survivors of domestic abuse.

Acknowledgements

Firstly, I'd like to thank my incredible agent Marilia Savvides for her acumen and her passion. I couldn't ask for a better advocate. Thank you to the rest of the team at PFD, particularly Alexandra Cliff, Rebecca Wearmouth, Jonathan Sisson, Zoe Sharples and Laura Otal. I'm so lucky to have you guys in my corner.

Thank you to Katy Loftus at Penguin UK, who understood this book and what I wanted to do with it straight away. Thank you for editing this book so wisely and sensitively, for caring deeply, and for being a joy to work with. Thank you Rosanna Forte for your insight and support. Thank you Shannon Kelly in the US for your enthusiasm and your perceptive editing. Thank you Ellie Smith for managing the editing process and Sarah Day for copy-editing. Thank you to all my fellow students and teachers at the Centre for New Writing in Manchester, and in particular to Beth Underdown for sharing your wisdom when things got overwhelming!

My deepest gratitude to Jeanette Winterson, a once-in-a-lifetime teacher and mentor. Thank you for believing in this book from the very beginning, and for your practical support in so many different ways. Your writing made me believe that it was worth it to pursue the life I wanted, and your confidence in me has given me confidence in myself. Thank you also to all my teachers over the years.

Thank you to the legendary Val McDermid for generously lending your time and eagle eye to read an early version of this book. It means so much for a writer finding her feet to have your feedback. To Grace McCleen for reading a draft that was mostly a mess and encouraging me nonetheless. Thank you to Natasha Green for sharing your expertise in domestic violence, to Josephine Knowles for your guidance with Jenny (and for your important work at Beyond the Streets), and to Assallah Tahir for your help with Nazia.

Thank you to all my friends and family. To Mum and Dad for supporting me in every way, for reading the book and helping me find my way forward with it (since that first long car ride, Mum!), and for never once showing anything but total faith that I could do it. I'm very, very lucky. Also Joe, Izzy, Granny, Grandpa and the rest of the clan (including the various cats, though frankly, overall, they contributed very little).

Thank you, Carys Lapwood, my dearest friend. For being my dearest friend.

And thank you, Jason Gwartz, for patiently tolerating every one of my various crises, for politely disagreeing when I insisted that the book was crap, for sticking by me through four cities, three countries and God knows how many homes. I couldn't do this without you. Love.

And last of all, thank you to all the practitioners working to end violence against women, and to survivors for sharing their stories.